Shots Fired in the Melting Pot

BY T. C. Clover

Cover Design by Tierney Roberts

Twitter account: **@isiahsskirmish**

THIRD EDITION

Dedication: For Tatyana Alexandra Khorishko, the desert rose that survived the blizzard; my inspiration, and someone I love very much.

To my father and siblings (in alphabetical order): Robbie Griffith, James Sellers, Jodi Sellers, and Shane Sellers.

To my mentors Jacque Turner-Schettler and Don Miles. I hope this work does justice for the wisdom that you have shared. I'm grateful.

To Lonna Marie for performing a beautiful, original song. Please visit: **www.LonnaMarie.com** for more great music.
Twitter: @LonnaMarie
Performance and Editing by Lonna Marie
Song Lyrics by Travis Adams Irish

To Tierney Roberts for your beautiful and inspired cover artwork. Please visit: **www.TierneyRoberts.com** for some incredible designs.
Twitter: @TierneyRoberts

iv

TABLE OF CONTENTS

TABLE OF CONTENTS

I. Flying Red Class

We create our own heaven; this is a thoughtless rhetoric and tired slogan of the optimist. Who are we to decide that our self-interests should be the way of the world? **-A Mother's Wrath.**

Litz Eliza Rack glared at the rocky face of a seventy-five-foot cliff with the austerity of a bullfighter. She felt the cool sting of winter air making its way through her loose-fitting orange tank top and a pair of black jeans. There were minuscule snowflakes stuck to the outer layers of her long brunette hair, and her Swedish-American complexion was pale and flaky. The fifteen-year-old could hear the sirens of fire trucks and police cars motoring up the winding canyon road to find her. Litz laughed them off with the tormented abandon of a broken heart, gazing at the sky with her eyes of oceanic blue. She could sense the cocaine and whiskey opening up her adolescent vascular system with adrenaline like an overheating engine.

The teenager glanced over her left shoulder at a charcoal plume of smoke twisting up through the snow-covered pine trees. Litz smirked at the thought of the black Chevrolet Corvette crumpled against a group of boulders in the river, invoking the drug dealer from whom she stole the car. Her ribcage was throbbing with sharp pain from when the young woman lost control of the vehicle, causing it to spin out on an icy bend in the road and crash into the riverbed. The impact had knocked her unconscious, but she awoke to survey her destiny through ice crystals on the windshield. A solitary cliff stood out from the mountains like an unneeded authority, forcing wildlife to go around and imposing its will on the area.

She had a fresh memory of what the car was like after the accident and took a moment to reminisce. Litz had taken a swig from a bottle of Jack Daniel's whiskey and poured the rest of its contents on the black leather passenger seat of the vehicle. The distraught juvenile then used a Zippo lighter to ignite the alcohol, which inspired her to vacate the car in a hurry. Upon exiting the Corvette, she fell backward onto a boulder with a thud, summoning immense pain from her back and spine. Litz rolled off of the rough gray rock to her right, landing knee-deep in the freezing waters of the river.

Despite the numbing effects of the cocaine, the teenager soon detected a sharp sting of ice water soaking her pants at the knees and all the way down into her shoes. Litz embraced each irritating sensation with a new level of defiance, slogging through the chilly waters like a child. She made it to the banks of the river and stood there long enough to delight in the splendor of the black sports car being consumed by fire.

The young woman shook off this memory during a moment of clarity, forcing herself to focus on the task at hand. She turned back to face the cliff, realizing that the sounds of rescue vehicles were growing louder. Litz had no idea where in the country she had crashed the car, or the names of the mountain ranges that surrounded her on all sides. The last sign that she read while sober had said 'Welcome to Park City,' which evoked childish excitement after driving all night. She embraced a newfound ambition inspired by the sirens, and the determined teen latched onto the dry, cold rocks with all of her upper body strength. Litz sought handholds without reservation and fumbled about for a few seconds, knowing that her fingers were getting cold. After multiple attempts, she gripped the rocks well enough to begin her ascent. The teenager had risen only a foot off of the ground when the cocaine demon on her shoulder applauded with orchestrated grace.

Litz sensed that the porous rocks scratched her left cheek as she reached for another handhold above her right shoulder. The torment of her weeks in captivity at the orphanage began to drift away with the freezing winds, and she refused to let herself fall. During the first thirty feet of her climb, she reflected on a heart attack and car crash that killed her father and brother when she was seven years old.

The audacious teenager continued to scale the cliff with sharp pains and aches from the bitter temperatures being reported by her skin. Although she dared not let the cliff win in her moment of triumph, the temptation to give up was enticing. Her entire body was shaking at the halfway mark, and she began to reflect on her mother for strength. The winds kicked up and swirled about the face of the cliff, threatening her with failure. She gripped the sandstone handholds with vibrant dissent, almost hissing through her chapped lips.

On the ground beneath her, Litz heard rescuers shouting upward for her to come down. The acoustics of the mountain range had a remarkable effect on their speech, allowing her to hear them with clarity. Litz thought of her mother's beautiful face and the tender way that she conducted herself. The woman was healthy and alive six months ago.

Litz noticed that she was on the verge of tears and stopped herself from slinking away into despair. She clung to the living image of her mother as her fingers shuddered to reach the next set of handholds. Her arms and shoulders were convulsing with each upward movement, but the juvenile held on with the perseverance of a wild creature. The cocaine demon on her shoulder had transformed into a celestial being, showing her the top of the cliff as a sanctuary from the suffering. She obeyed the mighty creature and its primal logic, hauling her body atop the gritty ledge amidst the hateful winds.

When Litz reached the top of the cliff, she bowed her head in a display of respect to the powers of nature. The teenager then curled her hands into fists of passionate rage and ground them down into the rocks at her sides. She twisted them until the jagged surface tore open the skin on her knuckles. Litz smiled with vindication and felt the agony that was her life dripping from her veins onto the frosted earth.

"I love you guys!" She declared to the heavens with her eyes shut, weeping as a sensation of peace radiated from the core of her body outward.

"I can't believe she made it!" A male rescue worker cried out from the ground, watching the young woman in awe. "Stay there. We'll be up to help you soon."

Litz opened her eyes but could not see the man. There was too much snow blowing about, and part of the ledge was in her way. She widened her gaze to reveal blue stones of hatred looking out upon the world, and the bloodshot white space that surrounded them. The vulnerable juvenile stood up tall and stomped over to the edge of the cliff, displaying the middle fingers on each of her hands. Litz had a sensation of triumph over authority but then found herself falling through the chilly air. Her gut wrenched with instant panic, unsettled by the lack of ground beneath her feet. The adolescent woman plummeted with a mixture of regret and exoneration, knowing that she would again see her family. A smile formed on her face as the cocaine angel abandoned her, shedding its celestial form to embrace a personification of darkness. Litz felt free from the bonds of the world, but her fall halted in an abrupt fashion, and a stream of warm blood began to trickle down her right cheek.

II. Hammerjack

How insane is the concept of sanity for those who must peer over the edge of a mountain to gain wisdom? When do the ripples in an ocean revert to the droplets of liquid from which they were displaced? **–A Mother's Wrath.**

TWELVE YEARS LATER

Litz Rack gazed upon New York City with familiar affection. She leaned further into her downward dog yoga stance, breathing in the fresh spring air. From the balcony of the penthouse, the city seemed tame and approachable, but a closer inspection would indicate otherwise. The twenty-seven-year-old glanced at a tattoo of an Irish car bomb on her right bicep, which depicted the popular mixed drink. It was a colorful illustration of a frothy beer with a shot glass inside, blending translucent yellows with auburn.

She sensed Richard's naughty schoolboy gaze tracing the curves of her body through the immaculate glass doors at her rear. Litz resisted the guilty pleasure of winking at her adversary, calculating that it would make her less goddess and more princess. The diva rose to a standing position with a rapid snap of her calf muscles, turned on her heel and marched toward the double doors with animal intent.

There was an awkward pause as Litz waited for the electronic motor to open the sliding doors, allowing her to invade the penthouse. She roused a wicked smile from her feminine lips, shuffling with effortless seduction in a pair of formfitting black tights. 'How does the shark pretend to be the noble dolphin?' Litz thought with deified rhetoric. The young woman leaned over Richard to see him reading obituaries from <u>The New York Times</u>. Her demeanor sparked as a smug fury, laced with a hint of girlish affirmation.

"Has anyone important died?" Litz asked in a coy manner, bending closer to Richard as if to advertise her creamy white skin and elicit a hungry glance from him.

She noticed a cameraman advancing to capture this moment for the show, and it seemed like a syringe of despair. The liberal woman had relaxed so much in her yoga regimen; she almost forgot about selling her soul to a television network. Cameraman Doug was approaching with the stealth of a black cat, despite his 300-pound body. He hovered over the back of a white sofa to get a shot of their faces. The heavy 3D hologram camera caused his elbows to impress the upright cushions like a wrestler strangling his opponent.

Litz switched her posture to a pinup girl pose and gave the camera a subtle half-kiss, something she had mimicked with her goldfish as a youngster. By comparison, Richard was ever the indigenous family man, refusing to pander to the camera in any situation. He had always treated the Shots Fired film crew like they were foreigners vying for the souls of his tribe.

"Everyone's death is important," Richard replied with nervous regret, swallowing hard as he realized that his chosen topic was taboo for 2056. "I was getting ready to check the sports scores." The thirty-one-year-old backpedaled, crossing his right leg over his left to seem more natural.

Litz opened her mouth at the Republican, wondering where to begin devouring such a fleeting opportunity. The shy man twisted his face in an awkward fashion, looking squeamish under the polarizing light of the camera. Although his tailored gray suit and black tie were doing most of the work to make him seem approachable, Richard managed to mess it up.

"I caught you staring at me on the balcony," Litz concluded with a wink toward the camera. "Why would you be doing that? I thought you were all about families."

"I – I wasn't staring at you!" Richard pleaded in a defense composed of broken English. "I was looking at the sunset."

"Oh, right…the sunset." She redirected with a raise of her eyebrows, biting her lower lip slightly as if to question his sanity. "So…does the sunset look amazing as is, or should it spend more time on abs?"

"It was a nice sunset," Richard declared in a dismissive tone, brushing his right hand through his short black hair.

"You're busted!" Litz stated with charismatic charm, grabbing Richard's sinewy shoulders and shaking them like a football coach.

"You had a phone call." He interrupted with a nervous glance at her satellite phone on the kitchen counter.

She released his shoulders and shrugged for the camera, ensuring that the audience empathized with her rejection. Litz then swatted Richard on the back of his head, restraining herself somewhat; making it look playful. The deified vixen stepped closer to the kitchen counter and retrieved her pink satellite phone from the white tiled surface. Richard grasped the back of his head as if the tail of a horse had just whipped him. He gave Litz a pouty look from his innocent blue eyes, and was surprised to see her return a gaze of innocence. Although it was brief, like the shadow of a firecracker exploding, Richard saw something deep and genuine in the eyes of the busty brunette.

Litz noticed an intimate longing creeping across Richard's adorable Scottish-American face as she finished listening to her voice mail with the stoicism of a true vixen. After a short pause for a girlie pose, she touched the screen to return the call.

"Hello, this is Great Rack Plumbing," Litz announced with seductive grace through her satellite phone. "How can we take care of your pipes today?" She watched Richard's predictable expression of disgust while tapping her right index finger against her lips with vulgar precision. "Oh, your kitchen faucet is leaking? That's so sad. Well, I can be there in an hour to take care of that for you. What's the address?"

"What the hell is your problem?" Jazzy Auburn Michelle roared as she exited the bathroom in a towel. "I told you not to shoot me in the shower!"

Richard turned to see paparazzi photographer Fassim Johnson running across the hardwood flooring of the penthouse with Jazzy in pursuit. He found himself tantalized by Jazzy's water-soaked legs, but glanced sideways at Litz and the cameraman; not wanting to send the wrong message.

Several locks of Fassim's blonde hair bounced here and there under her fuchsia headscarf, and she looked back at the pursuing comedian with gratuitous pride. The ambitious photographer winked at Jazzy with sisterly affection, and then disappeared into her bedroom at the far end of the penthouse.

After the door had shut, Jazzy seized the brass handle, tugging at it with vigor and staring at the painted oak as if to burn a hole in the material.

"You little mother-" Jazzy roared in a rush while pulling back her long orange hair and censoring what would have been a tirade of swearing on national television. "Don't ever shoot me while I'm in the shower again! I'm going to get some locks that you can't open with a butter knife."

Jazzy turned in the hallway to face Richard and cameraman Doug, checking her body to ensure that the towel was covering everything. The twenty-five-year-old Irish-American woman began to inhale an audible amount of air pressure into her lungs. Her eyes became like those of a boat captain seeking a port at which to dock her rage.

Richard shifted in his seat, feeling nervous that he might be on the receiving end of the famous comedian's wrath. He turned with desperate eyes to ask Litz for help, but she was no longer in the kitchen. Instead, he saw Cody K. Black, also known as CKB, and an attractive woman standing near the entryway. CKB was smiling at him in a manner that was typical of his demeanor, keeping his muscular arms folded to exempt himself from the drama.

"Oh, hey CKB," Richard began with a smile and nod. "Are you going to introduce me to your lady friend?" He asked with an overdone gesture while rising to his feet to greet them.

"Did you enjoy looking at my body, Richard?" Jazzy demanded as she entered the room, stomping over her previous watery footsteps. "Don't deny it!" She chastised with melodramatic outrage. "I saw your head turn like a sprinkler connected to a fire hose."

Jazzy's rage redirected with birdlike efficiency as Fassim's bedroom door opened, and the thirty-three-year-old Saudi Arabian photographer emerged with a triumphant smile. The bold woman then made graceful strides toward the comedian, wearing a blue blouse and moderate black jeans.

"You've got balls, girl!" Jazzy exclaimed with a hint of bewilderment in her light blue eyes, and pulled the towel tighter around her chest. "What did you do with that nude photo?"

CKB showed fresh interest in the conversation, and stroked his chin with his right index finger. The criminal's bald head exhibited a pale sheen under the kitchen lighting, which was enhanced by his rich African-American ancestry.

"That photo just paid my wages for the month," Fassim reported in a cocky manner, adjusting her rimless eyeglasses as she entered the kitchen area. "But don't worry, I was able to blur out your – nakedness."

"You people have no couth whatsoever!" Jazzy proclaimed to everyone in the room. "If you didn't have an immunity deal with the show, I would sue the pants off of you. Besides, I thought you don't believe in showing images of women?"

"That's true," Fassim asserted with the gaze of a friendly school teacher from her brown eyes. "Traditional Muslims do not like to show the naked female form."

"And?" Jazzy demanded with urgency, curling her petite right hand into a fist.

"I'm not a traditional Muslim, and therefore, I can make money with your naked photos," she explained with a shrug.

CKB snickered somewhat at this exchange, but stopped himself when Jazzy glared at him. The muscular man was clad in a white muscle shirt and black jean shorts that showed off his toned legs.

"Who is this short drink of sangria?" Jazzy asked through her teeth, lamenting the woman next to CKB for being more attractive than she. "Did she find her way up here alone, or did you have to guide her with duck calls?"

"This is Petunia, y'all," CBK announced in a bold way, sticking out his chest to silence Jazzy's verbal assault.

"My guess would have been witch hazel," Fassim teased with unusual determination, provoking a high five from Jazzy. "You're so beautiful! I would take your picture, but then I'd have to smash my camera to delouse the memory card."

"Well, I don't know about them," Richard began with a roll of his eyes, "but I'm pleased to meet you, Petunia."

"That's pretty offensive, Richard!" CKB mumbled in an aggressive manner, tightening the skin around his eyes. "Don't you come up to my woman all commando."

"What do you mean?" Richard inquired with an unbalanced expression. "What they said was ten times worse than-"

"Dude, just stop!" CKB ordered with the palm of his right hand held outward. "Jazzy and Fassim were just kidding. You came up to my girl like some dude with a plate of hot dogs, lookin' at her like she's your grill. Well, don't do it again, or I'll break your grill."

Petunia turned her head to the side in confusion and then gazed back at the small group of strangers with unshakable confidence. While she was not as busty as Litz, the rest of her body was something to behold, and her sense of fashion accentuated every curve. The Hispanic New Yorker wore a formfitting purple dress with black stripes, and a pair of yellow high heels adorned her small feet.

Jazzy and Fassim stared the twenty-two-year-old Hispanic woman down, enjoying that she was vulnerable and on their turf.

"Well, I'll be in my room reading with my hot dogs if anyone needs me," Richard interrupted with dispassion. "It was great to meet you, Petunia."

"Did anyone hear about the Mars mission?" Petunia suggested with inquisitive brown eyes. "They're going to fly to the moon for a few days and live there to prepare for life on Mars."

"This is New York, honey," Jazzy chided with her right hand on her hip. "If we can make it here, we can make it on Mars."

"Pretty lame, Jazzy," CKB sneered as he wrapped his right arm around Petunia's waist. "But I guess – just like your towel, you're only ten percent original material. Y'all have a wonderful afternoon."

"Oh yeah, well try not to bang her head into the wall; she doesn't seem to have any brain cells to spare." The comedian retorted with a winning smile, but conceded her position when Petunia issued her a fierce glare. 'I'm sorry,' she mouthed to the exotic woman in earnest, expressing a rare moment of guilt.

"How long are you guys going to be in there?" Fassim called out to the couple during their departure. "Should we plan on two minutes to cook a bag of compressed popcorn, or ten hours binge-watching a TV series?"

CKB didn't respond at first, but held up his right middle finger to the group while keeping his back to them. He grabbed Petunia by the hand and gave her a passionate kiss on their way to his bedroom.

"Should we put on some music?" Fassim suggested to Jazzy with a wink and tiger lily smile. "I don't want to hear animal kingdom all afternoon."

"That's for sure," Jazzy agreed with a frown, nodding at her co-star on the way back to the bathroom. "By the way, I'm pissed at you, Fassim; stop trying to suck up to me!"

"Hey, a picture is worth five thousand dollars." The paparazzo deadpanned without raising her eyes from the kitchen counter.

"When will I get a woman like that?" Richard obsessed aloud, biting his lower lip as he closed his eyes and waited for an inevitable response.

Jazzy sneaked close to the Republican with silent footsteps and put her face in front of his, staring at the man's closed eyelids.

"When CKB breaks her heart!" She shouted the moment Richard opened his eyes, causing him to slip and almost fall on the floor.

Fassim began to laugh, but Jazzy gestured at the wily Muslim with her left hand in a rattlesnake fashion. The peaceful photographer simply blew a kiss to the comedian, and then pretended to take photos with her empty hands.

"If they let any more women into this loft," Richard expressed with a guise of exhaustion, "then I'm going to jump."

As an editor for Feature Films for Families, Richard had a difficult time with the liberties taken by his fellow cast members. Their antics on the television show often caused him to cringe, and he yearned for more conservative company. However, Richard understood that the core concept of the show was to illustrate ideological differences between passionate people. In that regard, Litz was the perfect liberal adversary for him, providing the shock and awe desired by the producers of the show.

Richard gazed at the loft with fondness. He looked at the marble tiles leading to the rooms with bunk beds that were used by the crew. The living quarters on the south end of the complex were far less extravagant than those for the television stars. By comparison, there was gorgeous white oak hardwood flooring leading to the six bedrooms of the actors, and each of them had five times the space of any crew member. He recalled Mike saying that it took six weeks to refurbish the penthouse for the show. Richard scoffed at the fact that thirty crew members shared two unisex bathrooms while the stars and executives got deluxe accommodations. The conflicted man decided that if he won the grand prize at the end of the season, he would share it with the crew.

III. Waterboarding the Pit Bull

What is it inside of that covetous human gaze, causing everyone to tremble? Is it the preamble to a blood diamond; that rare gem perceived as sometimes more beloved than a child's life? After all, what am I to you and you to me, but a collection of synapses firing at random in response to the events of the day? The kids of this generation say shots fired when there is social turbulence and controversy or mockery. It is fascinating how opinion can be honed like an elephant gun and used to destroy the lives or careers of others. How unprepared the older generations must have felt when the latest barrage of social commentary let loose on the landscape like demons fornicating at sunset; their long shadows superimposed on all things tangible. One must feel like a ghost in today's world when the whole of humanity seems to abandon them for a single comment. It is such a perfectly flawed system of judgment, and yet so efficient and precise.

This crescendo is my weapon of choice, ladies and gentlemen. I am the pretentious Judas at the back of every room; the expert marksman who needs only a smartphone to destroy your reputation. Isn't it beautiful; the name of the smartphone? We have created these tiny devices that capture life's most uninspired moments. This data levels the playing field for those of us who know how to hunt, where to look, and when to strike. The battles of today are fought on the fronts of what you can capture. Because if I can get a photo, recording, or message from you at your worst; then your worst is all anyone will ever know. So I welcome you to my world; it is the palace of information capture and the battlefield of overexposure. We will engage one another as friends, but I will steal your most horrible moments and display them to the world – so that I may have my blood diamond.

Those who are powerless to say farewell to their innocence will always be victims. This precedent is as true in the new social landscape as it is the hunting grounds of the wild. I am unashamed to admit that my colleagues and I eagerly await your failure. I am also unafraid to tell you that I will dry your tears and give you comfort, only to capture you at your most vulnerable – for consumption by the other predators of the world. Welcome to the melting pot; I look forward to your trusting smile and the feeling of your fragile dreams in my powerful fingers. **–A Mother's Wrath.**

The air felt cold to Stoney Akuda as he entered the cavernous penthouse apartment community reserved for the television show. He shook this chill off as an arbitrary sensation, knowing that nothing was wrong with the temperature outside of his body. The twenty-eight-year-old New Yorker sensed a recurring anxiety that had been with him in the elevator. It tugged at the back of his mind with unsettling precision. Stoney scurried across the glossy marble tiles of the production offices like a frightened forest creature, hoping to reach a quiet place amongst the chaos.

A few members of the television crew waved to the Japanese man as he crossed their paths, and Stoney appeased them with a forced smile. Panic was building inside of him as he neared the crew's unisex bathroom, feeling thankful that it was unoccupied.

"Stoney, where are you going?" Jennifer Priest called out in a commanding voice over the second unit camera crew.

"I need the bathroom," Stoney replied to the woman without turning to see her face. "Just give me a minute."

"You've got five minutes." The somewhat chubby blonde stated as Stoney closed the bathroom door to cut her off from his ritual. "Stoney, we're going to be on the air in five minutes," Jennifer confirmed with her right index finger pointed toward the door. "Make sure that you're on the set when the count begins. I don't care if you have to skip a few steps!" She concluded this short rant by grabbing at her tight ponytail and clicking a pair of orange high heels on the smooth marble.

Stoney felt a queasy sickness rolling up from his esophagus. There was a building pressure that had engulfed his heart, causing him to sweat.

"The living victims are always the hardest to deal with," Stoney announced to the small, empty bathroom.

He reached out with his right hand and flicked the light switch off, causing the bathroom vanity and toilet to disappear from view. Stoney's breathing became heavier as he recalled a boy that ran toward him earlier in the day with a sixteen-penny nail sticking out from the right side of his head. The large nail was a punishment from his angry Taiwanese father, who was redoing the kitchen in their apartment. Apparently, the toddler didn't understand why he couldn't get a snack from the fridge. And instead of talking to the little boy, his father shot him in the right side of the head with a nail gun. Fortunately, the air compressor was low on pressure at the time, and the nail didn't penetrate far into the boy's skull.

Although Stoney was able to rescue the toddler from his psychotic father, he had no outlet to release his anger. Further, he had to be professional when arresting the perpetrator since the man surrendered. It was one of many times when he wished that a 'perp' would resist. Stoney closed his eyes to explore a portfolio of memories where innocent people had survived horrific events. He squeezed his hands into fists and exhaled with a mighty calm, allowing the visions to fall away in the blackness of his mind. After a few seconds of total silence, the police officer assimilated joy that came with predictable peace.

The Japanese man kept himself in this state of silence for a while, unaware of how much time had passed. In his mind, the world needed to go away for a few minutes, and he imagined it like a yo-yo on a string in the darkness. Stoney could expertly spin it away from his center, and leave it suspended, but could never let it hit the floor. The pensive man took in one last breath of loving relaxation and then flipped on the bathroom light.

Stoney opened his eyes to see himself in a police uniform and a mocking reflection of his vulnerability in the mirror. He closed his eyes again, knowing that he was unprepared to be on television. With a few heaves of his chest, the officer allowed his anxiety to come back. Stoney thought of his lover watching at home, and the good that this second income would do for their lives. The optimistic television star reopened his eyes to see a dashing Japanese person with short black hair in the mirror. He smiled like a proud convict, mimicking the empty confidence demonstrated by almost every person who entered a jail cell with other criminals.

With his confidence restored, Stoney turned about-face and used his right hand to twist the cheap bronze door handle. He pulled the door open to see Jennifer blocking his path. The German-American woman had her arms folded, and she was giving him a typical Hollywood stare from her dark blue eyes.

"Makeup!" Jennifer shouted to her crew, clapping her hands in the air. "Get his hair and face prepped," she ordered a youthful, African-American stylist who approached from a few feet away. "You have ninety seconds to get him on the set!"

The makeup technician's eyes widened after hearing this command, but then she became calmer, darting into the bathroom with eagerness and determination. Jennifer looked back at Stoney and shook her head in disgust, knowing that the logistics of their opening sequence might need alterations.

"Come on, people, we have a configuration change," Jennifer barked to the crew as she stomped to the far end of the penthouse. "Let's start with the other five and bring up Stoney in the final shot. Make it look like he's always been there."

"Go ahead and walk toward the set." The makeup artist instructed Stoney in a sweet voice. "I'm just going to rub some water through your hair and put some base on you. Come forward; don't worry about me." She urged him as her hands rubbed water over his dark hair.

Stoney walked toward the set slowly, but the tenacious woman prompted him to move faster by flapping her right hand in the air. To his surprise, she was able to brush his hair and apply a layer of makeup on his face while walking backward. She looked back every few steps to navigate obstacles on the set and moved her body in the direction of Stoney's assigned chair.

The Japanese police officer sensed the marble flooring turning to soft shag carpeting as he stepped forward. He was disappointed to see that Jennifer had placed him between Litz Rack and Richard Orton.

"Please smile," the makeup artist requested with a grimace, "you need to look happy and confident. My makeup can only do so much!" She added with a charming wink.

Stoney tried to smile and sucked in a deep breath as he and the makeup artist entered the massive living room for the opening shots. The officer was impressed with her spatial intelligence until she licked her right thumb and used it to straighten his bangs.

"All done," the makeup artist whispered as she departed the vast living room set. "Good luck."

"Stoney, take your seat for the Live Pod session," Jennifer ordered from the back of the set. "Mike, they're all yours."

"Thank you, Jennifer." The director muttered in an obligatory fashion, sounding distracted. "Everyone hold up your chins and smile for the narration shots. Okay, the narrator is ready to record; just hold it there until we get the green light." Mike Farr looked at his watch with impatience, wondering why he ever agreed to shoot a live television show.

"Welcome, worldwide viewers, to another episode of Shots Fired in the Melting Pot," the narrator opened with charisma in a baritone voice. "Tonight, you'll see six rivals attempt to coexist in one New York City penthouse. We've found three men and three women whose backgrounds are fundamentally incompatible. Watch as they compete for gold and silver coins to see who will win three million dollars during our final episode. Since each of our stars is required to work at least six hours a day, we'll be bringing you footage from their unique lifestyles. So grab your favorite cold drink, because the battle is about to heat up on the number one live show in America."

Stoney sat up straight on the tall, white oak barstool with a confident smile. He found this posturing difficult with a criminal smirking at him from across the room. Cody K. Black, also known as CKB, was Stoney's chosen nemesis for the show. The muscular African-American was tall and sported a smooth, clean-shaven head. He was wearing a black T-shirt and white cargo pants; both with no logos. A gold chain adorned his neck, and there was a tattoo on his right bicep that read: 'only fools die poor.'

CKB sneered at the New York police officer that sat across from him. He immediately pulled up a satellite phone and lamented his adversary with a message on his Live Pod account: 'Hotdog stand is here to play. Hope he twists his knee next time he needs to shakedown one of my boys.' The thirty-five-year-old criminal then smirked and folded his bulky arms, concealing the phone behind his elbow.

Fassim shook her head as she watched the exchange between CKB and Stoney. At the age of thirty-three, the paparazzi photographer was having a difficult time believing that CKB was older than she. The light of the camera panned across the Muslim woman from the right and surprised her. Fassim instinctively tugged at the edges of her pink headscarf, hoping that her hair covering was proper for public viewing. The photographer's beautiful face glowed with a charismatic smile as she waited for the narrator to finish introducing her.

Jazzy Auburn Michelle rolled her eyes as the predatory photographer was in the spotlight. She clenched her right hand into a fist beneath the oak barstool, hiding it from the camera. Although Jazzy had a flattering smile on her face, there was fresh tension from the memory of Fassim taking a picture of her naked bum in the bathroom. 'I hope she pigs out and gets a muffin top,' the twenty-five-year-old comedian thought. 'One picture of my butt is enough to feed her for a month - the little leech.' Jazzy took a deep breath and exhaled with a peaceful demeanor, remembering her mother's advice about not letting the public see anger.

"How does my chest look in this shirt?" Litz Eliza Rack asked her adversary with an exaggerated flutter of her eyelids.

"Three-dimensional," Richard Theodore Orton replied to the poisonous beauty at his right, refusing to fall for her trickery again.

"Thank you!" Litz replied with a glorious smile as the light from the camera displayed her Swedish features.

'Stop talking!' Mike Farr mouthed from the director's chair, his eyes locked on the mischievous Litz Rack. 'If you ruin my intro again, I'm going to take away a gold coin.' He finished in a pantomime of desperation, making a series of hand gestures with a reddened face.

Litz raised her right hand toward the camera and gave a seductive wave to the lens with the tips of her rough fingers. She smiled playfully and twisted her head to the side like a high school cheerleader. The twenty-seven-year-old plumber effortlessly displayed why so many fans of the show had become fans of her.

'All hail the whore of Babylon,' Richard thought as the camera panned from Litz over to Stoney. 'If we were lobsters, she would parade us in front of the cameras before boiling us alive.' The thirty-one-year-old Republican abandoned his scornful stare for a brilliant smile as the camera panned onto him for the final shot. He sensed that the exposure of this show could land him in a coveted seat as a United States Senator. Richard sat up straight and waved at the camera with his right hand as well, but put his arm down when he received a signal of disapproval from the director.

Mike Farr used his right thumb and middle fingers to touch the bridge of his nose. He shook his head at the awkward mess that was Richard, but decided to encompass warmth and maturity before signaling the Live Pod session to begin. The six participants raised their heads in affirmation; some of them with a bit of childish glee, pulling out their satellite phones to wage war.

Litz wrenched a large pink phone from her pocket and typed on the screen as if writing a distress call: 'Stoney looks like my legs last week, unshaved and pale with a baby fat reduction.'

CKB sneered at Litz with nuanced insecurity, wiping his nose like a caveman and 'podding' with pensive energy: 'My daddy told me that life is about… Oh, look, a dog rubbing his bum on the lawn. What was he sayin'?'

Richard pulled out his black reading glasses and listened to his fellow competitors tapping their screens with ravenous indulgence. Every second that his cursor flashed with nothing on the screen was a barnacle on his pride.

In a rare showing of her childish intensity, Fassim raised her shoulders and glanced hungrily from side to side while tapping with her thumbs: 'I once took a picture of Justin Bieber that was worth $500, but by the time I got back to the studio, it was worth only $50.'

Jazzy locked eyes with Fassim for a few seconds, then smiled and showed a softer demeanor: 'Watching Richard struggle to form a thought is like waiting for a gorilla to pick his nose at the zoo.'

Stoney seemed oblivious to the whole experience, branding it as high school drama, but he elected to engage for the money: 'Who wants to bet that Litz will shake her fists at some point tonight?'

Richard sensed that time was running out for him to put an iron in the fire and began tapping his phone with urgency: 'I don't believe in evolution, but when CKB walks in the room, he seems like the missing link.'

The Republican showed off a proud grin, feeling like a composer who finished a brilliant symphony just in time for the royal ball. One by one, each of his co-stars stopped typing and gazed at him with horrified eyes. Richard detected the brazen hand of disapproval emerging to smite him.

"Do you realize how f'ing racist that is?" CKB demanded with a deadly stare, standing up from his barstool with an impulse of fury to confront Richard. "Are you calling me an ape, son?"

The other performers and members of the cast all froze; not knowing how to handle this bold insult.

"That's not racist!" Richard responded with uncertainty, shifting in his chair as he adjusted his reading glasses. "I was just saying that you're like a-"

"Gorilla!" CKB interrupted, moving closer to the smaller man until Richard was sitting in his shadow. "Do gorillas wear clothes?" The career criminal asked as he gripped his black shirt by the collar and pulled it upward.

Mike Farr had no idea that his television show was turning into a war zone. He had locked himself in a small storage room with a courier who arrived moments ago. The redheaded bike messenger had a sizable afro of curly locks. His body was pale and lanky, except for a pair of muscular legs that protruded from his expensive blue biking shorts. The man wore a white muscle shirt but had no bicep muscles to display.

Mike's hands began to tremble as he gazed at the courier's threatening blue eyes, which were behind a pair of gold-framed eyeglasses. He plunged the fingers of his right hand delicately between his short strands of dark brown hair. Mike's left hand rested on a jade-colored box, and he tapped the lengths of twine that held it together. The box was nearly two feet tall and a foot thick. It seemed to have expensive contents based on its vibrant colors and golden foil corners.

"This is only enough for a month," Mike protested with peaceful gestures, tightening the muscles of his abs under his suit to speak with more authority. "I paid you for six months," he said with a deliberate smile, taking a moment to straighten his red and white spotted tie.

The courier sneered at the television executive and made a point of looking up and down his Armani suit with moral abandon.

"Our six-month price is now the one-month price." The shifty redhead replied without explanation, unmoved by Mike's plea. "You already know how things are, Mike; I shouldn't have to coddle you all the time. Jennifer didn't give me any grief. I can take it back if you want." He offered with a shrug, pulling out a white satellite phone with callous indifference and looking at a series of text messages.

"The six-month price will be fine," Mike agreed with reluctance, rubbing his upper incisor against his lower lip. "Wait a second," he said with another thought, placing his hand on the courier's shoulder. "What if I didn't like the six-month price? Could we meet and get things back on track?"

"These prices," the Courier began with a prideful smirk, tapping the box on the side with his free hand, "will continue to rise. If you don't like it, then you and Jennifer can learn to swim." He ended his statement with a rehearsed stare, demonstrating for Mike the blackness of his deeper self.

"Okay, well-" Mike began with an outstretched hand, but the courier shook his head with irritation, stepping toward the door.

The militant bike messenger opened the door and departed the area with almost silent footsteps, leaving Mike to hear the statements of outrage coming from his set.

"Look, I'm sure he didn't mean it!" Jazzy exclaimed with a bit of piety, keeping her body between CKB and Richard. "We all know you're not a gorilla-"

"Yeah, I was talking about cavemen!" Richard interrupted with his arms extended, standing upright to back away from the raging criminal.

"Why don't you just calm down, Mighty Joe Young?" Stoney prodded with a smile as he stood up and glared at CKB from less than two feet away. "We're not afraid of you."

CKB turned toward Stoney with simmering rage, recognizing that the man was trying to own him with a blatant insult. He let his posture relax to a casual coolness that would be welcome at a jazz nightclub. The devious criminal then summoned a smile for his antagonist and approached Stoney with elitist confidence.

Stoney snarled at the lack of a reaction from the man, unwilling to buy what his adversary's smile was selling. To his revulsion, the career criminal held out his right hand in a staged offering of peace. The police officer felt agitated at this gesture, knowing that it would make him look like a power-crazed public servant. He decided to play the game as structured and reached out to take CKB's hand.

The criminal latched onto to Stoney's hand with a grip like a rat trap, jerking his right arm backward to unbalance the police officer. When the Japanese man's body tilted forward, CKB used the index and middle finger of his left hand to dig into his armpit.

Stoney winced in pain, and his fair brown eyes expressed a feeling of shock and betrayal. The officer scowled at his attacker and produced a 45 caliber, semi-automatic pistol from the waistband of his pants.

"Whoa, God! Doug, pull the camera away!" Mike commanded his camera crew, knowing that the ten-second delay might save them from embarrassment. "Jennifer, make sure we cut that out of the live feed. Go to commercial now!"

The director took less than a second to gather his wits, pausing to glare at the cast as he would a group of misbehaving children. He then advanced toward Stoney with his palms facing outward, indicating a need for cooler heads and warmer hearts.

CKB released Stoney's arm and raised his hands in the air out of instinct, seeming uncertain and alert. He stepped backward on the shag carpet, moving only a few inches at a time and refusing to make eye contact with the gunman.

"Stoney, I need you to put that gun away!" Mike ordered with an authoritative voice as he navigated the furniture on the living room set. "We can't have any actual shots fired on this show. And let me remind you – that you've all signed contracts preventing you from pressing charges on one another. That means no jail time. It specifies no lawsuits. Our power of attorney even prevents you from going after the show or the network. So put the damn gun away right now!" The director shouted in a startling expression of his aggressive nature.

Stoney stared at the terrified faces of his fellow cast members for a moment, seeming to snap out of his frenzy. He put the pistol back into the concealed holster of his waistband and looked upon the set as if a bomb had almost detonated.

"Don't you ever bring a gun on my set again!" Mike lamented with a sober tone, pointing his right index finger at Stoney and shaking it somewhat. "Why don't you all grab some dinner? We're going to wrap up the shoot for tonight, and we'll start fresh after you get off work tomorrow."

CKB and Stoney looked at one another with distilled pride, each wanting the other to recognize that this dispute wasn't over. Jazzy grabbed CKB with a firm right hand and led him away from the fuming police officer.

"Live Pod is dangerous!" Richard declared with a hint of outrage, tossing his satellite phone hard into the white cushions on the couch.

Stoney wiped some sweat from his brow and blinked a few times as he waited for the living room set to be clear of other people. He thought back to his childhood on the gritty streets of Harlem, New York. At the age of eleven, he had become a superhero to his younger sister, and she often referred to him as Superman. It didn't take long for the siblings to notice that the world was in need of truth and justice, but both were in short supply in the impoverished neighborhood in which they lived.

There was a massive crime spree that took place during the years following The Passing of 2033, and people filled their pockets while the government wrestled with issues of food supplies and pollution. Stoney and his seven-year-old sister had spent those years with their parents in shelters that were run by righteous and stalwart people. The quirky Japanese boy had grown fond of a group of men who patrolled the streets around their shelter to keep them from losing everything to burglars. He and his sister would sit above the alleyways and giggle when members of the neighborhood watch shot at trespassers with rock salt. After a perpetrator had entered their outer perimeter, the children would make a game of counting down the seconds before the crook was hit with a blast of salt and ran away screaming.

The police officer gazed out the windows of the living room toward the city, recalling why he had chosen to stand up for those who were weaker. Without the service of the men at the shelter, he and his sister may not have survived those turbulent years in America. Although his childhood fantasy shattered when he saw the ugliness of evil, it never swayed him from his course. As an adult, Stoney decided that what made heroes superhuman was their ability to see terrible things and keep fighting to stop them. Each year of service on the police force created a mental burden that had become like a new pair of ankle weights for him to bear.

IV. Garbage Soup

'A beer would be great about now,' CKB thought as he traversed the streets of New York during a warm spring morning. Despite the potential for discomfort, he had left the loft dressed in a white Nike sweatshirt and black jeans. The career criminal was cautious when taking the subway to Brooklyn, wanting to appear soft and cuddly to 'appease suspicious white people.' He clenched a small brown grocery bag in his right hand, swinging it somewhat to give the appearance that its contents were trivial. Although each time the fifty thousand dollars shuffled about inside of the bag, it made him feel nervous.

Stoney kept pace a few dozen yards behind CKB with his face camouflaged in cheap sunglasses and a blue baseball cap. His body was concealed by an oversized gray T-shirt and blue jeans, giving him a casual exterior. The determined police officer tugged at a brown leather jacket that completed his ensemble, feeling it tighten over the folds of the T-shirt. Despite the warm April weather, Stoney knew that the jacket was required to conceal the shape of his body. He watched CKB progressing through the crowds of Brooklyn toward Canarsie Park on the waterfront.

Jamaica Bay wasn't visible through the crowd of pedestrians, but as the wind blew across his face, the disguised officer imagined its graceful blue waters. Stoney watched the bag of money swaying in CKB's right hand, and a smile emerged from his otherwise stoic face. The meticulous police officer had been curious about its purpose ever since he found the bag stashed away in the loft. Stoney felt his stomach growling and cringed at the thought of his body betraying him this close to victory. He shrugged off the warnings from his digestive system and pressed forward in pursuit of his co-star.

CKB glanced at the time on his satellite phone and quickened his pace. He took broad steps toward a playground where dozens of children were enjoying swing sets and slides. After inspecting the grounds, he strode with aggression toward a black wrought iron fence that surrounded the play area. The criminal then watched and waited near the fence as if expecting someone to meet with him.

Stoney observed the muscular black man from the edges of the park and sensed that an opportunity may arise to imprison his foe. He looked closer at the areas near his target and saw no immediate signs of an impending transaction. Despite his contract with the studio, no clause prevented him from having CKB arrested and brought up on charges by a friend.

CKB tilted his head forward when he noticed a chubby man of German descent watching the children at the playground. The television star's eyes seemed to flash under the modest warmth of the afternoon sun as if he took a mental picture of the stranger. Although the men stood on opposite sides of the same fence, more than eighty-five feet apart, CKB was worried about being discovered.

The mysterious German was pasty and clean-shaven: he loitered next to the three-foot wrought iron fence with two baseball gloves pressed against his abdomen. CKB watched in disbelief as the mothers in the area went about their business, unaware that a predator was only a few steps from their children.

The bullish crook grabbed the back of his neck and shook his head, wishing that the trees could tell the mothers what had taken place over the years. CKB recalled the first time that he saw the creepy outsider and picked up on his ulterior motives. It was easy for criminals to catch one another plotting their next misdeeds. He often refused to involve himself, but CKB had no patience when it came to acts against children. 'Everyone deserves protection from the streets,' he thought after concluding that the kidnapper would not be taking action today.

"I'll be here when you make your move," CKB said aloud to the fresh air of the park, "and you won't see me comin'."

The criminal tightened his hands around the top rail of the decorative fence, caressing the smooth welded metal with manipulative grace. He spied the short German tracing routes from the children to their parents, trying to determine who would let their guard down. After watching to ensure that the man lacked enough confidence to act today, CKB strafed left around the fence toward the shipping docks.

Stoney grimaced from the strain in his abdomen, regretting the big breakfast that he allowed Fassim to feed him. He observed CKB with halfhearted interest, wondering if this outing would produce a smoking gun. The crook had been acting strange all morning, but this venture into the park was the first real sign of intent to misbehave. His thoughts were interrupted when Stoney noticed that CKB was bolting toward the docks at an aggressive pace. He shook his head with a tormented sense of dedication, reluctantly jogging behind his adversary.

The television stars traversed the park in silence as CKB pulled several hundred yards ahead of his pursuer. Stoney felt agonizing pain in his right side and recognized that his body wouldn't allow this chase to continue much longer. He bit his lower lip and set his sights on a few possible shortcuts to gain ground on his co-star.

CKB made his way through the wide streets of a vast industrial district. He ran past warehouses that stored: amalgamated sugars, vegetarian hamburgers, and concrete mix. His breathing was becoming labored as he approached a modest sporting goods warehouse. The building had turquoise aluminum siding that was flaking off to reveal an earth tone primer. It featured a solitary door at the front with bulletproof glass that was tinted almost solid black. He retracted the brown bag in a protective manner and reached for the black steel door handle with his left hand. Upon entering the building, CKB noticed beads of sweat forming all over his shiny bald head.

The interior of the sporting goods warehouse looked nothing like its exterior. There were rustic hardwood floors of dark hickory and walls paneled in stained pinewood. A solitary staircase on the left side of the room led to a second-floor balcony. The circular set of stairs was stainless steel, and despite being designed for outdoor use, it looked attractive with the rest of the décor.

Although the front portion of the warehouse took up only one-third of the total space, it was still large enough to command respect. The layout was simple on the ground floor, featuring racks of clothing on the left and shelves with sporting equipment to the right. On the second floor, there were miscellaneous items like archery targets, kayaks, fishing poles and climbing equipment. His employer had a habit of keeping all of the guns in the back where he could see them.

CKB moved through racks of spring clothing that included camouflage jackets and black spandex outfits. He took a moment to gaze at the head of a timber wolf that was mounted above a doorway which led to the larger part of the warehouse. The taxidermist had done something unnatural to the eyes of the creature, making it appear alive to those who entered the building.

His gut trembled as he considered Mitch Gentile's need to use symbols in every aspect of his life. The wolf represented something obvious to those who served the warehouse under his employ. CKB twisted the cheap brass knob on the flimsy interior door, avoiding the rough birch surface as he entered the workspace of his boss.

The miscreant found himself in a small room where the warehouse seemed to end. There was a tall desk made up of glossy, painted concrete with a marble countertop at its front. It had a tacky, dark blue paint job, and the marble topper was a hideous quartz color; something that one would find at a discount store. A portly Hispanic guard sat behind the desk and watched CKB enter the room with disinterest. His fingers were intertwined, and his hands were resting on the back of his head, allowing him to recline on a padded swivel chair. The man wore a uniform that was a snug fit, and it featured dull colors that went well with the gloomy office.

CKB set the bag of cash down on the countertop and nodded to the security guard, waiting for him to reply. The man took a deep breath and released his hands from the back of his head, appearing lifeless and unhappy. He raised his eyes to CKB under a mass of unkempt black hair, coming to life for a moment with the charm of a judgmental mother.

"He wants to see you," the Hispanic guard muttered without making eye contact.

Before CKB could offer up an excuse, the man punched a six-digit code into a keypad, and a false brick wall behind him slid to the right. The television star observed the security gate fading away a few inches each second, as though it were feeding time for a prodigious predator. CKB snatched the brown bag from the countertop like a pouty toddler and walked with forced arrogance past the brooding security guard.

The greater portion of the warehouse shone brighter at its center with a sort of corridor leading up to Mitch Gentile's desk. On either side of CKB, men were unpacking boxes in the shadows on bare concrete. There were stacks of boxes and bags of various illegal goods almost all the way to the ceiling. Each side of the area was at capacity with freight to a level that would be the envy of a lifelong hoarder.

CKB moved across a length of short black carpet that covered only the center of the room. The corridor featured some wide stairs that rose five feet from the main floor, leading up to Mitch Gentile's pristine desk of stainless steel and decorative glass. There was a mural behind the desk that came into view as CKB climbed the stairs. It featured a white Chinese dragon that seemed to have snaked its way from the upper left corner of the wall to the lower right.

"You've pissed off a lot of people, superstar," Mitch Gentile stated with the tone of a disparaging father. "I don't know how all this attention is supposed to benefit me." He added, bending down to a small black refrigerator near the wall to retrieve a few bottles of Corona Light. "Just put it on the desk." The gangster ordered, noticing the bag swinging in CKB's right hand. "I just got off the phone with some guys that aren't happy about their faces being posted on the Internet."

Mitch sat down with a flustered look of confusion, glancing over the surface of his desk. His expensive black suit had been tailored a bit too tight, and CKB posited that drinking a bottle of beer might cause the top button to pop off of the jacket. The twenty-seven-year-old gangster seemed calmer when he located a bottle opener in the top left drawer of his oversized desk. He retrieved it with haste and snapped off the caps of the two beer bottles, exercising graceful authority. The man's eyes locked onto CKB for the first time when he reached across the desk to hand him one of the beers. His pupils had a quality that inspired dread in many people; a sort of assured damnation with predatory flair. Mitch ran his fingers through his long blonde hair, forcing it into compliance with the rest of his ensemble.

"So, what are we going to do about that?" The brash Norwegian asked in an urgent manner and leaned forward to snatch his beer from the desk.

"I guess they're gonna' have to deal with it," CKB answered with a devious smirk, taking a seat opposite his boss. "They do make for good entertainment." He quipped and pursed his lips, punctuating his sentence with a sip from the beer bottle.

Mitch set down the beer and rested his palms atop the transparent glass of the desk. He remained silent for a few seconds, leveraging an awkward moment to stare at his companion as if to clear his mind.

"I need you to do it again," Mitch said with conviction, looking away from his colleague to the right.

"Who and when?" CKB inquired with repressed enthusiasm as his left hand tightened around the bend of his knee.

"Today...now," the powerful gangster demanded without showing a hint of compassion. "It's going to be Hector Mescal. I need you to take him down a few pegs – let the air out of his tires."

"Mescal?" CKB confirmed with raised eyebrows and gripped his knee tighter at the mention of such a dangerous name. "Why are we antagonizing Mescal? You told me that would be a stupid move."

"Yeah, and it still is a stupid move, but it has to be done," Mitch asserted with a nod, exhaling somewhat with regret. "Sometimes we have to do stupid things, Cody; it's like setting off an explosion to put out a bigger fire."

"And how am I supposed to get away from that explosion?" He questioned with waning confidence, hoping that this was a joke with the punch line still pending. "Am I going to have any people?"

"No, it's just going to be you," the boss replied with a shrug as if to challenge his employee's manhood. "You know that you're always alone on these. If I recall, it was your idea to do this; you thought it was fun." Mitch expressed with impatience and tapped his right index fingernail hard against the glass.

"Okay, I'll get it done," CKB agreed with a deep breath, exhibiting a total lack of confidence in his statement.

"Good, the sooner, the better," his boss reiterated in a lackluster moment of victory. "When you're done with that, I need you to take Mayor Ackerman's daughter out for a fun night. Give her whatever she wants."

"I'm seeing someone," the astonished man protested. "Why can't George-"

"Because I want you to take care of her!" Mitch interrupted with blistering authority. "That damn TV show must have made you forget who you work for. I only allowed you to do that if it would give me some opportunities. Now that you're a celebrity, I'm going to whore you out to the city. Understood?"

"Understood," CKB acknowledged with disappointment, wishing he were almost anywhere else in the world.

"If she wants some Vitamin D, then give it to her!" His boss growled with frigid authority and glared at CKB like a malfunctioning vehicle. "When you work for me, Cody, you have to be a man! Hell, you have to be more than a man… I've got everything ready to go for Mescal. Get your gear and get out of my sight!"

Templar Drug Territory – Brooklyn, New York

CKB walked with a forlorn expression through the projects of Southeast Brooklyn. Dozens of eager faces surveyed his progress through the streets of the Templar's drug territory. Hector's spies seemed to hover in the space between the real world and that of the dead, eyeing him from basements and rooftops. This quandary was a part of town so corrupt that the residents would disobey the laws of physics if they knew how. The police rarely ventured into the area, and when they did, it was considered a rookie mistake.

A public swimming pool was at the heart of the projects where Hector Mescal liked to relax and conduct business. It had been abandoned by the city long ago as if the ghost of righteousness were exorcised by all the horrid events that took place. After passing through a few natural barricades and checkpoints monitored by the Templars, CKB found himself approaching the infamous swimming pool. There was a rumor that Hector often swam in the blood of those whom he had sentenced to death.

The fence that used to surround the pool had been removed and replaced with a ten-foot wall of concrete blocks. This wall had small portholes through which one might get a glimpse of the pool if they were close enough. One also may have met with the business end of a shotgun for doing the same.

CKB began his approach toward a black gated entrance of the swimming complex with a brown paper bag swinging in his right hand. When he was within fifty yards of the thick steel gate, four men appeared on the asphalt behind him, maintaining the same pace. He glanced backward to see that they were all armed, and ready to cut him down at the first sign of trouble.

Stoney was perspiring as he watched CKB getting escorted by armed men from an alleyway off to the right. His bowels were reporting severe discomfort from an urgent need to relieve himself. The stoic police officer glanced around the area in search of a reprieve, but there seemed to be nothing but low-rent housing. He knelt down on one knee behind a dark green dumpster. The smell of garbage made him want to vomit, and the troubling pressure in his abdomen was causing his legs to shake. Stoney took in deep breaths as his brow began to drip with sweat. The vengeful man thought himself crazy for venturing into this part of town, and the melancholy of regret was enveloping him like a cloud of poisonous smoke. All he had seen for the past few blocks were tattoos, guns and gang colors. If hell had a recreation center, then this would have been its swimming pool.

"What's your business with us, ese?" A Templar enforcer called out to CKB, prompting him to stop walking.

"I've got some flowers for Hector," CKB answered with caution, hoping that this code phrase was still correct. "He needed them from my mother."

The drug enforcer didn't answer, but walked over to CKB and snatched the bag from his right hand. He peered inside at the contents while another enforcer patted their visitor down in search of weapons. When they were satisfied with their search, the men signaled toward the gate and handed the paper bag back to its owner.

CKB watched the gate open as the men near him dispersed from the area. He approached the passageway with pessimism, hearing the sounds of adults frolicking and music playing just beyond the thick concrete. The watchful man sensed all manner of weapons trained on his body from high places and wished that Mitch never gave him this assignment. Upon reaching the gate, he noticed a six-foot-five-inch guard standing near it with his arms folded. Cody's strides quickened as he ambled past the three-hundred-pound muscular gatekeeper, knowing that there was no escaping this place.

The compound was friendlier inside, and CKB hardly noticed the gate when it closed behind him. There were blaring sounds of mariachi musicians, loud talking from a group surrounding the pool, and the occasional splash near the diving board. The whole interior was painted in distinct sandstone colors to mimic the red rocks of Arizona and Utah. It featured flowerbeds with hundreds of desert roses and various species of cacti.

CKB concluded that there were three beautiful women to every man in the facility, making it a misogynist's paradise. Most of the crowd was dancing or drinking as one would expect at any party, but something was amiss. As he glanced around, CKB perceived that there were no less than a dozen lounge chairs, and all of them featured men in their early twenties wearing dark sunglasses. The men were sporting identical bathing suits featuring an orange Aztec sun god symbol embroidered on a white background. Each of them had similar builds, and their haircuts matched as if they were clones.

The career criminal smirked at this deception, having already figured out which was the real Hector. His celebration was short-lived as he saw the gatekeeper following a few steps behind him with his arms folded. CKB did a double take at the bulky enforcer, jumping a bit at the sight of him. The man seemed to grow suspicious of this action, prompting Cody to attempt a more relaxed appearance. He turned his attention back to the men on the lounge chairs and spotted one surrounded by the most attractive and busty women in the area.

"I have something for Hector," Cody said to the behemoth guard, holding up the brown bag for him to inspect.

The gatekeeper stepped up next to CKB and snatched the bag from his hands, almost ripping the indented portions from the top. He looked inside the bag and shuffled the contents about, like a bear nosing around in a trash can. After a thorough search, he pointed a sausage-like finger at CKB, signaling for him to stay put. He then marched over to Hector Mescal with the prize, keeping his back between CKB and his boss. There was a short exchange between the two men, and then the gatekeeper motioned for CKB to approach closer. The defenseless criminal did as instructed, detecting unwholesomeness at the center of his stomach.

"You've got some special Mary Jane for me?" Hector asked from behind his sunglasses as CKB approached the lounge chair. "What's so special about this? I've been smoking it since I was twelve."

"Yeah, but this batch was genetically engineered to have a stronger effect on the brain," CKB stated with conceit, keeping a foot of space between himself and the lounge chair. "Be careful, though, it does leave a bit of residue since it's so potent."

"Is it poisoned?" Hector pried with suspicion, looking up at his guard in disappointment. "Why don't you try some first?"

Without another thought, the gang leader tossed a white marijuana joint at CKB and retrieved a silver Zippo lighter from a glass table. CKB caught the marijuana cigarette in his palm, and the lighter soon followed. He immediately stuck the end of the joint into his mouth and flicked the lighter a few times to ignite the tip, shielding it from the wind. The powerful man took two drags of thick smoke through his teeth and held it in his lungs for a few seconds. After pausing for a satisfactory amount of time, he blew the smoke out in a casual manner. Cody then held the cigarette at his side between the index and middle fingers of his right hand.

"All right! Let's party!" Hector announced in a lustful manner, passing joints to several of the women around him. "Give me my lighter."

CKB tossed the lighter back to Hector, allowing the marijuana cigarette to remain burning between his fingers.

Stoney peered through a square porthole on the west side of the complex, taking pictures with his satellite phone. He could see that CKB was smoking something, and it looked to be an illegal amount. Although he wanted a stronger charge than illegal possession of enough marijuana to distribute; it would be plenty to get even. The police officer could feel his hands shaking from a severe need to use a bathroom. Stoney decided that he would call in the bust and then make his way to the closest public place. He swore at himself for not using the alley but was fearful of getting caught with his pants down by drug dealers.

"Drop the phone and put your hands against the wall, officer." A male voice ordered Stoney from behind.

The Japanese man felt the barrel of a pistol pressing against his spine, and he turned around to see a street thug in a ski mask standing behind him. Stoney put his hands against the wall, horrified about being captured without police dispatch knowing his whereabouts.

CKB found himself swaying to time-honored Mexican music next to the glimmering swimming pool. He glanced down at the ornate patterns within the slabs of sandstone that surrounded the area. They featured engravings with a rich tradition of Aztec symbols from extinct civilizations. The television star watched one of Hector's guards grimace at his boss, and a smirk formed on CKB's face. He turned to surveil Hector, who was smoking with a satisfied expression in his deluxe lounge chair. Unbeknownst to the gang leader, the marijuana joint was gradually turning his mouth and lips green. The lower part of his face now appeared to have been soaked in forest green food coloring.

Cody steadied his body to ensure that the hidden camera on his chest captured Hector smoking and looking like a fool. His stomach became tense as he realized that the most dangerous part of this deception was about to go down. One of the ladies turned to give Hector a kiss, and he grabbed her jaw in a state of shock. The aggressive gang leader twisted his head from side to side, inspecting the green stains all over her mouth and lips.

"Yo, cut the music!" Hector shouted to a group of guards that were near the locker rooms. "Is my mouth green? Is my mouth green?" He asked several bystanders with an expression of betrayal. "What did you give me?" The powerful gangster shouted at CKB, moving with explosive energy to confront him near the pool.

"I didn't give you anything. It's just Mary Jane." CKB contended with a casual expression, holding his arms out to the sides in submission.

"Bulls***, you gave me something!" The fierce gang leader swore at CKB, snapping his fingers at the massive gatekeeper to fetch him a pistol.

"I told you that this stuff is strong, and it leaves a residue on your mouth." Cody proclaimed in his defense, attempting to sound innocent.

"Then why isn't any on your mouth, huh?" Hector redirected with outrage, swaying from side to side in front of CKB as the gatekeeper handed him a black, 9 millimeter semi-automatic pistol. "Why isn't there any on your mouth? Because you're a liar!"

"Look, I didn't smoke as much as you – okay," CKB reported with a troubled stare, watching Hector for any signs of aggression. "The more you smoke; the more it coats your face. It's the strongest pot in the world; what did you expect?"

"I'm gonna' drown you, bro!" Hector shouted as he gripped CKB by the front of his sweatshirt, smearing green residue on the white fabric. "I'm gonna' drown you here and now. You think you can make me look like a punta? Huh? Do think I'm gonna' let you get away with that?" He spat in CKB's face and slugged him hard in the stomach, watching with satisfaction as the man fell to the ground.

"Yo, Hector, I found this cop outside." One of the guards reported as he escorted Stoney to the pool area with a gun at his back. "I think he came with CKB."

"Did you bring a cop to my place?" Hector lamented in a fit of rage, kicking CKB in the stomach several times. "Are you with the pigs now, CKB? What the f*** are you doing, bro?" The gang leader swore again and continued to kick CKB until blood was seeping from his mouth.

Stoney stood stationary with his hands clenched into tight white balls of discomfort. The officer's body had nearly reached its breaking point, and his legs shook with a severe need to empty his bowels. Although he refused to give in to his colon, he knew that there would soon be no other choice. His baseball cap and sunglasses had been confiscated by the thug that caught him, leaving Stoney feeling overexposed under the bright sunshine.

"What are you doing here, cop?" The gang leader asked with outrage and prejudice. "I said what are you doing here, cop?" Hector lost his patience and struck Stoney on the right side of his face with the pistol.

Stoney felt his cheek tear open, and a fresh stream of blood ran down the side of his face from a small cut. He considered himself unfairly prosecuted, despite the situation, and the gang leader had nowhere near as much influence over him as did his bowels. In two quick movements, Stoney ripped the pistol from the gang leader's right hand and turned it upward against the man's jaw.

"I have to s***! I have to s***!" The desperate police officer shouted at the crowd as he took the gang leader hostage. "We're going to the men's room, and if you try to stop me, I'll do more than turn his mouth green." Stoney wrenched Hector in a forceful manner toward the locker rooms, determined to relieve himself.

Over a dozen gang members immediately pointed their weapons at Stoney; a collection of AK-47 rifles, shotguns, and pistols. The gangsters watched in calm silence as the cop dragged their boss toward the men's locker room.

CKB turned onto his side with one hand clutching his stomach to witness this spectacle, unaware that Stoney had followed him. His crazed co-star was now luring the gang into the locker room with their leader held hostage. There was a small army of men following his every step in a tight group. If Stoney were to so much as slip and fall, it would be the end of him.

The desperate police officer stared at the faces of every man that was threatening him with their weapons. He systematically let each of them know that he was serious about murdering their leader. Hector began to struggle under the grip of Stoney's left arm across his abdomen, but the Japanese man shoved the barrel of the pistol harder into his lower jaw. Stoney blinked as they made their way into the locker room, moving out of the sunlight and into the darker, confined space. Something was haunting about the eyes of the men threatening him, and regardless of his accuracy or agility, he couldn't escape the circle of death. This notion caused him to press the pistol deeper into Hector's jaw, leaving red marks all over the man's flesh.

Stoney was dripping sweat with a dire need to use the bathroom, and his body protested with every step. Each time Hector struggled, it was as if his guts were an overinflated animal balloon, and any movement would cause them to burst. He looked with exhaustion at the showers to his left and noticed that the privacy toilets were only a few yards behind him.

CKB remained outside near the pool. He had managed to stand up during the diversion, and his feet were shifting backward in a casual dance of retreat. There was a shotgun just seven feet behind him in a recessed portion of the wall, next to one of the portholes. Most of the people in the area were standing in a crowd around the locker rooms, appearing concerned for Hector's wellbeing. The career criminal knew that there was no better opportunity to procure his freedom than this moment. He saw a white towel on a round patio table just four feet from the defense porthole. His feet shifted in a natural manner until he was able to pick up the towel and use it to dab the blood from his lips.

"What are you doing over there?" A macho guard inquired in an unusually deep voice. "If something happens to Hector, you're going to be dragged behind a car, my friend." The man promised with an aggressive stare as he made his way over to the table where CKB was standing.

"I don't know why that cop followed me," CKB answered in a flustered manner, continuing to wipe his face and arms with the towel. "I just wanted to bring you guys some weed as a gift from my boss Mitch Gentile."

"Yeah, we know who Mitch is; he's the guy that's trying to embarrass all of the competition." The Hispanic man relayed with a clever gaze, allowing his eyes to wander over CKB's body. "Do you have a camera on you? Are you trying to make my boss look like an ass on the Internet?" He tightened his gaze, and his dark brown pupils reflected a person of high intelligence.

"Yep, I've got a hidden camera right here," CKB responded in a bold tone, pointing with his left hand at his right shoulder.

The guard turned his head to take a closer look, and a white patio chair exploded up from the sandstone toward his face. When he lurched backward to dodge the chair, he found his eyes covered by a blood-stained white towel.

Cody had let out a muffled grunt when he raised his left leg to kick the chair at the guard, and his stomach muscles reported back in protest from the beating that he took earlier. The savvy criminal then tossed the towel over his foe's face and twisted his body toward the outer wall. CKB took a few giant strides to the recessed shelf and snatched up the shotgun with both hands. His body then twisted around in an awkward manner as he lowered the shotgun to threaten the guard near him. This action was well-timed as the man had recovered already and was just three feet from pouncing on CKB. Despite this victory, the criminal felt something pop in his right ankle and sensed that he had twisted it too far.

CKB faced the guard with a demeanor of irreverent poise, attempting to conceal the pain that he was feeling. He then gestured with the shotgun toward the gate and jutted his chin out. The guard sneered at him with contempt and folded his arms, refusing to move. CKB dipped the barrel of the shotgun below the man's waist and fired an earsplitting round at the cement between his feet. In a state of shock, the man began to inspect his lower legs and pelvis, feeling grateful that his stance was wide when the gun went off.

Most of the people in the crowd turned their heads and ducked simultaneously, glaring back at CKB like a herd of startled livestock. A few guards started advancing with their weapons but stopped when they saw their comrade in jeopardy.

"Hey, Hector, CKB is getting away. What do you want us to do?" A bearded guard shouted from the pool area to the locker rooms. "He's got Miguel held hostage."

"Hector, CKB is escaping, and he has Miguel as a hostage." Another guard relayed from the entrance of the locker room to his boss.

"Let him go!" Stoney ordered as he kicked backward at an open bathroom stall, being careful not to strain himself.

"Let him go," Hector conceded in a halfhearted tone, hanging his head in shame.

"Hector wants you to let him go!" The guard near the locker room shouted to his comrades and shrugged in a confused manner.

"Thank you, Stoney," CKB whispered under his breath as he moved with his captive to the gate. "Keep your body between me and the guns, or next time it'll be your kneecap." He threatened the clever guard to maintain control of the situation.

CKB slid sideways on the sandstone with his twisted ankle, grimacing with each lateral movement. He was able to prop himself against the wall as the guard fiddled with the gate for a few seconds. After what seemed like five minutes of bumbling, the gate finally swung open.

"Get me to a car," CKB ordered with the shotgun pressed against the guard's head. "You're going to drive me home."

"Close the door," Stoney threatened with a shaky right hand as he aimed the pistol at his adversary's heart.

"Oh, dude, I'm not gonna' be in here wit' you while you do yo' business!" Hector protested with a frown of disgust. "Hell no!"

Stoney unbuttoned his pants with his left hand and unzipped the zipper, feeling his bowels tighten in a way that caused him to grit his teeth. His legs trembled like a massive dog as he peeled off his boxer shorts and lowered himself onto the toilet.

"You have three seconds to close the door, or I'm going to empty this clip into you." The desperate police officer warned with a gaze of pure psychosis. "One. Two."

Hector closed the bathroom stall door, pretending not to notice the disappointed expressions on the faces of his men. He covered his eyes and turned his head to the right as the police officer unleashed his biological payload.

"What should we do?" The massive gatekeeper asked his colleague from their position immediately outside the bathroom stall.

"I'm not sure. We could jump up and shoot him in the head." His senior colleague replied in a muffled voice, grabbing at his short black hair with wild confusion.

"I can hear what you're saying!" Stoney growled in a hateful tone after the whispers echoed over the top of the bathroom stall.

"Don't do anything stupid! You let me handle this!" Hector announced to his men with overcompensated masculinity, trying to regain some dignity.

After several minutes of silence, Stoney felt the relief that he had sought with so much passion. However, the veteran police officer raised his head to recognize the conundrum that his passion had bought him. He sat in a bathroom stall with his pants on the floor, afraid to flush the toilet at the risk of inciting a gun battle.

"What do we do now?" Stoney submitted to Hector with reluctance, unable to figure out a way forward from the madness.

"Are you kidding me, bro?" Hector snapped at him like a bewildered child as he held his nose from the fumes. "Flush the damn toilet! I'm not talking to you with all that…"

Stoney moved the pistol to his left hand and used his right to flush the toilet as requested. There was an unmistakable whooshing sound as the area was cleared of all human waste. Hector raised his head high when this happened and stared at his enemy with discontent.

"Why did you come here?" Hector solicited with a wise stare, seeming noble despite the green residue that covered his mouth and jaw.

"I wanted to get payback on CKB," the officer replied with total honesty, keeping the gun trained on the gang leader. "He's been making a fool of me on our TV show, and I'm sick of looking at his snarky face."

"What TV show?" Hector bemoaned in confusion. "Never mind; we don't watch TV. We entertain ourselves in other ways." The gangster stated with a dismissive wave of his right hand. "Do you really want payback on CKB?"

Stoney nodded in affirmation and leaned backward, hoping that this would come to a peaceful ending.

"Well, I don't need a dead cop around here; it's bad for business," Hector concluded after a moment of consideration. "I tell you what, officer; if you want to walk away from here today, I can make that work. But you need to forget that any of this ever happened."

Stoney glanced down at his naked legs and nodded with enthusiasm to accept this condition.

"Just one thing, though," Hector began by holding up his right index finger in a warning, "if CKB posts any of this on the Internet, then you're done. I don't care if I have to take out everyone at your station; I'll get you. Do you understand?"

"Yes, I understand," Stoney confirmed with reluctance, hoping that CKB wasn't already on his way to doom them. "Can I go?" He asked with a faithful expression, lowering the pistol to his lap.

"Yeah, one second," Hector offered with a smirk for the first time, "I'll have one of my boys give you a sat' phone. If you really want to get back at the man, then call the number on that burner, and we'll work somethin' out."

The police officer felt calm throughout his body and was so satisfied by this result that he offered Hector his left hand to seal the deal.

"Wash your damn hands, man. That's disgusting." The gang leader responded with outrage, turning to unlock the stall door and exit the bathroom. "Peace out, officer."

The Shots Fired Loft – Manhattan, New York

Mike Farr sat on a tall cloth chair behind his desk in the production office portion of the loft. For the past half hour, he had been listening to a wild tale that Stoney was offloading like a hyperactive child. The director kept his fingers pressed together in a pyramid shape and twisted back and forth in his seat. He was clad in a formal black suit with a salmon tie that made him appear approachable.

"So I need to make sure that CKB doesn't upload that video, or we're done!" Stoney reiterated for what must have been the seventh time.

The Japanese police officer used his shaky right hand to drink from an open water bottle that had been left by an intern.

"I haven't seen CKB-" Mike began to repeat himself but was cut off again by the frazzled policeman.

"When is he getting back?" Stoney asked in a rush, gazing at the director with panicked eyes. "I need to stop him from uploading that: these guys aren't screwing around!"

"Yeah, but this can't be the first time that you've been threatened by criminals." The director chastised with a subtle grin, attempting to jar Stoney's sense of pride. "I mean, what is so different about these guys?"

"The Templars? Are you serious?" The officer replied with a stare of betrayal and dumbfounded shock. "These guys are...the guys that you should fear. Look, there is what we call a tradecraft criminal, and then there are real psychopaths. This is a hornet's nest...that I might be able to survive, but I don't want to find out." Stoney finished with a disgusted scowl and raised his hands in the air as though Mike were the manifestation of incompetence.

"Okay, I know that CKB is at the hospital having his ankle looked at," Mike offered with a hint of mistrust. "We'll make sure that video doesn't get published." The director turned left in his chair and crossed one leg over the other. "I'm glad you're all right. We'll get this handled. On another topic, we have your big reveal coming up in the next few days."

"Oh, Mike, I can't do that right now." The Japanese man protested with a wave of his left hand as he set the empty water bottle on the desk.

"Look, I know you had a tough day, Stoney," Mike waxed sympathetic with a Hollywood smile. "But let's get serious here; you've had much worse in your years of law enforcement. And I know that this isn't something that is easy for you to reveal to the public, but that's why we have contracts. If you don't go through with this, and put forth some showmanship, then I'll sue you for breach of contract. In other words, you'll get nothing for your time on this show, and we'll go after your wages – maybe even your pension."

"You really are a snazzy little prick of an opportunist," Stoney patronized with a demeanor of pride and hostility. "Fine, I'll be your dancing bear for one episode." He lamented with a blistering sneer and stood up to make an exaggerated exit from the office.

"Stoney, I just want to remind you that your contract prevents you from taking any personal actions against me." The television guru announced with a twisted smile, failing to maintain a poker face.

The exhausted officer turned abruptly and raised his right hand toward the director in a handgun pantomime. He then fanned his left thumb repeatedly over the top of his right thumb like a gunfighter of the old west. This gesture was fast enough to force Mike to hold his breath, and he exhaled with the caution of a nuclear engineer upon seeing that it was a joke.

"That's how fast action can be taken on the streets." The tormented police officer whispered to his colleague with an unexpected sadness in his eyes. "You don't have time for paperwork in those moments. You only hope that you're alive to do the paperwork later."

Mike nodded to show respect and felt guilty for misreading the alpha protector.

Pier 94 – Hell's Kitchen, New York

Litz let her long brunette hair hang loose atop the smooth wood of a public picnic table. Her body was stretched across the extended burgundy planks in a relaxed pose as she discussed the mysteries of the universe with her friend Oslo Norway. There was a folded, brown paper sack on the table next to her right hip along with a half-empty bottle of water. She had gone for a run earlier in the day wearing black tights and an oversize pink T-shirt, which were now somewhat damp with sweat.

Her longtime friend and mentor, Oslo Norway, had been named as such by his parents since his birth had disrupted their plans to travel to that city. Litz didn't know the man's last name but was aware that he had been homeless from the age of sixteen.

Oslo sat on the edge of a pier just ten feet from where Litz was resting. His full beard seemed rugged and natural in the presence of the Hudson River. He was swinging his feet in the cool water as the sun warmed his pale, hairy legs. Oslo wore a red 'Sunshine State' T-shirt that someone had discarded long ago, and a pair of gray cargo pants that were rolled up to each knee.

"Do you ever wish that you had kids, Oslo?" Litz wondered aloud as she stared up at the clear skies above New York.

"Yep, the ransom money would do me good." The homeless man said in jest without interrupting his playtime in the water. "I could live like a king for a few months if I got past the FBI."

"What is it about a man that makes them occasionally necessary?" She asked with an innocent smile.

"Sometimes you just want someone there…to wash your windshield," Oslo redirected in a positive tone. "I tried it last week on Broadway, but those people have no sense of humor. The ambulance driver told me to let him pass and didn't offer me a tip."

"Why did my mother die?" The volatile woman questioned in a sad way, pushing her chin closer to her chest.

"You know why," he replied in a more serious tone and turned to confirm the expression of pain on her face. "There was no good explanation, Litz; it was her time."

"You're not going to leave me, are you Oslo?" She teased her friend with the innocent voice of a 1920s movie star.

"I might if you keep asking these stupid questions," Oslo answered with a roll of his eyes as if the river were listening. "There's nothing to worry about, Litz, I'm forty-three-years-old."

"What happened to your dog?" Litz inquired as she raised her head from the picnic table and sat facing the sunlight.

"He got laid," Oslo responded with a shrug. "I guess that b**** had more to offer him than me, but I keep a plate handy for him. Are they gonna' just stand there all afternoon?" The man inquired as he rolled his left hand into a fist and pointed his index finger at her security guards.

Litz turned toward her security detail with the poise of an adventurous celebrity and placed her feet atop one of the benches. There were two men in navy blue suits that stood over twenty feet from where she and Oslo were talking. They remained silent and watched the surrounding areas, facing in opposite directions.

"Oh, that's just bulky Kevin and William," she said in a casual manner and reached down to take a sip from her water bottle. "All female stars of the television show get a security detail when we're filming during the week. There have been a few overzealous fans. What do you make of people these days, Oslo?"

"I think they're amazing and warm," he retorted with a wide smile. "Everyone has been so generous and open with opportunities. Nobody is greedy, heartless or shallow. I walked into town the other day and this guy said, 'Here, have a job; you seem to need one.'"

"Wow, that is amazing!" Litz erupted with a genuine chuckle. "I love how they are – out in traffic. There is so much warmth, and not a hint of hubris among them. They're so caring and full of life. One man even offered to take me home the other night. Isn't that sweet?"

"Yeah, I've found that ample-chested women usually have a hard time finding their way home," Oslo confirmed with a nod. "There are always twenty or thirty men that insist on getting you safely to your door, whether you like it or not. It's like that rap music they play late at night about women like you. They're always talking about your personality and intelligence – in complex metaphors, of course."

"It's all far too complicated for us to understand," Litz expressed with a smile.

"Yes, we'll never get the lonely nuances of the aggressive orange collar male." The bearded man added with a slight chuckle as he stood up from the river and walked toward his shoes.

Litz jumped down from the picnic table and snatched the brown paper bag from its surface. She was careful to remove a sandwich wrapped in cellophane from within the bag, which she presented to her friend.

"I told you not to feed me!" Oslo argued as he slapped the sandwich out of her hand and watched it land near the edge of the river. "You know that I need to stay strong to survive. I can't be depending on anyone."

"It's just one sandwich," the idealistic woman conveyed with apologetic eyes, appearing heartbroken by this rejection. "I wanted to show my gratitude."

"Well, don't show your gratitude to me!" He growled with a callous expression, turned on his heel, took a few steps and began to put on his shoes. "Look, Litz, I think you're a dynamite gal, but don't cheapen our friendship with gestures. You and I…are better than that."

"Yes, we are," she agreed with tears streaming down her face. "But I thought that-"

Oslo got to his feet and began to stomp away, but stopped after a few steps and turned back toward the erratic woman. He then sighed with fatherly exasperation and approached Litz with his arms outstretched, giving her a loving hug. Litz could smell his foul body odor, and his beard scratched her face, yet the television star enjoyed the embrace like a spiritual awakening. She started to weep in the midst of their closeness, but Oslo shook the diva to make her stop.

"Your mother would be proud of you, Litz Rack." Oslo foretold with a righteous tone of voice. "And I'm proud of you."

Litz became lost in this embrace despite the snickers that echoed from her security detail. She felt that Kevin and William were remiss in their prejudices, and asserted that men like Oslo were invisible to them.

V. Deviled and Overeasy

"Have you seen CKB?" Stoney asked the key grip on his way to the formal area of the set.

The bewildered employee responded with a shrug as though refusing to claim guardianship of the criminal. He clutched a camera rigging tight in his left hand and departed from the desperate police officer toward the living room. Stoney saw the dietician moving along the hardwood flooring of the hallway toward the kitchen and pointed his right index finger at her, preparing to ask a question.

"No, man, I haven't seen CKB!" The tall, blonde woman blurted out before Stoney began to speak.

Stoney grimaced and patted down the tufts of hair that were sticking up from the back of his head. He glanced down at his white long underwear and gathered that his results may have been better if he had freshened up and gotten dressed.

"I saw CKB earlier this morning," an eighteen-year-old intern declared as he stood with his left shoulder against the hallway wall in a forced pose, attempting to be mysterious.

"Did he say where he was going?" Stoney assimilated with reluctance and took the bait. "Do you know where he went?"

"He was headed to..." The young man paused and sighed at his coworker, displaying an expression of longing. "You know, I always help you guys with all of these crappy tasks, and you never pay attention to me, and rarely say thank you."

"Well, what do you want?" The officer asked in an irritated tone, biting his lip and resisting the urge to make a fist with his right hand.

"I want you to put in a good word with the director for me," the teenager requested with a snarky smile. "It's time for me to move up in the world."

"Fine, fine," the Japanese man agreed in a hesitant manner, showing off a disgusted gaze. "Where did he go?"

"He went down to the park to stretch out his sprained ankle," the intern touted in a coy manner, nodding at the floor like a rock star.

"And…you're fired," Mike chimed in with an aggressive handshake to the intern as he darted between the youthful man and Stoney. "What are you waiting for? You're done. Get your stuff. Get out!" The director reprimanded in an elite manner, delivering his messages before the teenager could speak. "Security, please escort this young man – I don't know his name. Just get him out of the building. He tried to extort one of my actors." Mike turned to a security guard on the set and bid farewell to the intern before pivoting back to Stoney. "So talk to me, big daddy, I thought we had this all worked out." His posture became friendlier as he put his arm around the policeman and began walking him toward the kitchen. "I told you that I took care of the video situation, so why are you trying to track down CKB?"

"I can't trust you on this one, and I sure as hell can't trust CKB," Stoney protested with aggression, pointing his right index finger at the director's chest.

The director paused and looked down at the sleek black jacket of his pinstripe suit to wipe away some dust from the right sleeve. He took a bit longer to straighten his gold tie and seemed to be considering what Stoney had said.

"Yeah, but if you did get the camera from CKB, there's no way you'd know if he had another copy of the video somewhere." Mike confided with a sober smile, trying to help his talent cool off and relax. "Look, I've got a big announcement today, and NASA has sent a group of caterers to surprise us with an amazing meal...or allegedly an amazing meal. It probably sucks; I won't lie."

"That's a first," Stoney grumbled with his arms folded in a disenchanted pose. "Look, dude, I won't let this drop until I get to talk with CKB, okay? So get us in a room together, and I'll stop poking around your little...whatever you call it here."

"Is that what you're wearing for the show tonight?" The director critiqued with a pouty exhale from his lips. "This is New York, and you're in television now, officer. Let's put on some clothing that doesn't scream poverty to the world."

"I want my meeting," the Japanese man reiterated in a forceful manner, breathing heavily through his nose.

"Okay, done. Just get out of those...rags." Mike accepted with a perturbed glare and shook his head in disgust. "Please get a shower too, the NASA people will be here soon. I'll call CKB and get your meeting. That video is not going on the Internet."

"Jazzy's in the shower...again," Stoney said with a chuckle as he departed from the kitchen toward his bedroom.

"I'm gonna' have to add our water bill to her contract." The director muttered to no one in particular, gripping the back of his head with malcontent.

"Give it back to me, Richard!" Litz cried out from the hallway as cameraman Doug filmed her from the right. "My mother gave that to me! It's all I have left!" The tormented plumber shouted through the thick wood of her co-star's bedroom door. "Don't barricade yourself in there like a coward. Come out and be a man!" She pleaded with building rage as tears streamed down her face.

'What's going on?' Jennifer Priest mouthed to Doug from off camera, gesturing toward Litz with her right hand. The cameraman shook his head and shrugged with caution as if to avoid shaking the camera. 'It's good TV; just keep filming.' The producer cheered in silence with a thumbs-up from her right hand, inspiring expressions of disbelief from her team members. She then made her way to the kitchen for a scheduled announcement.

"Richard, I'll give you a gold coin for that frog; I swear to God," Litz submitted with a defeated expression.

"Oh, look, I just accidentally ripped the head off," Richard teased in a callous voice, "and the little Styrofoam pellets inside are spilling all over the place."

"Richard! If you don't give that frog back to me right now, I'm going to rip this door down and use it to crush you!" Litz screeched in an operatic tone, hitting notes that were audible throughout the complex.

Members of the camera crew shook their heads when she screamed, showing genuine concern for her mental state.

"Do you know what I'll do to you if you destroy that?" She threatened in an almost demonic voice with her mouth next to the doorframe, feeling ashamed when some spittle dripped to the floor. "Do you have to film me right now?" Litz turned and interrogated the camera crew with a shameful demeanor. "Seriously, right now?"

Richard opened the door a few inches and was amazed when Litz slammed her right shoulder into it several times. He backed away and let the door come open to avoid injuring her body. She moved toward him like an enraged spirit in a horror movie, and the camera crew followed behind her in a religious fashion. The bashful conservative felt shocked by her ferocious attitude and fell backward with an unexpected bounce on the corner of his bed.

"I'll give you a silver coin and a gold coin," the intense woman proposed with a hurtful expression as tears dripped from her cheeks onto his black microfiber shirt.

Litz was wearing a formfitting white dress, but it didn't stop her from climbing atop the shy conservative. The ethical man squirmed in his tight black jeans when she squeezed his chest with her hands as if to beg for mercy. Richard looked down at the frog and then up at the face of his adversary. She seemed innocent and vulnerable at the moment, and he acknowledged her love for the strange heirloom.

The eager Republican reacted with instant remorse from this display of emotions. While it felt good to knock Litz off of her soapbox for a few seconds, he had no intention of wounding her to such an extent. She reminded him of a fierce beast in the wild, with the penetrating eyes of something that refused to give up, but had no alternative. Her gaze pleaded with him in vain, and he saw something more beautiful than ever before in his lifetime.

"Give me the coins tomorrow. I didn't do anything to damage your frog." The compassionate man gave in with a sudden feeling of inner peace, wishing that the camera crew hadn't been there to cheapen the moment.

Richard raised his right hand from his waist in a ceremonial fashion and returned the small stuffed frog to the plumber. Litz reached for the frog with tenderness and reverence, breathing in with relief when it touched her skin. She got up from the bed and turned the object over in her hands like it was a rare treasure.

The satisfied conservative also got to his feet and joined her in admiring the simple toy. It was an unremarkable frog with long, rectangular paint on its eyes and small webbed feet made of felt. Litz massaged it in her hands as though it were conjuring up a time in her life of great sorrow and joy.

"Get out!" Richard scorned the camera crew with a wicked stare from his pure blue eyes. "You got your footage; now get out!" He repeated without hesitation and ushered the men away from his bedroom before closing the door.

Richard then stepped up behind Litz and put his arms around her soft, feminine stomach in a silent apology. She clasped her free hand over his masculine hands in acceptance of the gesture.

"Harry got up…dressed all in black." [1] Jazzy sang along with a recording of The Eagles that was playing from her personal stereo in the corner of the bathroom. "Went down to the station…and he never came back." [2]

---

[1] Henley, Don. *New York Minute.* © 1989, 1994. The Eagles.

[2] Henley, Don. *New York Minute.* © 1989, 1994. The Eagles.

Fassim used a butter knife to slide the bathroom door open and proceeded inside with her phone set in video record mode. She knew that a video of Jazzy singing in the shower would yield big money, especially from such a well-known song. The crafty Muslim pulled an orange hijab tight around her head, straightened her eyeglasses, and returned the butter knife to the left pocket of her beige pantsuit. She then crept in a clandestine manner toward the shower, keeping her satellite phone ready for action. After a few steps, Fassim's feet began to slip, and she tried to balance herself by grabbing the toilet, but the floor was too slick. The photographer felt her feet shoot out from under her in a whoosh of energy, causing her back to slam against the white porcelain tiles.

"Oh, I said, somebody going to emergency; somebody's going to jail." [3] Jazzy sang as she threw the shower curtain aside to catch her assailant in a compromising position. "Did you know that tiles become really slick when you coat them with industrial soap and water? Well, look at what we have here; it's a sat' phone." The wrathful comedian reached down past the shower curtain and scooped up Fassim's satellite phone from the floor. "This is an expensive sat' phone." She relayed with a smirk, holding the unit between her index finger and thumb. "Well, I guess you can't prosecute me for destroying property, huh?" Jazzy dropped the red satellite phone into the basin of the shower and watched it become submerged in water with elation.

"You know what, Jazzy?" Fassim replied with a wounded scowl, trying to maintain her composure despite the pain in her back. "A real comedian…would have said something hilarious just now, but I guess that's why you're a reality TV star instead."

---

[3] Henley, Don. *New York Minute.* © 1989, 1994. The Eagles.

"Close the door," Jazzy berated with a roll of her eyes. "The weather forecast predicts perverted men with a high chance of catcalls. There's also a high douchebag index today, so you better wear a darker headscarf." She finished with authority, pretending to drop a microphone by letting a bar of soap fall from her left hand in a dramatic display. "Get out and let me shower in peace!" The diva issued a final warning before clutching the shower curtain and flinging it shut. "In a New York minute...everything can change." [4] She continued to mock her rival through lyrical bliss.

Canarsie Park – Brooklyn, New York

CKB traversed through the park with a noticeable limp, having ignored Petunia's advice to get a walking stick. His body was a bit too warm clad a black hoodie and faded blue jeans. Cody moved with meticulous determination, knowing that a predator was watching the children, and he had to do something. The career criminal felt grateful toward Stoney for being a man under pressure during his confrontation with Hector. But he presumed that it was a fleeting moment at best, and wouldn't expect kindness in the future.

"Why didn't you take this guy down when you were healthy?" He asked himself as the asphalt parking lot and concrete paths gave way to trees and swing sets.

---

[4] Henley, Don. *New York Minute.* © 1989, 1994. The Eagles.

It had taken a labor of passion for CKB to make it to the park, but he was glad that the journey wasn't wasted, noting that his target was right on schedule. He made his way to the wrought iron fence that enveloped the play area and craned his thick neck at the creepy German stranger, attempting to get the man's attention. Cody licked his dry lips at the onset of raw pain from his wounded right ankle and considered his options.

The short, pale German turned toward CKB with a sudden and intense stare of hatred. He watched the black man with the contempt of a sociopath and shook his head, signaling a possible retreat.

CKB smiled at the odd stranger and made a fist with his right hand. He then slammed the fist into the palm of his left hand and wrapped his free fingers over the knuckles.

"Jimmy, come here!" A startled mother called out to a four-year-old boy that was playing in the sandbox just ten feet from where CKB was standing. "Get away from that man! He's not having a good day."

The thirty-one-year-old blonde mother stepped with aggressive poise through the sandbox to position herself between CKB and her child. She then pulled out a satellite phone and twisted her head so that the agitator could see her making a call. In another protective move, she escorted her little boy away from the sandbox, causing a little girl near him to cry and hold up her hands. CKB bit his lip when he saw the youngster lose her playmate for the day.

'Bye-bye,' the self-righteous German mouthed to CKB as the mother's actions began to influence the situation.

CKB was thunderstruck by this development and wanted to accuse the woman of racism, but he knew better. His threatening actions near the children had been less than glowing. The mothers would alert the local police, and they would be keeping an eye out for him in the future.

"Unbelievable," CKB stated to an empty corner of the sandbox, keeping his eyes fixed on the predator that stood across from him.

He leaned back with his hands still clasping the iron railing. Every muscle in his body wanted to stay and protect the children, but it wasn't a part of town where the police would show him any kindness. CKB let his fingers slip from the railing in a slow and humiliating defeat. He turned his back on the children, despite knowing that something terrible could soon take place.

His defeat worsened with every step, and the criminal hung his head. The pain from his twisted ankle was now like the wailing of children screaming for his help. He thought of the horrid disappointment exhibited by the little girl in the sandbox and presumed that the stranger could evoke despair a hundred times darker. In a moment of inspiration, he fished a satellite phone from his right pocket and dialed a recent contact from his list of friends.

"Hey, Petunia, how you doin', baby?" CKB began with a smooth tone of voice, despite the pain in his foot. "Yeah, I'm sorry I haven't called you. No, no, I've been busy. Look, I need a favor... No, this is somethin' important to me. Look, just listen, I need you to take your lunch hour at Canarsie Park every day. It would be great if you could keep an eye on the kids... No, I don't have any kids. Look, I just need someone to keep an eye on these kids. Okay, you're gonna' be like that? Fine, we're done! 'bye!" He ended the phone call with a contemptible sigh, wishing that someone could understand what he was trying to get done.

The Shots Fired Loft – Manhattan, New York

"I'd like to propose a toast to our friends from NASA for providing this scrumptious catered meal," Mike Farr pandered to the television cameras like a bonafide Hollywood peacock. "And although none of it falls into my current diet, I'm sure that no aliens were harmed in the making of this food." The director quipped as he stood tall in his black designer pinstripe suit with a gold tie.

With the exception of CKB, every other member of the Shots Fired in the Melting Pot cast was present in the kitchen for the director's announcement. While they had delayed fifteen minutes to give him a call, the cast and crew decided to proceed without the career criminal. Litz was wearing her formfitting white dress, and Richard stood at her left in his black microfiber shirt and jeans of the same color. Fassim had changed into an American flag hijab that stood out from her navy blue pantsuit, and Jazzy was clad in a red cocktail dress with matching high heels. Stoney had gotten the director's approval by exhibiting a sleek black suit with a dark blue tie. And Jennifer Priest wore an elegant light blue, floor-length gown.

"I wanted everyone to be here today as I announce that we'll be filming on location in Houston, Texas with the fine people of NASA," Mike continued in a robust voice. "Our popular cast members will be hosting a fundraiser for NASA to help them get the Mars mission off the ground. We'll be given exclusive tours and VIP access to the space shuttles and other equipment, in preparation for the upcoming mission to the moon. This mission, of course, is in advance of a more exhilarating second mission to Mars. On behalf of the Shots Fired crew, we look forward to being your honored guests – at least for the first day. After that, I'm sure we'll have the same naughty antics that make our show one of the highest rated in the country. So without further delay, I'd like to kick off this party and welcome you all to get full…of booze." He finished with a debonair wink and grinned at the sound of obligatory applause.

Litz noticed a handsome astronaut that stood out from the others in the NASA group. The forty-two-year-old man had a distinct swagger, and something about him screamed for her attention. She wandered over to the mysterious stranger in her best impression of Scarlett from the film Gone With The Wind. Richard held his breath as he observed the gratuitous pursuits of his co-star. The conservative knew that Litz was flocking to the astronaut based on the cut of his jib, but elected to ignore this event, surmising that the man was hardly a stuffed frog.

CKB entered the room with a moody expression, and upon seeing the catered event, wished that he could limp to the solitude of his bedroom. Stoney noticed his adversary and nearly knocked Jennifer Priest over when his feet trudged forward to the entryway of the loft. Mike Farr saw the police officer approaching CKB and excused himself from a boring conversation with a NASA physicist, signaling the producer to take his place. He pushed air through his nose like a bull snorting at a bullfighter, hoping that the men could play nice until he got to them.

"Where's that video?" Stoney questioned his co-star with a desperate expression. "I've been looking all over for you, and need to get that video for the Templars, or we're both done."

"Look, man, I'm not in the mood to do this right now," CKB growled at his interrogator, giving off the social signals of a desperate man. "Shouldn't you be like – face down in a donut somewhere? Or maybe shooting your gun at cartoon crooks that never move?"

"Okay, that's enough," Mike interrupted as the men stared at one another with malignant disdain, "let's go to my office. Come on, CKB, you asked me to handle this thing, and now I'm getting it done."

Stoney grimaced at the director for taking the side of his natural enemy, and something changed in the way he carried himself. The police officer seemed volatile and filled with distrust. Mike placed his hand on CKB's shoulder, but the man shrugged him off and limped toward the office like a rebellious teenager. The Japanese authority figure felt wounded as he followed behind Mike and CKB. There were explosions of doubt in his mind that resembled the cavitations of heated steam in a nuclear power plant – melting down without any coolant.

"I'm glad you guys are doing this," Mike began as he watched the two men enter his office and closed the door, "it's important to get things-" The director went silent when he noticed that Stoney had drawn his pistol and was pointing it between CKB's eyes.

"The video; now!" Stoney exclaimed with his head tilted forward in a macho display of control.

"What are you gonna' do, cop?" CKB challenged with his arms extended to take up space on both sides. "Have you lost yo' mind, Cracker Jack? It looks like you let Hector get into your head."

"Is that right?" The policeman asserted by sticking out his chest at the criminal. "Hector is going to do us both if I don't get that video back to him. Besides, I don't know why this is on me; it's your fault for uploading all of those videos. You can't be making an ass of every thug in the city. Eventually, it's going to be..."

"Well, we all gotta' die of somethin'." The criminal boasted in a childish manner, dipping his right wrist down a bit to emphasize his point. "Maybe we should die right here."

"Okay, that's enough!" Mike intervened with authority, raising his hands and shaking them in annoyance. "You guys need to start saying something concrete, and stop posturing, or I'm gonna' push us all out the window."

CKB smirked at the director for his attempt at mimicking a street gangster and began to chuckle. Stoney had a similar reaction, and both men shared a glance of streetwise solidarity. They smirked at Mike as though he were a domesticated dog that was trying to threaten the hounds of hell. Stoney lowered his pistol and began to laugh heartily, and CKB soon joined in as their nervous energy dissipated.

"I'll tell you what, brother," CKB touted with a gaze of genuine affection, "you helped me get out of a tough spot the other day, so I'll help you out. If you get your boys in blue to watch the kids at Canarsie Park for the next couple of days, then that video won't make it anywhere."

"Why do you want us to watch the kids at the park?" Stoney inquired with a puzzled expression.

"Because the kids are very entertaining; they're like an improv group on Broadway. Does it matter?" The criminal reasoned with a hint of sarcasm and disbelief.

Stoney and Mike exchanged bewildered glances, having been unaware that their colleague possessed such depth.

"Okay, I'll go with that for now, but we need to talk again when we get to Houston." The Japanese officer agreed with a sigh of relief.

"Wait, why are we going to Houston?" CKB asked with a look of surprise.

"Mike can explain all of that, but let's talk again soon," Stoney conveyed with a smooth voice, reaching out with his left hand toward CKB.

The director watched CKB hesitate and felt that the fragile peace in his office was in danger of fading away. But the criminal reached up and took Stoney's outstretched hand, and their eyes met with the masculine version of a smile. Mike exhaled with renewed confidence in this delicate balance between the men and retreated to the party with a grin.

Litz devoured the astronaut using a pair of wild eyes and strutted forward with her right hand wrapped around her stomach. She hit him with a smile first but pulled away after a two-second count to keep it playful.

"Everything looks delicious, doesn't it?" The audacious brunette flirted with blatant desire. "My name is Litz Rack." She continued and stood tall in her white high heels to appear statuesque, lowering her right hand in a dainty way to invite their first contact.

"Oh my hell, you're Litz Rack!" The middle-aged man responded almost a second too late. "I've seen you on the show - you're hilarious. My name is Jason Harrington." He said and gave a weak tug to her hand.

'Game, set, match.' The disenchanted woman thought to herself as the astronaut exposed his soft white underbelly. She gazed at his gray suit and crimson tie, assuming that the body underneath may have been worth exploring. Litz decided to radio his manhood again to check for signs of intelligent life. Although the terrain looked inviting, it would be a short stay if there were no one with whom to discuss her travels.

"You know what I've been craving all week?" She offered with a wicked grin, feeling her body heat up in the most wonderful places.

"I don't know…probably chocolate." The astronaut answered with a blank stare, proving that he was no rocket scientist in the bedroom.

"Look, I've gotta' go, there's this thing I have to do for some starving children," Litz fibbed with an incredulous stare. "It was nice meeting you. Please tell your mother hi for me."

Jason seemed amused and clueless as the dashing beauty abandoned him to talk with the other NASA visitors. She began counting the number of seconds that it would take for him to realize the opportunity he had just lost. The man scratched his head for almost a minute, pretending to listen to a female colleague as he considered what Litz had to say. When his mind finished piecing together the hidden meanings of her flirtations, Jason's eyes locked onto the shaggy, gray carpet beneath him. He then slowly moved his gaze up her luscious body and closed his eyes for several seconds in anguish.

'And we have lift off,' Litz chuckled to herself as she maneuvered to the far side of the kitchen where Richard was hiding next to the catered food.

"Nobody's touching it," Richard reported to his co-star as she joined him in a quiet corner of the room.

"I know what you mean," the diva replied in a devilish fashion, wishing that she wasn't wasting her best lines on such fence posts. "It's frustrating, but you can survive if you have the right kind of rabbit."

Richard watched her like a teenager who just got assigned to be her science partner for the day. Litz looked down at the Texas food that littered the long table near the outer wall of the complex. Everything was either fried or covered in corn and chunks of red and green peppers. There was almost nothing on the tablecloth that a New Yorker would consider being good social fare.

"Do you hear that?" Litz asked her co-star with a coy smile and leaned closer to the table of catered food. "There's something coming from over there."

Richard leaned forward to listen near the table and closed his eyes to tune out distractions from the party. When he inched closer to the food, something bounced off the right side of his neck and again across the tip of his nose. The film editor opened his eyes to see Litz holding a plate of fried shrimp near her chest and flinging the breaded appetizers at his face. His body went numb with excitement as he checked the room to see if anyone was objecting to this behavior. But the barrage of shrimp kept coming, and the enthusiastic man felt obligated to pick up a tray of breaded veal to mount a defense.

Mike Farr pursed his lips together when he saw Richard and Litz battling each other with the catered food. The director held his breath and watched the NASA people for a moment, deciding that it was too late to ask the actors to behave. Joseph Kerr, the Vice President of Operations for NASA, watched the impromptu food fight with intrigue and began to giggle when witnessing Litz Rack at her jovial best. Mike brought forth a savvy business smile after reading this reaction, feeling grateful that the food would be of use to someone.

When Litz ran out of shrimp, she used the empty aluminum tray to shield herself from flying cutlets of veal. Her eyes scanned the table to a plate of more than a dozen caramel apples, and she grinned with childish anticipation. Richard was out of veal cutlets and decided to pick up a red plastic rack of hard-shell tacos from the far end of the table. His female co-star grabbed a caramel apple by the wooden dowel that stuck out from its center, which caused the whole plate to slide off of the table. Litz shrugged and dropped to her knees as lettuce, tomatoes, and taco meat rained down upon her from the opposite end of the kitchen.

Jennifer Priest stood with her mouth agape as she watched the two adults engaging in a food fight, and felt a piece of taco shell bounce off of her hair. She blew air out of her mouth in a haughty manner, and was about to yell at the television stars, but the director signaled her to let them alone. The producer raised her eyebrows at Mike Farr as if to ask if he was certain, and received back a wink from his right eye. Jennifer returned her gaze to the kitchen and saw Litz trying to hit Richard in the head by lobbing caramel apples at him. She then snapped her fingers, signaling for cameraman Doug to capture the moment with his equipment.

Litz was running out of caramel apples as she dodged the onslaught of taco fodder that fell from above. She inspected the table for something with more texture and found a fruit salad covered in whipped cream. The lively woman ran to the table like a comic book villain toward the decorative, red glass serving bowl of fruit salad. Richard noticed that Litz was upgrading her arsenal and tossed the four remaining tacos from the tray all at once.

Litz had maneuvered through the taco onslaught as well as her dress would permit, but not without getting tomato squares between her breasts and chunks of beef under her collar. She sidled up next to the hefty bowl of fruit salad and slid it to the edge of the table. Richard dropped the empty taco tray and snatched up a medium-sized silver bowl of pudding. He scooped up some of the chocolate pudding and whipped cream into a trembling mound in his right palm. The excited man then waited to look Litz in the eyes, and she obliged him with an adventurous scowl.

The feisty plumber tossed a black plastic serving spoon out of the fruit salad when she saw Richard manhandling the pudding. As her right hand plunged into the fruit salad, Richard pelted her with thick droplets of chocolate filling. She felt a stinging sensation as some pudding got caught in her right eyelash, but most of it hit the abdominal section of her white dress. The unabashed woman refused to back away and flung a softball-sized wad of fruit salad at her co-star. Her first shot covered the left side of Richard's face, forcing him to set down the bowl of pudding and clean out his eye.

All of the NASA executives and staff had crowded into the living room behind the safety of the sofa and were enjoying the spectacle. Cameraman Doug was sending everything to the network television feed as he filmed the comical exchange.

Litz surmised that Richard was unarmed, and took advantage of the situation by pelting him in rapid fashion with wads of fruit salad. She closed in on his position and continued to hit the conservative with accuracy. In a final aggressive move, Litz scooped up two handfuls of the sticky material and used her fingers to rub it into Richard's hair and all over his face.

"Oh my gosh; I'm so sorry!" She exclaimed with a reddening face and hysterical laughter. "Here, let me help you."

Spectators were enjoying the show with mixed reactions from the living room; most of which involved uncontrollable laughter. Litz grabbed a towel from the table and began to clear off sections of Richard's face. She couldn't help laughing at the man because he looked sad and cute with his eyes covered in marshmallows and whipped cream. Richard wore a boyish gaze of rebellious satisfaction as his co-star cleared the mess from his eyes and cheeks. Litz admired him with considerable affection for shedding his formal mask and leaned in for a passionate kiss.

Everyone in the loft went quiet at the same moment as the two natural rivals engaged in unexpected romance. The frenzied woman enjoyed the softness of Richard's eyes as her lips met his, but the taste of fruit salad was overwhelming. She gave him a rough embrace and drank in a moment of elation with her co-star, attacking his mouth with selfish indulgence. Although the kiss lasted just a few seconds, it seemed to make up for weeks of lost intimacy. Litz realized that the room had gone as silent as a church, and felt the eyes of the world bearing down upon her. She pushed against Richard's chest with both hands in a display of rejection. The diva then straightened her arms at the elbow, seeming to awaken from a dream. Litz turned toward the small crowd to her right and saw the power of her actions reflected in their awkward faces.

The confused woman closed her eyes with disbelief and dropped to her knees in shame. She hung her head and stared down at the messy white tiles of the kitchen floor. After taking a proper moment to reflect, Litz followed an impulse to punch her co-star between the legs. Richard, and those who witnessed the events in the loft, all seemed to gasp at the same moment. The incapacitated man gazed at his co-star in shock and fell sideways onto the serving table, knocking it over against the wall.

Litz brought her hands up to her mouth in dismay and shook her head, exhibiting vulnerable embarrassment. She looked to Mike Farr and Jennifer Priest with an awestruck demeanor, seeming to ask them what she had just done.

VI. Sloppy Bird

"You know, we all do things that we don't like, Jazzy," Mike Farr massaged his actor from across the room, keeping his hands flat on a dark walnut desk. "I remember a time when I had to go to a Mötley Crüe concert, and there were tons of screaming metalheads – it wasn't a good fit." He leaned back in his padded black leather chair and stared at the ceiling of his office.

"I thought you were around thirty-nine?" Jazzy surmised after a bit of calculation, raising her tearful face to confront the director. "If you went to a Mötley Crüe concert, that would make you around fifty."

"Look, I don't really remember who the artist was..." Mike remarked with a posture of cynicism. "Stop trying to take the focus off of yourself. We have a contract that says you'll be sharing a specific story with our audience. If you don't share that story, then I'll bring out the recording that we have on file from when you auditioned for the show. And then I'll take legal action against you for breach of contract. Besides, you know the bounty for winning at the end of the season, right? Whoever has the most value in coins by the time the show runs its course gets the three-million-dollar prize."

"Why do you have to be so cold to me, Mike?" She pleaded with a sullied demeanor. "There are hundreds of stories that I'd be more than happy to share on your show. This one happens to be very-"

"Exactly!" Mike concurred with a snap of his fingers. "It is very, which is what makes it very… If we decide to use a story with less emotion, then we lose an important and unintelligent modifier. I want people to describe this story the same way that you're describing it now. When they see our episode that night, they need to walk away and say, 'that was very…' Do you understand?"

"No, I really don't feel comfortable-" Jazzy started to elaborate but was cut off by her colleague.

"Okay, I'm going to bring the war hammer down on you then," he threatened with a blank stare, trying to maintain control of the conversation. "Do you think that you're the only one on this show who has to share something painful from their past? All five of your co-stars signed the same contract as you, and they'll be giving us the gritty details of their most painful experiences. I need you to understand that you don't have a choice on this one. The only thing you can do is control the narrative of the story when you're telling it live. So why don't you go think on that for a few days? There's a way to present yourself as the hero somewhere in all of this. You just need to reach deep inside of that little gut of yours and pull out the version you want to share."

Jazzy got up from her chair and stared at the director with an expression of hatred and confusion. The comedian folded her arms with angst and walked over to the windows at the corner of his office.

Mike looked thinner than normal in a tan leisure suit with a green silk tie. The director watched the comedian as she pouted in a striped blue and white blouse with her back turned halfway toward him. Jazzy stood tall in a pair of purple high heels, which were somewhat obscured by her faded blue jeans.

Mike felt his secondary phone ringing in a hidden pocket of his jacket, causing his neck to tingle with the dangers that the call might manifest. He retrieved the unit and looked at the black screen of the phone, seeing a dreaded call coming in that he could not ignore.

"Look, Jazzy, this is our pilot for today's flight," Mike announced with a phony smile and dismissive hand gesture. "You have a lot to think about. Why don't you take some time before we leave?"

"I can wait," the perceptive female insisted, turning to look at the black satellite phone in his right hand with curiosity.

"Look, I need you to take some time to yourself while I handle our travel arrangements," he said with growing eagerness, gesturing for her to depart from his office.

"That's not our pilot, is it?" She asked with a piercing look in her eyes.

"No, it's not!" He agreed with reluctance. "Now get out of my office and give me some privacy! Hello." The director answered his phone and stood up to walk Jazzy out of his workspace.

When the comedian was just over the threshold, Mike slammed the door and locked it behind her, and she heard him begin a muffled conversation through the thick door.

Jazzy saw Jennifer Priest after exiting the office, and she glared at the producer with concentrated rage. This awkwardness caused the tall blonde to show confusion, and she marched toward the television star with an air of concern.

"What's going on, Jazzy?" Jennifer pried in a condescending tone, sounding like a firefighter that was hoping to combat a light blaze.

"Mike is talking on his secret black sat' phone," Jazzy conveyed with irritation as she continued to move towards her bedroom. "You know, the secret sat' phone that everyone knows about?"

"He got a call on the black phone?" The producer inquired with a gaze of suspicion as she stopped walking.

"Yes, what is it with you guys and your couriers and sat' phones?" The comedian demanded as she halted to confront the blonde, placing her hands on her hips in disgust.

"I don't know what you're speaking about," the producer lied without much effort, seeming preoccupied with the news of the phone call.

"Oh seriously, Jennifer, you think we all don't know about that creepy redhead who comes here once or twice a week?" She began a torrent of accusations. "You get packages and phone calls at all hours-"

"Look, I'm sure this may come as a shock to you, Jazzy, but Mike and I are adults," Jennifer stated to diffuse the conversation before it could mushroom any further. "Why don't you get ready for our trip to Houston? Our jet is leaving the tarmac in about three hours. In the meantime, unless they create laws against receiving phone calls and packages, then I'll thank you in advance to mind your own damn business! Thank you." The tall blonde stomped away from Jazzy en route to Mike's office, touting an expression of wickedness as she went to emphasize her point.

"This is frickin' fantastic!" Jazzy announced to the television crew in the hallway as she stared at the blank walls. "I'm working on a show with a couple of urban drug dealers. 'Just get on the jet everyone and be ready to bare your souls to the world. By the way, we're making a quick stop in Colombia – not the university,'" she mocked with a clenched fist and struck a pose for those watching at home.

LaGuardia Airport – New York

One could not have wanted a sexier private jet for luxury travel. The television network operated under a parent company with assets in excess of a hundred billion dollars. Therefore, the company jet was a sleek, black model that seemed to have been designed by the makers of Ferrari sports cars. The cast members were in awe as they rolled their suitcases across the runway on the private side of the airport.

Litz was wearing her best black Audrey Hepburn throwback gown as she strutted through the vast outdoor space of LaGuardia Airport. All three of the men from the show were dressed in matching black suits with orange silk ties to impress the NASA people upon arrival. However, the three women had refused to wear similar outfits, so the director gave them a stipend to buy new clothing. Jazzy had selected the latest fashion, a baby blue dress that featured a furry hoodie, which was preferred by many younger girls. As her polar opposite, Fassim had chosen a lime green pantsuit with matching hijab. Despite their varying styles, each of the women agreed upon wearing a new line of high heels called Snarky Nitch, in colors that matched their outfits.

"I can't allow these on the plane, sir," a gray-haired pilot said to Mike in a respectful manner. "They don't have any tags to prove that they went through TSA checkpoints." The older man finished his statement by gesturing with his right hand at ten black freight containers that were stacked on the runway.

"Okay, no problem," Mike reassured the pilot as the group of cast members wheeled their suitcases past the two men toward the plane. "Just get into the jet and start prepping us for our flight; I don't want to be late for NASA. Please remember that we need to be airing the show live from Houston right on time."

"All right, I'll get us ready," the pilot replied with a smile of relief, "and I'm sorry about you having to leave your freight behind."

"No worries, brother, just get my show off the road," the director mused with a wink and a handshake.

The eager pilot followed his orders and jogged ahead of the cast to ascend the stairs and enter the jet. When the man disappeared into the aircraft, Mike whistled to their security detail and signaled the men to begin loading the freight. Jazzy thought about protesting, but then remembered the threat that Jennifer had issued regarding privacy.

When the cast members entered the jet, they were immersed in a world of luxury and style. There was a full bar in the back that was visible from the seating area. Each of the sixteen seats were overstuffed and upholstered in tan leather. The rows were also spaced far enough apart to allow for reclining leg rests. Their accommodations included a 3D hologram movie theater screen, digital real sound speakers, personal music players, and various refrigerators filled with gourmet snacks. On either side of the cabin were two small desks with reading lights and computers that had Internet access. The carpet was made of a white plush material, and all of the controls in the cabin were inlayed under shiny black carbon fiber coverings.

Everyone appeared thrilled by the accommodations except for Jazzy and Stoney. The two stars seemed preoccupied with something regarding the trip, and the comedian kept glancing out the window at the freight that was being loaded.

"What the hell are we carrying?" The skeptical woman asked with a sneer, wondering if she should have made a bigger issue about the freight, or alerted the pilot.

Ellington Airport – Houston, Texas

The weather in Houston was hot and humid, and the weekly forecast didn't offer much hope of a reprieve. All six cast members were met at Ellington Airport by two NASA road shuttles; no doubt labeled as such for the simple irony. They took a short twenty-minute drive from the airport to the space station and were dropped off at the executive offices of NASA to begin their tour. Litz froze when she saw the ominous Memorial Towers that dominated the Houston skyline, casting shadows over the city during the early afternoon.

Joseph Kerr stood just inside the lobby of the Space Center Houston executive offices with his hands on his hips. He displayed a nervous confidence as the television stars filed in through the glass doors of the NASA executive office complex. Litz bit her lower lip when she noticed that Jason Harrington was standing to the right of Joseph. The attractive astronaut kept his hands clasped together over his pelvis with a professional smile that one might see in a stock photo or shopping catalog. His senior-level colleague had selected a much more chic suit than the younger astronaut, wearing a cream-colored Italian ensemble with a cranberry silk tie. The older man's hair was graying in a healthy pattern, but still short enough to pull off the spiked style that he had chosen.

"Welcome to Houston, everyone," Joseph greeted his guests with a throaty Texas accent and inviting blue eyes. "I hope ya'll don't mind if Jason gives you the tour today; I'm afraid I have some meetings that couldn't be rescheduled." He gestured toward his colleague before shaking the hands of all six cast members. "I'm pleased to see y'all again and hope that you enjoy learning more about us over the next few days. NASA is a, well; it's a heck of a place. But I'll let Jason get to the rest of that, and you give me a holler if ya'll need anything." The savvy executive finished their abrupt meet and greet with a wink, taking the time to smile at everyone before retreating to his office in a brisk manner.

"Well, why don't we get started?" Jason asked as he opened his hands in an awkward fashion and let them drop to his sides. "Oh hey, food fight, how are you doing?" The astronaut addressed Litz in a tone that sounded too happy for the New Yorkers after their long flight.

"Yeah, lead the way, Buzz Lightyear," Litz quipped with apprehension as his lack of tact once again ruined her appetite for man candy.

CKB noticed the tension between the astronaut and Litz, which prompted him to lean forward and whisper into Jazzy's ear.

"Oh totally!" Jazzy agreed with a delicious grin as she winked at the career criminal.

The comedian bent forward and whispered into Fassim's ear, and the moderate Muslim giggled as she walked through the offices with the group. Fassim then whispered into Litz's ear, and the plumber opened her mouth in silent, hearty laughter.

"Wow, Jason, that navy blue suit is really doing it for me today," Jazzy expressed with a naughty wink as the man led them through the office complex toward the space center.

"Yeowwww, boy," Fassim half-shouted an aggressive cat call at the astronaut, "I'd like to get into some deep spaces with you."

"Hey there, Mr. Astronaut," Litz began with a seductive voice of ownership, "my engines are hot, and you still haven't boarded me yet."

CKB and the other two men started to chuckle at Jason as the women taunted him like sex-starved construction workers. The criminal made a fist over his mouth and enjoyed their retribution on the astronaut after absently calling Litz 'food fight.'

Jason showed some discomfort but regained his composure in a prudent display of confidence, which silenced the laughter of the three men. He straightened the jacket of his navy blue suit and checked his black tie for stains.

"Okay, the first thing I want to show you-" the astronaut began, only to be interrupted by Fassim.

"Yessss, what would you like to – show us?" Fassim teased in a tawdry manner with hungry eyes.

"Jason, do you know where our luggage went?" Jazzy prodded with an innocent smile.

"Your luggage should have been delivered to the hotel," the astronaut reassured her. "It will be in your room when you get back tonight."

"Oh, geez," the comedian answered in a plastic manner with a snap of her fingers, "and I was hoping to put on a bra and panties – just in the event that we have to climb any ladders. Well, I guess it's okay if you guys see my girl. We do it all the time in New York anyway."

"Oh yeah, we love to just leave our stuff hanging out," Litz added with a clever smile, twisting her head to gaze into Jason's eyes. "I mean, New Yorkers in spring have the tannest genitals in the wild kingdom. It's like going to the deli and seeing all of the meat on dis-" she stopped speaking when their guide interrupted her.

"Okay, what's going on?" Jason asked the group as he placed his hands on his hips and stood up straight to confront them.

"CKB offered us a hundred dollars to see who could embarrass you the most with innuendo," Jazzy replied with a sheepish smile, looking away from Jason as she finished her sentence.

"You snitch," CKB said with a playful grin as he moved his right arm over his stomach and rested his left hand under his chin.

"It was her," the astronaut confirmed as he pointed at Litz. "Now, let's head this way, I want to show you the chest... I mean, the water tanks," the man corrected himself in a helpless show of frustration. "Follow me."

Litz stopped and snapped her fingers at CKB in a silent demand for payment on their wager. The rest of the group moved on as she and the career criminal settled their debt.

After a long walk across the concourse, the television stars found themselves standing above a large water tank. There was an astronaut in a suit submerged in the water, and Jason explained how the tank was used to simulate weightlessness. The New Yorkers looked at one another with cynicism and raised eyebrows, as though they wanted to ask if the tour was for eight-year-old children. Most attractions within the space station gave off this level of excitement, and after their first four exhibits, CKB and Litz began to say 'wow' with little emotion at everything they saw.

Jason detected the group's apathy toward the more pedestrian areas of the tour and decided to cut it short with a rocket propulsion demonstration. He guided the television stars to a large concrete launch pad at the far end of the complex. They walked up a flight of stairs to an observation catwalk in front of a massive rocket exhaust port. The New Yorkers seemed to show respect for this monstrosity of engineering as Jason led them and their camera crew toward a control panel for the test.

The rocket was at least as wide as a small house, and it would have taken several seconds to walk up the exhaust port and into the unit. Richard gazed down the length of the rocket to its tip, noting that it ended fifty yards to their right in a steep point. The white surface was made up of tempered steel and had all manner of safety stickers on its outer layer.

"Okay, so I need you all to step back to the edge of the observation deck as we get ready to ignite this unit," Jason instructed as he started to flip switches on the control panel at the front of the platform. "This is a special demonstration that we're staging for you and the television show. So, since it's not part of the regular tour, I need to take a few extra safety precautions. First, the blast is going to blow off at our left, so if you stay at the right side of the platform, you'll be more insulated from the heat. Second, I want you to avoid staring at the flames for too long in case I need to signal you to evacuate the platform. We'll have a hard time hearing when the rocket ignites, but you don't need hearing protection. Does everyone understand?"

Every member of the cast nodded and shifted to the rear right of the platform except for Stoney. The police officer was preoccupied with the control panel and rocket exhaust port in the background. 'I don't want to do this, Mike,' he thought to himself as his stomach began to burn with anxiety.

"Okay, I'm going to begin a countdown, and we'll ignite the rocket when I get to zero," the astronaut instructed with a confident smile, knowing that this test would likely shock even the strongest among them. "If I signal with both hands in an urgent manner; that means you need to evacuate the platform. Okay, is everyone ready?"

'It's your time, Stoney,' the Japanese officer coaxed himself as he exhaled through his nostrils, 'you need to make it happen now.'

"Okay, counting down," Jason informed everyone and flipped a switch to begin the ignition sequence after confirming that the observers were ready. "Ten. Nine. Eight. Seven. Six. Five-" He stopped the count as one of the cast members stepped up behind him.

"Hello, my name is Stoney Akuda," the law enforcement officer began as he stepped between the astronaut and his co-stars to face the television cameras. "I'm a New York City police officer and a gay man."

The oxygen seemed to get sucked out of the area in a rush as the rocket ignited with a brilliant and sustained wall of yellow and orange fire. Jason was trying to say something to everyone, but the sound of the blast drowned out everything else. Stoney looked at the faces of his colleagues after the announcement, trying to detect any negative reactions. Litz gave him a thumbs-up and smiled, and Jazzy soon followed with the same reaction. CKB also smiled and winked, but the two conservative cast members folded their arms in silence. Fassim and Richard looked like they wanted to ask a few questions; however, the sound of the rocket was too overpowering.

Stoney looked dismayed but tried to appear positive for his lover that was watching at home. He had hoped to use the reactions of his co-stars to determine how the officers at his precinct would respond. Since forty percent of his colleagues from the show seemed to harbor some reservations, it made the battle at his day job seem more daunting. He glared at the cameras with the wall of fire glowing behind him and hoped that Mike was watching. This fiasco was not how he wanted to come out to the world, regardless of what his contract required.

VII. Headfirst Feedback

The Wednesday afternoon crowd in the bar at The Hilton Hotel was subdued. A few travelers were seated in the serving area watching a baseball game on a sixty-inch 3D hologram television while a young couple played pool in the far corner of the room. A heavyset man hovered over a jukebox in the corner opposite the couple but seemed too drunk to make a selection, and had been there for over ten minutes.

Every cast member of <u>Shots Fired in the Melting Pot</u> was seated at a wide rectangular table, sans the camera crew and executive staff. Stoney glanced down at the glossy surface of the white oak table. He felt as though his stomach had been opened with a scalpel, and those gathered around him were going to roast his insides. The police officer sat at the end of the table with Richard and Fassim on his right, and Litz, CKB, and Jazzy on the left. Nobody had said much after his bold announcement near the fiery rocket, except when Jason concluded that the test was successful.

Stoney panned his head from left to right, looking at the faces of his companions. Their expensive suits and fancy gowns made his moment of truth feel like something out of a high school prom. He wondered if Mike and Jennifer were back at their room celebrating his humiliation with a bottle of champagne. It wasn't hard to imagine the mysterious duo as a pair of soul-sucking chupacabras, but Stoney decided that it would be less vivid after drinking some alcohol.

"Pick a song already!" Richard insisted with restraint; not speaking loud enough for the obese drunk to hear him. "How long has he been hogging that jukebox?"

"Maybe he thinks that he's already listening to something," CKB offered with a smirk as he turned to gaze at the bar patron.

"That would be amazing!" Litz echoed her support with a demeanor of playful excitement. "Which drink makes you hallucinate that you hear music? More of that please."

"What can I get for you?" A tidy, twenty-two-year-old blonde waitress asked in a rich Texas accent as she held a digital tablet in front of her to take their order.

"We want three Long Island Iced Teas on this side, and one at the end of the table," Litz requested in a way that was pure business. "I'm not sure what they want," she added with a disenchanted stare, folding her arms to display strength.

"I'll have a Coke," Richard said in what sounded like a moment of grief for his lack of access to the jukebox.

"Get me a copper camel," Fassim answered as she stared at Litz with disapproval.

"I thought you don't drink?" Litz asked the paparazzi photographer.

Fassim didn't bother justifying the inquiry with an answer and turned up her nose at the plumber. The waitress looked somewhat uncomfortable with the apparent conflict at the table. She stared at the floor and then elected to seek sanctuary behind the bar without attempting to confirm any orders.

"I don't understand why you won't just support Stoney; it's not up to you to tell other people how to live," Litz argued with her conservative co-stars across the table. "I mean sex is only one percent of your life – at best. How can you judge a person based on one percent of their life?"

"It's just not what we believe in," Richard stated with a shrug, "and I don't have to support things that aren't part of my belief system."

"Look, I didn't even want to come out like that; it was part of my contract with the show," Stoney said with contempt as he felt the corrosive gazes of Richard and Fassim eating away at his identity. "I also know that every one of you has a skeleton in your closet. Mike said that before the season is done, you'll all have to reveal something from your past."

The other actors looked away from one another in a silent confirmation of this claim. After a short pause, the waitress interrupted them by setting down drinks on the table with the efficiency of a naval officer.

"Let me know if there's anything else I can get for you," the youthful Texan offered with a forced smile, noticing that her patrons had become more awkward than before.

"Do you have a big rainbow flag that we could borrow?" Jazzy quipped with a wink and a smile, causing the server to pause and twist her head to the right. "No, I'm just kidding; we're fine."

"Do you see this drink in front of me?" Fassim asked Stoney as she placed her hands on her knees, taking up extra space with her elbows bowing outward. "I could drink this down and enjoy all of the warmth that it has to offer, or I could dump it out on the floor. When you run into a man, and you're craving his touch, you don't have to partake. It's your choice if you want to do those things. I know, because I also like men, and I have the ability to say no."

Litz was about to respond with a myriad of witty retorts and facts but was shocked to hear slow clapping from Richard. The undaunted plumber glared at the film editor with a vivacious demeanor of betrayal. Richard stared back into her eyes and continued to clap, confirming that this was not an area where he would be willing to budge.

"I can't believe that the two of you won't support Stoney in a time like this!" Litz growled at the conservative pair through gritted teeth. "We've all been tolerant of your religious crap, and now you can't even be decent. Oh, and by the way, Fassim; what a clever way to set up your argument. I'll order a drink and sit here like a crocodile until I have a prop in front of me to make my case. Why don't you go out and buy some poster board and markers? Then you could draw pictures of penises and vaginas, and let us all know how they're compatible. I can't believe that you think your religion should matter to all of us."

"Yeah, I'm with Litz and Jazzy on this one; you don't need to be tellin' our boy what he can and can't do in the bedroom," CKB added and shook his head.

Stoney felt conflicted as the criminal stuck up for him with genuine passion. He was perplexed that one announcement could cause such a divide among a group of people. His sexuality had become like a genie lingering over the group, refusing to go back into its bottle.

"Well, who says that we need your approval anyway?" Jazzy prodded with a serving of sarcasm. "It's not like he needs to call you and ask your permission next time he decides to have sex. Besides, Fassim, with all of the naked pictures you take of me, I wouldn't be surprised if you're a secret lesbian."

Fassim knocked the copper camel over in Jazzy's direction and spilled some of the liquid onto her expensive outfit. The comedian then jumped up from her chair with instant rage, bolting around the left side of the table to confront her colleague. In a moment of fight or flight, the paparazzi photographer was quick to react and sprinted toward the exit with her co-star in pursuit. Most of the bar patrons watched the women as they raced through the establishment to the entryway of the hotel. Jazzy swore several times on her way through the hotel hallway, gauging that the other woman was much faster.

Stoney exhaled in a moment of social disdain and snatched his drink from the table. He then gulped the Long Island Iced Tea down as though it would erase the past few hours, and didn't come up for air until only ice remained in his glass.

"Can we get our check?" Litz called out to the waitress when the woman began to approach their table.

"Don't worry about your check, they told us to bill it to the room," the waitress said with a wave of her right hand. "Is everything okay over there?"

"Everything is just fine," the unwavering plumber answered as she stared Richard down and stood up from her chair. "I'll get you for this, Richard. There are a lot of shows left in this season, and you'll regret making Stoney feel this way." She moved her body between CKB and Stoney, gripping their shoulders in a display of solidarity before taking her leave from the bar.

Richard looked down at his Coke, an empty, bubbling black mass on the table, and felt the same way on the inside. Although he didn't hate Stoney in his heart; there were too many lessons from church and his childhood to let something like this slide.

"Mike shouldn't have made you do it that way," Richard stated in a small peace offering and began to depart from the establishment. "But if you ask me to repeat that on camera, I won't support you." He shrugged and moved faster toward the exit, somehow feeling better about the situation.

"I need some time alone," Stoney whispered to CKB as he felt the sweet warmth of the alcohol dulling the pain from his recent announcement.

The career criminal got up from the table and patted his co-star on the shoulder. He then departed the bar with a somber expression, thinking about their return to New York.

Litz was flustered as she stomped through the hallways of the hotel, snarling at other patrons on her way back to the luxury suite. When she got to the elevator, her satellite phone showed a text message that she had missed while in the bar. The flustered woman tilted her head back in confusion after reading the sentence. It was as follows: 'Hey this is Jason Harrington from NASA; I got your number from Jennifer and was wondering if I could pay you a visit?'

She exhaled in a manner that was slow and sustained, wondering if company would be a good idea right now. Although the message was a bit on the creepy side, it did show off a bold part of the man's personality that had been lacking before. Litz decided to respond with: 'What did you have in mind?'

The television star waited for several seconds before finally receiving a reply: 'I heard you were staying at the Hilton. Could I see you in your room?'

She smiled and began to chuckle, surprising the other three passengers in the elevator. Litz ignored their passive-aggressive responses and bit her lower lip as she considered his proposition. After a few seconds of thought and allowing the alcohol to kick in, she replied with: '718.' The diva breathed in as much oxygen as her lungs could hold, and then exhaled with the burden of preemptive regret. She knew that the chance of this turning into a positive encounter was rare, but it couldn't have been worse than her last interaction.

When the elevator doors opened at the seventh floor, Litz evacuated the unit as if she had ridden in it with her friend's parents. Several of the passengers were also relieved by her departure. The young woman made her way back to the hotel suite in a brisk effort to freshen up before Jason arrived.

Litz spent the next ten minutes getting ready for a romantic adventure. She went to the luxury bathroom and used a bar of soap to clean all the parts of her body where heat could have produced odor. After that, she teased her hair in the mirror several times, attempting to find a look that was acceptable. The thoughtful vixen then changed her panties from the pink nightmare that she had worn all day to something smaller, black and silky. As a final touch, she sprayed her neck twice with some alluring perfume and changed into a pair of black high heels.

The television star felt like a full diva as she let her heels click on the marble tiles throughout the suite. When she was about to adjust the lighting in the room for a better mood, there was a knock at the door.

Litz checked her body one last time as if she were a race car that had pulled in to get some work done by a pit crew.

"Everything is fresh, the hair is fine, and the attitude is ready for action," Litz said to herself in a whisper before pulling the door open.

As the door swung inward, she was surprised to see Jason standing in the hallway wearing a black tuxedo and matching bowtie. The middle-aged astronaut had an enormous black hiking backpack slung over his shoulders and smiled like a tour guide when he saw Litz.

"Come on in," the mysterious woman invited with a puzzled expression. "Are we…going hiking tonight?"

"Actually, I have a surprise for you," the astronaut said with a wink and smirked as he trod across the threshold into the entryway of the suite.

Litz admired Jason's black designer shoes as he made his way into the hotel room. Some part of her didn't like the idea of a surprise, which caused the reluctant woman to regard the backpack with a degree of mistrust.

"So what's the surprise?" She asked without much thought, wanting to get past this unknown factor.

"Come with me," Jason replied with a mysterious smile, taking her by the hand and leading her toward the sliding glass doors. "I think you'll like this."

He slid the door open in a bold fashion and led his younger date out onto the balcony. Jason then removed the backpack, unzipped its zipper in a hurry and pulled out two black leather and vinyl harnesses.

"What...are we doing?" The television star demanded in a soft manner, indicating that his actions seemed bizarre.

"Oh, well our surprise is seventy feet below us," he answered with a wry smile and began to prepare a harness for Litz.

"Can't we just take the elevator?" Litz suggested with a cute blinking gesture from her attractive eyes.

"I thought you were adventurous?" Jason challenged with another playful look of banter. "Astronauts are not as boring as you make us out to be," he added and slid the harness over her dress, fastening it to a snug fit around her shapely body.

Litz glanced over the railing and saw a glowing blue swimming pool seventy feet below the balcony. There were three flags in the pool area, and the wind was whipping them back and forth. She swallowed hard and closed her eyes, leaning away from the railing for a moment to regain perspective. Jason was oblivious to her plight and brought out two lengths of black rope, which he set on the concrete near their feet.

"See, if the police were chasing after us, we'd be arrested by now," he joked with a wink and delicately ran a length of rope through her harness. "We'll tie this off really snug, and it should hold you just fine." He secured the shorter end of the rope to the railing in a square knot and gave it a tug to test the hold.

After checking the knot for strength, he put a harness around himself and secured it over his tuxedo. Jason repeated the process of weaving a rope through his harness and tied another square knot to the steel railing. He then double-checked the harnesses for a secure fit and pulled the knots again to verify their stability. To the diva's delight, Jason tossed the lengths of rope over the railing in a reckless display of his intent to have fun. As a final precaution, he removed two pairs of leather gloves from the backpack. The couple then smiled at one another as they pulled their gloves on for the fun to begin.

"Are you ready?" Jason prompted with a forced schoolboy smile.

"Whatever is down there had better be worth it," Litz declared as she got in a position to climb over the railing.

Jason helped the novice to maneuver her body for the descent, coaching her on how to drop lower in a safe way. The dashing astronaut then climbed over the railing to join her as they began to move downward a few feet at a time.

Litz could feel her heartbeat increasing to new levels of terror when she realized that her body was dangling in the air. She closed her eyes and recalled being fifteen years old the last time her body was up this high. The wind was not making anything easier as it tugged at the folds of her dress and tossed her hair about at random.

"Hey, hey, look at me," Jason spoke in a soft voice, placing his right hand on her shoulder.

Litz opened a pair of fearful eyes to see the kindness of his face staring at her, and made an effort to show bravery.

"Put your feet against the cement and use them to stabilize yourself," he instructed in a calm manner, returning his hands to the sections of rope above and below him. "Now kick off from the wall and let yourself drop a few feet, then tighten your grip again."

The stubborn woman worked on her form in a clumsy way, and had a few scares, but was finally able to control her speed. After dropping the first ten feet, she had confidence that the rope would hold, and the chaotic experience became more natural. Litz enjoyed the freedom of their rebellious path to the pool, knowing that they were probably the first guests to venture down this way. When the couple got past the halfway point, she was able to relax and laugh with her date. The inspired star wondered why she considered passing up this experience. It took them less than fifteen minutes to reach the pool area, and Litz felt the exhilaration of accomplishment when her shoes touched the concrete.

"Go ahead and drop your harness right there: I have someone who will take care of it for us," Jason conveyed with a hungry gaze of admiration and began to remove his harness.

"That was awesome!" Litz exclaimed as she stepped out of the harness and looked back up to the balcony from whence they came. "I can't believe we just did that! Did you get permission from the hotel? Never mind, I don't want to know."

"Well, my dear, our table is ready," he announced and gestured with his right hand to a table with a white linen topper.

The energetic woman felt new warmth in her face as she spotted a table with a pair of long white candles, and a bottle of champagne chilling in an ice bucket. There was a middle-aged hotel waiter with white gloves standing next to the table, and his smile added to the ambiance.

"Oh my God, this is so cool!" She responded with unbridled desire and made her way to a solitary table next to the illuminated swimming pool.

"This is Jack," the astronaut stated as he joined her at the table, "he's a friend of mine that I just met tonight. It's thanks to him that we were able to pull this off." He shook the waiter's hand before taking a seat opposite his date and paused to savor her expression of enjoyment.

"Wait!" Litz interrupted as though there were something urgent on her mind. "Before we start with dinner, I want to dance. Let's dance next to the pool." The enchanted woman waited for a moment, unaware that she was holding her breath.

"Okay, let's dance," Jason agreed after a short pause, standing up tall to escort his date to the concrete near the pool.

Litz was swept up in a second round of exhilaration as the astronaut began to lead her in an improvised classical dance. She admired his moves, and he smelled great, which allowed her to become lost in the moment.

Richard watched Litz dancing with the astronaut from within the hotel and clenched his right hand into a fist. He felt the cold, dry bite of rejection combined with having to observe how happy she was making Jason. His insides started to tremble as he envisioned what the two might wind up doing later that evening, and decided it was futile to pout. The adventurous bombshell had chosen someone else. Richard heard the wail of police sirens broadcast over the wall near the pool and saw the couple stop dancing. Jason took Litz by the hand, and they laughed like escaped convicts, sprinting away from the authorities towards the hotel. Richard continued to observe until flashes from red and blue lights were visible from the parking lot, and he prayed that the police could capture them in time.

Fassim returned to the bar with a desire to learn what had happened to the rest of their party. She had led Jazzy through the hotel for the better part of twenty minutes before the security desk told her to stop running. At that point, she realized that her pursuer had given up with less of a battle than expected.

When she reached the familiar wooden rectangle table, Fassim was amazed to find Jazzy sitting back in her original spot. However, the comedian was no longer full of strength and energy. Her eyes were puffy, and makeup was running down her face. The paparazzi photographer noticed three empty beer bottles in front of her co-star, and another that was being drunk.

"Go ahead and get your photo, you selfish b****!" Jazzy challenged with a defeated gaze and raised her head. "I don't care what you do anymore. Go ahead and make ten grand off of my shame."

"What's going on?" Fassim asked as she sat down opposite her adversary, lowering her face to look into Jazzy's eyes. "Are you okay?"

"Do you really care?" The comedian prompted in a threatening manner. "I have a hard time believing that."

"Yes, I really care, but I'm unhappy that you injured my back," the photographer answered with innocence and honesty.

"Sorry about that," Jazzy said with a slight smile, attempting to hide her enjoyment. "You know how Stoney said that Mike is making us tell something terrible about our past on the show?" She inquired as her face melted back into a portrait of sadness.

"Yes, I think he's done that to everyone," Fassim confirmed with raised eyebrows, leaning closer to her co-star. "What is he asking you to do?"

"He wants me to tell everyone about when I was raped by a billionaire." The distraught comedian erupted in a fit of tears, shaking from the emotional scars of her past.

Fassim got up from the table and walked around to sit next to Jazzy. When they were close enough together, she placed her right arm around the horrified woman and rocked her from side to side.

The insightful Muslim recognized this fit of agony and recollected her time helping other victims of abuse when she lived in Amman, Jordan. Fassim closed her eyes as Jazzy's wails of hysteria took her back to the war-torn landscape of the Middle East.

At age seventeen, Fassim found herself counseling women brutalized by soldiers or their husbands. The teenager built up a sprawling hatred for men during the first six months of conflict between Jordan and Israel. She had formed a group of women called Sisters of Love, but it was shut down by bureaucrats before she could accomplish anything.

For several weeks, she anguished at the sight of repeated violence against females of all ages that often led to death. The spiritual woman prayed to Allah for strength one evening and felt inspired wandering into a market the next day. She came across a Chinese-made camera with a powerful analog lens that could zoom in close from over a hundred yards away. Although the device seemed useless, Fassim felt an urge to buy it, and found herself walking away from the store having spent half of the money she needed for food and rent.

After purchasing the camera, the teenager returned to the shelter where women were recovering from their attacks. Fassim felt as though the hand of the creator was pushing her forward when she began snapping pictures of the horrid scenes. It took her an hour to capture the faces of all the women, and she kept a journal containing the names and descriptions of their attackers.

Two days later, the youthful activist was walking through the market when a pair of American soldiers hollered for her to join them at an outdoor table where they were eating lunch. Fassim was cautious of the Americans, having heard stories of their bloodlust and desire to reign supreme over the world. But when she approached the table, the soldiers seemed friendly, and they asked her to take their photo. Although she felt mistrust, the teenager snapped a few pictures of a man called The Pale Horse and his friend Jose.

The Pale Horse was a muscular Native American man with short dark hair and deep brown eyes. He asked to see the photo on the preview screen and Fassim handed him the camera. His demeanor was content until he scrolled too far through the collection of images and saw the battered women. The soldier then became reverent and asked Fassim who had abused the victims.

As a devout Muslim, she was hesitant to trust the men, but they seemed upset and genuine. Fassim did her best to explain the attacks in broken English, and the men listened with horrified expressions. After taking the time to hear her story, The Pale Horse asked if she could get detailed pictures of the men who hurt the women at her shelter. The teenager felt afraid to believe her enemies, but there was something kind in their eyes. Fassim agreed to provide The Pale Horse with images and locations of the attackers, and he promised to end the suffering of her beloved sisters.

VIII. Alphabromeric

Litz awoke from a deep sleep following a satisfying evening of intimacy with her new lover. Despite having a severe headache from a hangover, she turned over to indulge in a good morning kiss. When the amorous brunette rolled from her right side to her left, she recognized that Jason had gone during the night. Her first instinct was to inhale with a forlorn expression and stare at the ceiling. The television star then began to justify his departure with a multitude of valid excuses.

"Good morning," Jason called out to the preoccupied woman as he strutted out of the darkened bathroom and into the bedroom.

"Oh, dear God!" Litz shrieked in a tone of uncoordinated panic, flailing her arms in the bed like a morbidly obese woman. "Turn the light on if you're going to use the bathroom – for hell's sake." She grabbed her forehead in contempt and closed her eyes, but a smile formed across her face. "I can't believe they called the cops on us. How did you sort that out?"

"Sorry, I just had to pee," he explained with embarrassment, sensing that this was too much detail for a new romance. "The cops recognized me from the news and decided to let me off with a ticket for reckless endangerment."

"I'm glad that we didn't go to jail. By the way, is peeing in the dark part of your astronaut training?" The audacious woman teased with a dismissive wave of her right hand. "Jason, we want to know if you can pee in the dark. First you'll get a glow stick, and then you'll have to build a fire."

"Fire is no bueno in space; it uses up all of the oxygen," he reported in a snarky fashion and climbed back under the covers with her.

"You know what; I'd prefer that your mouth be used for things other than talking," she proposed with a naughty grin, keeping her eyes shut to deny that it was morning.

"I want to show you something," Jason announced in a sober tone, waiting for his companion to act her age.

"I'll bet you do!" Litz exclaimed with a warm expression as she opened her eyes and submitted to his morning person charm. "Why don't you go play with the other morning people for a few hours, and let the rest of us adults sleep a little longer?"

"Get up, lazy bones," he demanded with masculine affection and grabbed her wrists to pull her into a sitting position. "Come on, we can't stay in here all day."

"I hate you," she blurted out with her eyes still halfway closed and a wavy mass of hair that was sticking up from the right side of her head. "Okay, okay, I'm up, and we're going to do…something." Litz forced her eyes open and turned her head from left to right, attempting to regain her bearings.

"You know, I'm surprised that Jennifer gave me your number," Jason said as he got up from the bed and walked back into the bathroom. "Most women wouldn't give out their friend's sat' phone numbers."

"So where are we going today?" The boisterous plumber asked as she blew a tuft of hair out of her eyes. "What's this thing that you want to show me? Do I get to see the alien craft now? Are you going to parade me around in front of the office executives?"

Litz got up from the bed and began to dress herself from a black suitcase near the wall. She stretched a gray tank top over her bare abdomen and pulled on a pair of black running shorts. Jason stepped out of the bathroom wearing a pair of black boxer shorts and seemed dismayed that he didn't get to see her naked again. He was in good shape for his age with a tanned stomach, and abdominal muscles that showed partial definition.

The crafty woman looked up long enough to see that he had been combing his hair and chuckled at his formal nature.

"I want to give you a better tour today," he admitted with a glowing grin of satisfaction. "There are a lot of things that you didn't get to see."

"Well, it had better be more than my wildest dreams," she challenged with a smirk, "because you just interrupted some of my wildest dreams."

"Why don't you pretend that you're dreaming now?" The astronaut proposed with a bold gaze of desire.

The agreeable brunette smiled as Jason began to savor her face and neck with selfish kisses. She was soon confident in the knowledge that whatever he had planned for their day; they were going to be late.

"So what did you want to talk about so early?" CKB prodded as he flipped a chair around near the rectangular table, and sat down with his arms hanging over its back side.

Jazzy and Fassim continued to loiter on the opposite side of the serving table that they had used the previous night. CKB blinked a few times and looked at the troubled women with irritation.

"Have you been in the bar all night?" He inquired with a judgmental stare. "Why would you want to stay at a hotel and not sleep?"

"Jazzy and I have been talking all night," Fassim informed him with a demure attitude. "We need to get your advice about something."

"Okay, that's cool," CKB stated with a yawn and scratched his chest through a light blue running shirt. "You've gotta' buy me some coffee, though."

"I'll go get your coffee," the paparazzi photographer agreed with a forced smile. "Go ahead and tell him what happened," she instructed Jazzy and gripped the comedian's hands in a loving gesture, "and I'll be right back." She paused long enough to make eye contact with her co-star before getting up to retrieve some drinks from the bar.

"So, what's goin' on, Jazzy?" The criminal prompted with an even stare, shifting in his seat in preparation for a heavy emotional burden.

"Sorry, I'm just really tired," she answered from a dry throat, pausing to cough and clear her airway. "Almost a year ago, a billionaire named Ned Jones invited me to a party on his yacht." Jazzy breathed in deep and looked at the ceiling, trying to decide if she wanted to continue. "He was handsome and sophisticated, and I had just broken off a relationship, so I was looking forward to having some fun. Anyway, when we got to the yacht, everything seemed great. There were loads of people all over, and the atmosphere was perfect. So after having a few drinks, Ned came up to me and asked if I wanted to be part of the mile-below club. Of course, I laughed like an idiot and said, 'Don't you mean the mile-high club?' Well, apparently this yacht had a submarine, and he took me down there to show me some of the controls – ballast and down bubble, or whatever."

Fassim returned to the table with three cups of coffee, which she distributed among their party without interrupting Jazzy. CKB took the brown disposable coffee cup and kept it dangling from the fingers of his right hand. The muscular African-American grimaced as though he knew where the story was going.

"Thanks," Jazzy emoted with genuine appreciation as she paused and took a few light sips from the steaming container. "I don't know why I thought I was safe, but he slammed the hatch shut and screwed it down tight like they do in the movies. After that, he punched me in the side of the face and was smiling." She began to cry as the terror of the visual memory resurfaced. "He forced me into the captain's bed, or bunk – I can't remember. And there was nothing I could do. I screamed the whole time, but nobody could hear me. After it was over, he took us down into the ocean and threatened to drown us both if I said anything. He put his hand on the hatch and kept spinning the wheel: I thought we were going to die. So I agreed never to say anything to anyone, and he told me that it was my fault. He said that I should've known better than to come to his yacht party. And that's it..." The celebrity said as she closed her eyes, attempting to dismiss all the unpleasant thoughts.

CKB looked down at the floor and took a drink from his coffee. He then twisted his head from side to side and massaged the back of his neck with rigorous strokes.

"So what's your advice?" Fassim inquired with a gaze of concern, seeming worried that the criminal might hurt Jazzy's feelings. "How can we get this guy without Jazzy being harmed?"

"Let's see," CKB began with a gleam in his eyes as he stared up at the ceiling. "He's a billionaire with a yacht and his name is Ned Jones? Does he live in New York?"

"Yes," Jazzy confirmed with an enthusiastic nod.

"Let me handle it," he said with a confident grin and stood up from the table to depart with his coffee. "Thanks for the drink."

"Wait a minute," Fassim demanded with an expression of disappointment. "What is your advice?"

"Let me handle it," CKB called out as he continued to walk away from the table without turning back.

"What do you think he's going to do?" Jazzy asked with an expression of concern.

"I'm not sure, but it's time for you to get some rest," the photographer replied with a demeanor of building confidence. "Let's get back to our rooms, and I'll take you to get a massage later."

Building 8 – Space Center Houston

"Stop, they're going to catch us," Jason warned his lover with an affectionate giggle. "We shouldn't be fooling around in here anyway."

"I thought you said that the cameras can't see into this area?" Litz pressed with a stare of lust and youthful adventure.

The astronaut was lying on the floor of the space shuttle with the gorgeous reality star straddling his pelvis. He looked up at the roof of the cockpit and felt a shudder of guilt pass through his body. Jason sat up and signaled Litz to get off of him, deciding that they were too close to being discovered.

"So no more playtime?" She asked with a wink as Jason pulled up his pants and secured them around his waist. "Are you worried about the security cameras?"

"No, I'm not worried about the cameras," he said with an exasperated shrug, "because NASA doesn't have enough funding to put proper security in this area. I'm just worried that a technician will come back here and find us…"

"And find us doing what?" The perceptive woman taunted with a brilliant smile, leaning forward to kiss her companion with warm affection. "So tell me more about how the shuttle works; you said that reentry was the most dangerous part, right?" Litz questioned with a smirk as she stood up and began to inspect the instrument panels.

"No, that's not right, naughty girl," Jason reminded her and got to his feet, placing his arms around her flat stomach. "The launch sequence and reentry are both equally dangerous."

"Tell me what could go wrong," she prompted in a loving tone of voice as his arms seemed to melt around her.

"Well, the biggest danger on takeoff is having the boosters explode, which has happened a few times," he professed with a soothing voice. "But when you're coming back into the atmosphere, a lot can go wrong. For example, if some technician put clear tape over our sensors, and forgot to remove it, we wouldn't come through earth's atmosphere at the right angle. Another problem would be a malfunction in the integrity of the vessel. If the outer shell were compromised, the heat of the atmosphere would cut us open like a grapefruit. We could also have a failure of our life support, a fire, or any number of incidents."

"Is this the shuttle that's going to be keeping you safe during the next mission?" Litz suggested with wide eyes, showing concern for her new lover. "I don't want anything bad to happen to you. Who will I climb down the side of hotels with? And if you're not around, I may never get out of bed in the morning."

"You're such a ham," Jason concluded as he bent down and kissed the beautiful brunette on the right cheek, "let's get out of here before we wind up in trouble."

"No, I want to stay and learn more about how this thing works; maybe they'll let me go with you," the television star boasted with a smirk. "Besides, I'm a plumber, and I went to college to become an engineer. So I'm not just some idiot woman that doesn't understand what she's looking at. Hell, I installed a furnace for a guy last week, and all I needed was a few teenagers to help me with the heavy lifting."

"Okay, miss engineer," he replied with a gaze of amusement, "let's go down into the belly of the beast and see if you can understand how the systems are run by the circuit boards."

"Game on, mister romance," she accepted with raised eyebrows, "and if I can explain everything back to you that you mansplain to me, then you have to buy me dinner. Also, just to clarify, by dinner I mean an upscale restaurant – not Famous Bill's barbecue shack."

Jason adopted a more competitive ambiance as he reached out with his right hand and led the brunette to the center of the craft, just behind the cockpit. He then removed a maintenance hatch and helped her to descend a ladder to the control systems. Litz was in awe at the number of systems that the crew could control from one small room. Everything had labels for ease of use and seemed to have enough safety overrides to make a successful journey possible. She rewarded Jason with a passionate kiss each time he described something that would make his return trip home safer.

Hilton Hotel Lobby – Houston, Texas

"Look at all of these young people having fun!" Robert Duerdin shouted through the hotel lobby as he pranced defiantly across the carpet with a metal baseball bat.

The retired soldier looked ragged with a long graying beard, and his brown eyes gleamed with murderous desperation.

"Are you getting some good vacation time?" The tall forty-four-year-old asked as he raised the bat above a glass table.

Robert drove the thick end of his baseball bat through the glass top of a black coffee table in the waiting room near the front desk. Three people in their early twenties had been sitting near the table and remained motionless, pretending not to notice his antics. However, when the table erupted into shards of glass, the trio of two men and a woman vacated the area with exceptional speed.

Robert raised the steel bat with his right arm above his head like a combat victor. He was dressed in a skin-tight brown and orange bowling shirt and a pair of comfort-fit khaki pants. The man seemed to glow as the younger people dispersed, and he glided across the carpet in a reckless display of aggression. His brown loafers and other attire had caused people to think that his actions were a staged prank until he proved otherwise.

Richard watched this latest display of Sunset Syndrome from the safety of a second-floor lounge with muted interest. The man had entered the hotel talking about the end of the world and quoting passages from the bible. But his actions escalated to a violent tantrum when he realized that most people were ignoring him. Although the soldier carried only a baseball bat, he had the menacing eyes of a trained killer, and not someone that hotel security wanted to infuriate. One member of the security team had already been hit in the kneecap and was still rolling around in pain near the front window of the waiting area.

The conservative film editor let his gaze drift to the front desk, where he saw the hotel manager speaking on a satellite phone in a whisper. Richard chuckled when he noticed that the man's eyes were wide with terror; as though a baseball bat bully was something much deadlier than a nuisance. He looked at his watch with a degree of impatience, wondering how long it would take for the police to arrive and subdue the crazed intruder.

On the main floor of the lobby, the soldier charged through a group of people who were wheeling in luggage from the parking lot. They abandoned their luggage for safety, and the attacker was able to hit two small bags across the room with his weapon. Richard rolled his eyes at this ridiculous display, confused as to why hotel security staff refused to let a drone handle the man. It was all grand entertainment until Richard noticed that Litz and her new boyfriend were making their way into the hotel through the massive sliding doors. He glanced down to see that his co-star was on a collision course with the dangerous soldier and wanted to warn her, but something hateful simmered in his core. Richard gripped his forehead at the onset of this dilemma, and couldn't decide whether there was a greater chance of Litz being harmed or her astronaut lover.

"He's a man," Richard concluded aloud to the other patrons in the lounge, "he'll have to stand up for her."

"Are you coming to the party tomorrow?" Jason asked as he escorted the beautiful television star through the lobby of her hotel. "I'd love to spend some more time with you," he added with the gaze of a person wrapped in the bonds of love.

Litz frowned upon Jason for investing in her at such an early stage. She thought he would have been more of a conquest, but regardless of his semi-clingy nature, the man would be traveling to the moon in less than a week. Therefore, the beauty took his advances as an opportunity to make him work harder.

Jason felt awkward after Litz gave a negative response to his affection. He was about to conclude that she had problems with intimacy when the top of a baseball bat came swinging down at his face. The astronaut's forearms shot forward in a defensive posture, and the metal bat struck hard just below his left elbow. In a moment of protective instinct, he sidestepped to the right with his arms still in the air, and then pushed off to his left. This maneuver caused his attacker to lose his footing and fall almost onto his face. The soldier released the baseball bat and used his hands to keep his nose from smashing into the carpet.

Litz and Jason watched the event unfold in a surreal state of shock, unaware of what circumstances had led up to this moment. The steel bat bounced a few times on the carpet, and Robert reached out to grab it, but Jason stepped up and kicked it across the room toward the front desk. Litz admired this move by her lover, but she cringed when the metal object clanged hard against the lobby tiles a few times.

"What the hell are you doing?" Jason shouted with a baffled expression as he gripped more of the man's shirt than his left shoulder.

"Sweetheart, I think he has Sunset Syndrome," Litz thought aloud as she took the age of the man and his appearance into consideration. "I mean, let's not be stupid; he could be a total psycho, but don't hurt him if you don't need to," she instructed with hand gestures that embodied a level of calm and wisdom.

"They want me out!" Robert decried to the hotel lobby from his position on all fours. "I don't understand; I just don't understand why it has to be this way."

"Litz, are you okay?" Richard asked as he approached the couple in a pretentious manner. "Did he scare you?"

"I'm the one who almost got brained!" Jason expressed with a fiery gaze, showing his disapproval for Richard's contrived gesture.

Litz glared at Richard and wanted to spit on his green turtleneck sweater. She hated him from his black wingtips and matching dress pants all the way to his foolish schoolboy haircut. Her right hand trembled when she thought about how Richard had shunned Stoney on perhaps the most vulnerable day of his life.

"This is the man who wants you out; he hates older men," Litz said to the soldier who had moved to a kneeling position on the carpet and was looking them over.

Richard and Jason gawked at their companion with dumbfounded faces. Neither of them believed that anyone could be so irresponsible and unpredictable. The soldier leapt from his kneeling position and waylaid Richard with a tremendous right-handed punch to his jaw.

"That's for Stoney, you bastard!" Litz announced as she stood over Richard and shook her fists. "You should have supported him for being gay."

"You lied to me!" Robert snarled at the pretentious woman as he bolted across the entryway carpet to get in her face. "You lied!"

"No...yes, but you still hit him for a good reason." She held out her hands toward the enraged soldier and felt dread creeping through her veins.

Robert got within a few inches of her body before Jason tackled him and wrestled him to the floor. Litz began to back away in her high heels and raised her elbow above her face in a defensive position. But when the attack didn't come, she lowered her arm and observed Jason in an uncharacteristic fit of aggression. The astronaut grappled the soldier like a murderous jungle cat and was able to subdue him with his right elbow against the back of the man's head. Jason pressed his elbow down with extreme force until he was confident about pinning his attacker's face to the floor.

In less than a minute, the police showed up to escort the man away, and several people in the lobby applauded Jason's bravery. Richard was sitting on the carpet with his knees bent in an uncomfortable position. He glared at Litz and rubbed his sore jaw, dismayed that this opportunity had turned into such a loss. His heart sank as Jason reached out and offered him a hand. Although it was the last thing he wanted, the spectators in the hotel would never approve, so Richard accepted his help and rose to his feet.

"You don't deserve him," Richard declared to the bold vixen after Jason pulled him to a standing position. "He's too good for someone as soulless as you, Litz." The irritable conservative then shook Jason's hand and turned on his heel, vacating the lobby with the remainder of his dignity.

Litz breathed out through her nose with a sigh. She knew that her actions had lost points with both men, but decided that it was necessary for justice to have its moment.

"I think it's time to say goodnight," Litz stated with a frown as she watched Jason come in for a kiss, pushing him back with a firm right hand. "Maybe I'll see you at the fundraiser tomorrow," she conveyed in a hollow fashion, refusing to look into his eyes.

"Maybe..." Jason replied in a disenchanted tone as he turned and strutted away without another thought.

The astronaut expected a cold reception from his new lover at the NASA fundraiser and wondered if he should avoid her altogether. He clenched his right hand into a fist and then thought better of this action, wanting to appear collected and mature during his exit. As a middle-aged man, he was empathetic toward the rebellious guy who smashed up the hotel with a baseball bat and wondered if he would do something similar in the future.

Jason gazed up at the sky when he emerged from the hotel to the beautiful outdoors of Houston, Texas. He remembered dreaming about space from the time he was a boy. It seemed like a fantastic escape from a world that featured such unnecessary drama. Everything about space was the opposite of the bustling cacophony of modern life. For those who were unafraid of being inches from death at every turn, the universe provided a means to gain an ultimate perspective.

The frustrated astronaut snorted when he thought about Litz and the erotic adventure upon which they had embarked. He had no illusions about his motivations but detected nuances of love in the television star. There were short flashes of eternity that came to light when she let her guard down. However, Jason realized that he may as well have been picking flowers during a tornado. His mission to Mars had a ten-percent chance of survival, and he knew that the second shuttle would be his vehicle to the grave. Despite the glaring finality of this mission, Litz Rack had given him something that he could cling to without fear. With her raucous nature of disobedience, she had shown Jason how to 'face death like a rock star and ride his motorcycle to hell.'

IX. Blister

For the first time in seven years, Richard felt tempted by a glass of red wine. His eyes were fixed on the brilliant crimson liquid as it whirled around inside a wineglass made of fine crystal. The golden rim of the glass seemed to tempt him, giving off an allure like something holy and comforting. His hands shook when he turned and saw Stoney and CKB carrying on like a couple of war buddies twenty feet to his right. They had carved out a territory near the stage where a band was playing festive country dance music. The cop and criminal were dressed in black tuxedos, which matched in color and style. Other than their obvious distinction in muscle mass, the only difference between the two was CKB's bright yellow tie that contrasted with Stoney's navy blue bowtie.

Richard pounded his fist on the banquet table in front of him during a moment of clouded desperation. He saw Jazzy and Fassim standing near a makeshift bar fifteen feet to his left, and was awestruck by their platonic attitudes during an energetic discussion. The conservative film editor peered down at his lap and wiped his forehead, sensing that he was sweating. However, when his hand brushed over the skin above his eyebrows, it came across completely dry.

He glanced at the wine again, swirling in a pristine glass wielded by the intricate hand of a beautiful redheaded woman. Richard made an O shape with his lips and blew out a stream of cool air, shifting his gaze away from the wine. The troubled man regretted this when he saw Litz and her new boyfriend Jason come into focus just beyond where he was staring. Litz was wearing a tight lime green T-shirt to show off her bust, along with a black leather skirt and lime green high heels. Her debonair companion was masculinity incarnate in his black designer suit and orange tie.

Richard tightened his right hand around his knee, sensing that his brain was screaming for alcohol. Over the past few days, he had become an island in relation to his fellow cast members. While the trip had helped the others to grow closer, Richard managed to have social sanctions applied against him. The actions of his co-stars, in preparation for the farewell fundraiser at NASA headquarters, had been nothing less than an embargo of affection.

"And here we sit, my old friend," Richard said to the red wine as it rocked hypnotically back and forth in the young woman's glass ten feet away. "Everyone else has someone tonight; maybe I should too." The film editor experienced coldness at his center that was worse than hunger, and the alcohol cried out to ease his pain like a siren in a pirate's tale.

Jason observed his new companion with mixed emotions as Litz waved to him on her way to the ladies' room. He returned the wave and blew her a kiss, attempting to suspend the regret that would follow in the next few days. Although their love affair had been ethereal in ways, his first test mission to the moon in preparation for Mars was in less than a week. If that mission went well, the engineers would give them another month, at best, before sending them up to take on the real thing. The astronaut smiled as he realized that, were it not for the deadlines, they might never have made up so fast after fighting the previous day. He shook his head after considering the horrid state of the man that had attacked them at the hotel. Jason took a moment to reflect on how many cases of Sunset Syndrome had been reported in the news each day. Dozens of men and women would break down and live out a fight or flight reaction to their fate.

The astronaut saw Richard glaring at him from the center of the room and raised his eyebrows in an expression of offense. He put his hands into the deep pockets of his black Armani suit jacket and decided to stroll over to where Richard was sitting. Jason watched the orange tie bouncing under the fabric of his high-thread-count suit jacket and smiled at the thought of a little competition. His better senses told him that making peace with everyone before going on a mission was good luck.

The excitement of the party was building throughout the cavernous meeting hall at the NASA executive office complex. Jason was careful to navigate through round tables with elegant white toppers and guests from all backgrounds that were enjoying the event. He noted the live music and full bar as signs that private investors had made life at NASA more enjoyable. The executive staff had also taken the time to add some mood lighting and a temporary dance floor to host the television stars. It was an enchanting event with only the finest accommodations.

Richard saw the astronaut coming toward him and wondered why he seemed approachable to the last person with whom he wanted to speak. The television star locked his gaze on a half-emptied glass of white wine on the table. He presumed that it was abandoned by one of the couples that vacated the table to have fun on the dance floor. The beleaguered man mustered all of his strength, but it wasn't enough, and he reached out for the glass of wine like a tattered life jacket in a raging sea. His fingers gripped the glass with the methodical muscle memory of a longtime addict, and the alcohol tipped down his throat as if it were yellow kerosene running into a furnace.

Jason paused when he reached the table where Richard was seated. He noticed that the television star had an unruly glow in his eyes. It was as though someone had just given him a beating, and Richard was doubling up his fist to come back at them.

"Look, I just want to say that I empathize with your position," Jason offered as he stretched out the fingers on both of his hands and flexed them in the air. "I know how women can lead a guy on – maybe with a passionate kiss." He paused and took a moment to deliver a charming smile. "Sometimes they do things out of emotion and have no idea what consequences will come about. That's why it's important for us to be adults about this whole arrangement."

"You're going to be on a rocket in a few days," Richard began as he snatched an almost full mimosa from the table and gulped it down. "There's a twenty-percent chance that your rocket will explode before you get into space. Once you go to the moon, there's a thirty-percent chance that you won't come home. There's another five-percent chance that you won't survive your reentry," the film editor announced with frivolous nuances of contempt. "I learned about that on the tour. But after you survive all those things, you'll have to turn around and do it again on a planet farther away."

"So your brilliant plan to get the girl comes from winning a death lottery?" The astronaut asked with a spirited chuckle. "Do you know how many missions I've survived? Are you aware that the stats they use on the tour are from the late Twentieth Century so that we can get more funding?"

Richard didn't respond to the challenges offered by Jason. Instead, he decided to inspect the table for more alcohol, finding a Bloody Mary that was melted to an almost inedible mess. Jason shook his head as the man opposite him seemed poised to drown himself in alcohol, even if it meant drinking from a urinal.

"You know the cops told me the other day that the guy with the baseball bat...had been there for a while." The astronaut accused his companion with a self-righteous gleam in his eyes. "It wouldn't surprise me if you saw him coming my way, and didn't bother to give me a heads-up."

"So what if I did?" Richard inquired with a bit of macho posturing. "What if I wanted him to crack your pretty little head open?"

"It would have been a tragedy; that's why," Jason answered in revulsion as he started to turn away from his adversary.

"Oh, really? Why?" The conservative asked with a bold stare, leaning toward the table with his abdominal muscles tightened.

"Because I have a girlfriend and kid!" Jason exclaimed in a heated display of outrage, signaling with his hands for Richard to stop speaking. "Look, I'm gonna' head out to my office. Go ahead and tell Litz whatever you want," the middle-aged man added as he tilted his head down and stepped away from the table in a rush.

Richard watched the astronaut depart in a state of panic, wondering whether he had heard the man correctly, or if it was the alcohol speaking to him. He stared at the tablecloth in a daze for a few seconds, and then decided it was time to get a fresh drink.

"So did you hear the one about the comedian that took home a lonely Texas boy?" A lanky Texas millionaire prompted Jazzy with a brazen smile.

"Oh, you mean the one that wound up pregnant and single, living alone on welfare?" Jazzy retorted with an unflattering squint at the end of her sentence. "Yeah, that is an awesome story! Thanks for playing; now get out of my face!"

The thirty-seven-year-old oil tycoon was undeterred by this statement. Instead, he took a moment to consider her sentiments and blew them off with gruff laughter. He then straightened his cream-colored pants by tugging on a thick, black leather belt. The man was clad in a soft white button-down dress shirt with silver TX cufflinks and a pair of pale snakeskin cowboy boots. Jazzy shuddered at the sound of his laughter, wishing that she were back in New York where men recognized rudeness.

"Look, Texas Jack, or whatever your name is," Fassim hissed at the lonely stranger, "I need you and your penis to step back five paces so that my friend and I can breathe. No, don't make a joke about your manhood; that wasn't an invitation to be raunchy. Just get out of our space, okay?" The paparazzi photographer put her hands on the man's shoulders and gave him a light shove, hoping to breach his alcoholic haze.

"You're one of them Muslims, aren't you?" He asserted by pointing his right index finger at Fassim's orange headscarf. "Well isn't that just fantastic?" The millionaire paused and shifted his stance to admire the photographer's beautiful face. "Have you ever heard about the Muslim woman who took home a lonely Texas boy?" His face lit up with excitement as he made this offer, and he began to imagine what the woman looked like in the nude.

"Do you see this thing around my head?" Fassim demanded with a hint of proud feminist rhetoric. "This is supposed to send a message to all of the men in the area. It's hot and uncomfortable, but not as bad as getting hit on when you aren't looking for anyone. Now, I understand that you have physical needs, sir. So may I direct your attention to the blonde over there that is speaking loudly and showing off her cleavage? She would be more in the market for what you're offering. Now have a good night!" The fiery Muslim pointed to a blonde woman over thirty feet away who looked as if she was falling out of her red dress.

After the man had spotted the blonde that Fassim was pointing out, he nodded and returned a warm smile. His appreciation reminded her of stories about Sacagawea guiding Lewis and Clark through the barren wilderness to sustenance.

"Deflection is always better than rejection," Fassim said to Jazzy as the man walked away in a hurry. "They think you're their hero and don't blame you if the next girl shoots them down."

Jazzy smiled at her companion and realized that it was the first time a paparazzo had ever protected her from harassment. The comedian had picked a low-key black gown for the event, and her hair was tied up in a ponytail to combat the famous Houston humidity. Fassim had chosen to wear a blue and white flower print blouse, along with loose-fitting blue jeans to go with her headscarf. They stood near a bar that the NASA employees had fashioned from the reception desk and a white bed sheet.

The skillful Muslim had been surpassing Jazzy's expectations all week. Her actions could almost justify the comedian forgiving her for the collage of nude photos that were published in various tabloids. It was a bittersweet sisterhood, but after the support shown in her time of crisis, Jazzy considered the woman her 'bitchy little sister.'

Jazzy watched the country musicians on the stage with an unusual amount of reverence. Her father had been a music teacher, but after three bouts with cancer, the family had nearly gone broke. Although he survived his long battle, it came with an impossible price tag. She had to drop out of high school to get a job at age fifteen, and found herself serving tables at a local nightclub in Chicago, Illinois. There was a terrible snowstorm on Open Mic Night, which kept away most of the scheduled acts. Jazzy had been coerced by the club owner to take the stage and tell a few jokes. Although she was nervous, it wound up being one of the best nights of her life.

The impressionable woman lowered her head as the best night of her life wound up reminding her of the worst. She glanced over at CKB and traced the contours of his muscular body in the stylish black tuxedo. Although the comedian had made several attempts to find out his plans to 'take care of' the billionaire that attacked her, he had only responded with winks or smiles. There was a nervous energy brewing within her lower abdomen. On one hand, she welcomed swift and fierce retribution for the violence that had been visited upon her, but on the other, it could backfire into something worse. CKB could get hurt or killed, and the man might seek vengeance of his own against the entertainer.

"Where is Litz?" Richard barked as he approached the two women like an overzealous bloodhound. "I need to tell her something."

Jazzy was startled by her co-star when she saw him encroaching on the sisterly space between her and Fassim. Richard was wearing a black button-down shirt with matching dress pants, and a shiny pair of noir wingtip shoes. He had been as approachable as a cactus since Stoney made his announcement, and the all-black ensemble wasn't helping.

"You shouldn't talk to Litz right now, Richard," Jazzy instructed and placed her right hand on his left bicep to caution him further.

"Are you drunk, Richard?" Fassim asked with wide eyes as she took in his stuffy mannerisms and slurred speech. "What are you trying to do, win the hypocrite of the year award?"

"I need to tell Litz something…important," he continued in an awkward fashion and spun around counterclockwise a few times, looking in all directions.

"Look, Litz went home with Jason," the comedian began in a noble moment of tough love, "you should try hitting on that loud blonde over there."

Jazzy and Fassim looked at one another and shared a delinquent laugh. They had lost count of how many men were sent in the direction of the blonde in search of love. It had made for good amusement when the men discovered that her husband was seated right beside her. The smile left Jazzy's face when she noticed that Richard was poking her bare shoulder with his right index finger.

"What? What do you need to tell Litz that is so important?" Jazzy shouted at her co-star in a moment of severe annoyance.

"Jason is standing right there," Richard said as he turned his finger over and pointed it at the dance floor.

Jazzy screwed up her face when she noticed that Jason was waiting near the corner of the dance floor wearing a white dress shirt and orange tie. His suit jacket was wrapped around his arms, and he seemed to be bothered by something.

"Look, Richard, I need you to go with Stoney and CKB," Jazzy instructed her drunken co-star, tapping him on the shoulder in a gentle way with her right hand. "Fassim and I will go find Litz, and we'll let her know that you have something important to say."

Richard held up his right hand with the index finger and thumb pressed together as if to say 'okay.' Jazzy and Fassim then made their way through the partygoers towards the dance floor, watching for Litz as they went.

"Where's our girl?" Jazzy inquired when she and her co-star were within five feet of Jason.

"I don't know," the astronaut said in what seemed like a lost and hopeless state. "She might be in the bathroom thinking about things, or maybe she talked to Richard and went back to the hotel."

"Why? What does Richard want?" The unshakable woman pried with a hint of concern. "How long ago did she leave for the bathroom?"

"It's been about thirty minutes," Jason replied in a forlorn manner as he listened to the rebellious notes of the live country music.

Jazzy turned away from Jason upon hearing this news and made her way over to their security detail. A bullish Hispanic man was standing near the door in a light gray suit. His hands were clasped together over his abdomen as his body swayed in time with the music.

"Jose, where did Litz go?" Jazzy requested when she reached the double doors of the meeting hall.

"She went to the bathroom, but I haven't seen her for a while," the twenty-five-year-old bodyguard announced with a shrug.

"Call the hotel and see if she's there," the comedian ordered with alarm as she and Fassim made their way out into the hallway.

"Why are you so worried about Litz?" Fassim asked during a spirited dash through the dark and desolate office hallways.

"I heard Jennifer and Mike talking about a guy who is obsessed with Litz from watching our TV show," Jazzy responded in a hurry as she burst into the ladies' room with Fassim in tow.

"You mean she has a stalker?" The paparazzi photographer attempted to confirm in a whisper. "But why would he be down here in Texas?"

The flustered comedian ignored this valid question and elected instead to trust her gut. She maneuvered through a handful of women in their early twenties and began to inspect the areas under the bathroom stalls.

"Look, if she has a stalker, it's unlikely that he took a flight down here," Fassim offered with a shrug of impending disappointment.

Jazzy knelt down like a crab and reached under one of the stall doors, grunting somewhat from the strain. She then stood up tall with a pair of lime green high heels clutched in her right hand. The photographer opened her mouth in shock and closed her eyes with a feeling of shame.

X. Diving into Concrete

"There are 1,600 acres of grounds to search at the space center," Jason concluded with a desperate gaze as he ran his fingers through his hair. "And she's not answering her phone?" He asked the security guards and actors that were standing before him.

"She may not even be here," Jazzy speculated with her arms folded tight in a display of concern.

"Well, if she's not at the hotel, then where else would she go?" The astronaut asked with impatience. "I mean she is old enough to make her own choices, but nobody is going out on the town without their shoes. So why would she leave?"

"Look, Jennifer and Mike have been getting death threats for Litz every day," the comedian explained with a demeanor of exhaustion. "Someone is obsessed with her, and they've been sending letters to the television station. I think the producers even got the FBI involved."

"I don't want to think that way!" Jason exclaimed with a scowl as he began to pace back and forth through the conference room. "The chance that some creep followed her here is unlikely, so I'm going to assume that she's on the grounds. We'll get some people on our trams, and I'll help to coordinate the security camera footage. There are two-and-a-half square miles to cover, so the best thing we can do is to get started. You folks can wait in here or back at the hotel; I'll call you when we know something."

"We want to help with the search," Fassim offered with a desperate gaze, turning her hands over with both palms upward.

"No, I'm not allowed to have anyone on the grounds that isn't authorized to be there," Jason answered in a prompt manner. "There are some real dangers out in the field here. This place is full of rocket fuel, ignition systems, and vehicles of all types. It's best that we only have one missing person in potential danger. Please stay here and I'll update you as soon as we know something. In the meantime, I need someone to get a piece of her clothing; we're going to use some police dogs to track her down. They'll be here within the hour."

Jazzy glanced around at her co-stars with a feeling of helplessness. Given the fresh knowledge that their colleague was missing, the NASA conference room felt small and surreal to the actors. CKB, Stoney, and Richard were standing at the back of the room speaking to one another in whispers. The comedian decided that it was in the nature of men to speculate on a solution.

"I'll go get something from her hotel room for the police dogs," Fassim suggested as she stroked her orange headscarf in a display of nervous energy. "It should only take me forty minutes to get back from the hotel. No, wait, we have her shoes right here; the dogs can use those. Don't mind me; I'm just tired." The weary Muslim used her index fingers to massage the bridge of her nose.

"If it's okay, I think we should wait here until they tell us something," Jazzy suggested to Fassim and her male co-stars.

Everyone nodded in agreement and Jazzy glanced around the oak conference table at the padded chairs, searching for a place to get comfortable. Jason and the other NASA people vacated the room in a hurry. In their haste, they gave the impression that certain details were confidential to the television stars and their security staff.

Jason followed Brian Mahoney through the hallway during their journey to the security offices. Although there were over a hundred cameras on the property, finding someone could be a cumbersome task. He swore to himself as he considered the possibility of NASA executives seeing him and Litz fooling around in the shuttle bay. It would be even worse if they saw them during their multiple instances of naked fun. Brian was a short twenty-four-year-old man, but he had a rapid gait, and it was difficult for Jason to keep pace with him. The five-foot-three-inch technician was a bald man of African descent. He wore thick eyeglasses that went well with his plain white T-shirt and black trousers.

After three minutes of silent walking, the two NASA employees made their way into the security control room. There were six rows and twelve columns of monitors embedded in the far wall of the room. Each monitor had at least eighteen inches of diagonal viewing space. Three tall benches were positioned just eight feet behind the wall of monitors, and each had a comfy padded swivel chair. Jason elected to stand stoic behind the bench at the right side of the room. His colleague began turning on computer monitors and pulled up some software to search the archived video footage.

The astronaut felt useless after a moment, and his heart began to pound when he thought about someone abducting his new girlfriend. He inhaled with repressed emotions, deciding that it would be better to maintain his wits.

"Let's start with the bathrooms," Jason suggested in a state of fear as he abandoned his stoicism and took a seat to the right of Brian.

Litz awoke to the brilliant glow of the Houston sky at night. There were dozens of stars shining down on her, and she could feel cold metal beneath her back and legs. The early morning was deceptively chilly in Texas, and the small leather skirt provided little cover. Her legs were shaking and covered in goose bumps. She had cried herself to sleep, which caused makeup to run down the sides of her face in thick lines. The disoriented plumber held up her bare arms and saw smudges of something black all over them.

Litz decided to retrace her steps from the party, remembering that Jason had waved to her before she went to the bathroom. When she got to a stall and sat down on the toilet, her forehead broke out in a profuse sweat. The memories of her family tragedies began to surface, and a panic attack ensued. She took off her shoes due to the sensation of heat. Her body was dripping with perspiration and it felt like something terrible was happening. Litz recollected running out of the bathroom as fast as she could manage. It seemed like all of the darkness was chasing her through the hallways, and she couldn't escape. There were memories of her father's heart attack and the subsequent car crash that killed him and her little brother. She saw the death of her mother played in a sadistic loop as if Satan was the emcee of her memories. This sickening display eventually gave way to her time at the boarding school and the abusive teenagers that persecuted her there. Litz recalled spending several years with her head buried in books, learning about all manner of philosophy and engineering. But the teenagers went too far one day and the abuse was unbearable. She escaped the boarding school and spent several days on the streets until she found a predatory drug dealer. The fifteen-year-old accepted his offer to take a joyride, and she abandoned the pervert at the first gas station.

Litz remembered how powerful the black Chevrolet Corvette felt under her rear end. It was the first time she had taken power back from the universe. But it ended when the car hit a patch of ice in Park City, Utah and crashed into a riverbed. The young woman was so high on cocaine and drunk on whiskey that she decided to go rock climbing in the snow. Although the boarding school had taken the students out and taught them to climb with the proper safety equipment – that was not her concern. She wanted to scale the cliff and show its broad face of authority that it could not win. After ascending seventy-five feet onto the ledge of the prominent rock formation, Litz Eliza Rack took a leap of faith and landed in the outstretched branches of a large pine tree. It was as though she was caught by her mother in midair, and told never to give up fighting for her beliefs.

"I love you, mom," Litz said to the calming air of the Texas sky. "I miss you!"

In the distance, there came the repetitive sounds of dogs barking. Litz raised her head somewhat but decided to put it back down when a throbbing pain erupted through her right eye. The young woman felt severe dryness in her throat and closed her eyes for a moment to quell the pain.

"Litz! Litz!" Jason's voice called out from the distance. "Oh my God! She's in the flame trench. Litz, hang on we're coming."

"Flame trench?" Litz repeated as she rolled onto her side and felt her right hand snag on a steel cable.

The agitated woman started to wrestle with the cable and twisted sideways to get it away from her face. Litz felt the steel drop out from underneath her body. She grabbed the cable tight as her bare feet and legs dangled into a vast dark space.

"Oh my God!" The television star exclaimed in terror as her hands tried to get a stronger hold on the cable.

She kicked in desperation at the air and reached out with the ends of her toes to find a foothold, but there was nothing beneath her other than blackness. The black smudges on her arms were greasy, and she was slipping off of the cable a few inches at a time. Litz wrapped her left arm around the cable and felt a sliver of steel repay her with a deep wound. The panicked woman cried out and stopped kicking her legs. She realized that her poor upper body strength was the only way to prevent a treacherous fall.

"Litz, don't let go, you're fifty feet over a concrete channel," Jason reported through heaving breaths. "I'm almost there, sweetheart, just hold onto that cable."

Litz could see that the horizontal cable was part of a walkway that went across a massive concrete channel. She had been lying on her back at the center of the maintenance catwalk, which had three lengths of cable on either side to prevent workers from falling.

Her breaths came out in desperate gasps as she clung to the safety cable for life. But the greasy substance on her hands and arms was causing the cable to slip away, regardless of how Litz tried to maintain her grip. She could hear Jason's heavy footsteps ambling across the walkway as her left wrist began to slip over the top of the cable. The middle-aged astronaut dove hard, and Litz felt his body crash into the steel floor of the catwalk. He grunted to indicate a fresh injury and reached out to help the television star.

"Careful, my hands are covered in something slippery," Litz pleaded with the astronaut as his efforts caused her to slide faster.

Litz felt her body dropping and saw Jason lunge with his arms toward her from the catwalk. He managed to grab her underneath both arms, but his body was hanging halfway off of the walkway. She began to tremble, noticing that he was hanging upside down beneath her and wondered if they were falling. Her arms wrapped tight around his abdomen, and Litz prepared for the precious final seconds of her life.

"What are you doing?" Jason protested in earnest at her reckless actions. "Climb up my legs and get back on the walkway."

Litz raised her head in extreme confusion and saw that Jason had wrapped his legs around the steel cable to keep them from falling. He was hanging upside down with his arms wrapped around her torso, using the joints of her underarms for leverage. If he were to release his legs, they would both plummet to the concrete fifty feet below the catwalk.

"You should let me go," Litz pleaded with the astronaut when she saw how much he was risking to save her. "Jason, you should just let me go; it's too heavy for both of us."

"Just climb my damn legs! Now!" Jason shouted in a throaty and masculine voice. "We can do this if you hurry!"

Litz reached between his legs and used the back of his right thigh to pull herself up. Fortunately, the fabric of his dress pants absorbed most of the grease, and she was able to pull herself high enough to reach the cable. The cautious woman paused to wipe her free hand on his pants before grabbing the lowest cable. She then gripped the next cable up with her other hand and climbed steadily until her body was balanced above the third cable.

Several rescue workers from NASA arrived on the catwalk and knelt down to assist Jason up from his dangerous position. A bearded man in his late thirties stepped over to Litz and helped her down from the top cable. The young woman began to cry when she felt her bare feet touch the cold steel.

Jason got to his feet with the help of his comrades and wiped some sweat from his brow. He then let his colleagues walk past him single file so that he could be close to Litz.

"I don't know what's wrong with me!" Litz admitted in a moment of vulnerable innocence as tears ran down her cheeks. "I had some kind of panic attack and wound up out here. Thank you for saving me! Thank you so much!"

Jason embraced his younger lover with unabated affection. He kissed her passionately and ran his fingers all over her body as if to confirm that she was real. Litz felt the power of his arms around her and gazed down at the darkness beneath them. She was trembling at the sight of the cavernous concrete channel into which they almost fell.

"This is the flame trench," Jason said as he led her by the hand off of the walkway. "It's used to keep the heat away from the space shuttle so that it can lift off without blowing itself up."

"I don't care what you call it. I hate it!" She said in a manner that was half joking and somewhat truthful.

As the couple stepped across the last few feet of walkway, Litz glimpsed a flashlight from someone who was moving through the bottom of the trench. Her eyes glazed over with renewed fear when she understood the scale of the massive structure.

"How did you wind up out here?" Jason asked once they made it to the safety of the solid concrete pads. "Everyone was worried that you'd been abducted. Why did you leave your shoes behind?"

"Something horrible happened to my mother when I was younger," Litz confessed with reluctance. "If I have enough to drink, it causes me to have an episode. I hope you don't think I'm crazy."

"No, I'm just glad that you're okay," he answered with a suave smile. "But the police are going to have some questions for you. It should only take a few hours."

Ellington Airport – Houston, Texas

Litz stood atop the tarmac on the private side of Ellington Airport, waiting for Jason to show up and say goodbye. After the police had finished questioning her, the couple had stayed up all night talking and caressing one another in her hotel room. She recalled looking down at the pool seven floors below, and the railing from which they had rappelled. There were many magical moments and all of them had ended too soon.

The pensive woman pushed a pair of dark sunglasses firmly against the bridge of her nose. She licked her lips as a dry breeze kicked up and whisked past, leaving her feeling ridiculous in a sexy white dress.

"Five more minutes, Litz," Mike Farr shouted from the steps near their private jet.

Jazzy shook her head in defiance as she took in the spectacle that had become Mike and Jennifer. The director and producer seemed pale and strung out, like two teenagers that had been partying for two weeks. Their hair was stringy, and they wore wrinkled clothing, which contrasted with everyone else that worked for the show. She saw Mike wince several times and grab at the back of his head as if he had a hangover. Jennifer had similar tics but was able to keep them under better control. The comedian wondered where Mike and Jennifer had gone during their whole trip. They didn't bother to do more than a meet and greet with the NASA people. Their behavior aroused further suspicion when they didn't show up to help find Litz; nor did they seem to care about her near-death experience.

Jazzy breathed out a sigh of frustration. She felt alone in her thoughts, but then CKB signaled with the middle and index fingers of his right hand that he was also watching the mysterious duo. The comedian smiled at ebony Hercules for his incredible gesture and was feeling grateful to have supportive friends in her life.

Richard watched Litz waiting on the runway with a mixture of relief and distress. After what she described of her ordeal during the night, he decided to let Jason have his secret. It seemed to him that the lie needed to remain intact to keep the fragile woman from having another episode.

A black Lincoln Navigator pulled up on the visitor side of the fence, and Litz began walking towards it with a grin. However, she stopped after ten feet, noticing that a brunette woman was in the passenger seat next to Jason. Her center went cold as she saw a little boy leaning between the two front seats from the middle seat. Jason took a moment to rub the boy's hair with his right hand and gave the woman a loving kiss.

Litz rediscovered the penetrating sting of romantic betrayal. Thoughts were racing through her mind, but the anger that she wanted to express was somehow blocked. When Jason got out of the vehicle and said hello, her brain seemed to short circuit. She stared at the woman and looked away, repeating this process every few seconds. The television star couldn't imagine what her colleagues felt as they witnessed this revelation from the jet.

Her hands began to shake with an involuntary rush of rage that refused to come forth from her lips. The forlorn beauty thought about all the intimate time she had spent with Jason and realized that he was just having fun. Litz closed her eyes and tipped her face toward the ground. She had prepared a small speech to ask the man not to go on his mission, but that was before he turned her world upside down. The slighted woman opened her eyes and breathed out a slow, steady stream of air. Litz then gathered strength from within and tightened her stomach muscles as she spoke.

"Goodbye, Jason," the television star said with deep sadness and turned to walk away without waiting for him to respond.

Litz kept from hanging her head as she moved and smiled at Jazzy when approaching the private jet. Never in her life had she been more ready to return to New York.

XI. Selfie in Stripes

"Did you know that people who eat leftovers from the garbage are happier than most of their Homo sapien cousins?" Oslo Norway mused as he swung in a heavy green canvas hammock beneath a bustling New York City overpass.

"That's so totally true," Litz replied with a smile from another army green hammock just a few feet away. "You get more nutrients from the surprises in every trash can. Do you know what they should do, Oslo?"

"Yeah, but they don't," the homeless man offered while thoughtfully stroking his beard.

"They should come out with a new line of garbage cuisines," she professed with a smile of relaxation.

"But then what will they do with the leftover garbage cuisine?" He posited in an urgent tone. "They can't mix garbage cuisine in with new garbage; that would create dark matter garbage." The middle-aged man sat up in his hammock with excitement like a child getting ready to tell a bedtime story. "Hey, Litz, I have a great idea!"

"Oh, really?" The thoughtful woman prodded with a coy expression.

"Why don't we go cut up some wolves and try to feed them to sheep?" Oslo proposed with a broad smile, showing that he had only three molars remaining in his lower jaw. "We'd turn them into wolf juice and let the sheep slurp it up instead of water. Do you know what that would eventually create?"

"Wolf-sheep?" The television star asked and turned her head to witness his theatrics. "Ouch!" Litz complained after one of Oslo's shoes hit her in the forehead, indicating that he disliked her response.

"No, you idiot," he lamented with a smirk of enjoyment. "They'd be sheep-wolves. Then we'd get a big white piece of wool and wrap it around a sheep-wolf, which would make a…" Oslo paused and held his hands high in a grand gesture, waiting for her to finish his sentence.

"A sheep-wolf in sheep's clothing?" Litz suggested with vigorous laughter.

Oslo didn't respond but turned his head to the right as if her answer offended him. He then spun around and dropped his hands to his sides, which allowed him to recline in the hammock and pull the loose fabric around his body.

"Are we pouting now?" The vivacious woman pried with an innocent chuckle. "You know, Oslo, I think I just met a sheep-wolf in sheep's clothing," she said with a bittersweet sigh.

"So you rubbed his magic lamp, and after the genie popped out, it wasn't ready to go home with you?" He quipped with a measure of sincerity. "Every man is just a little boy, and every little boy plays with things and forgets about them."

"Yeah, but that man saved my life," Litz retorted in a moment of romantic reflection.

"And that boy broke your heart," Olso responded with a subtle warning in his voice. "Now you're one and one, and no one can replace the other one. Do you know what you need?"

"What do I need, Oslo?" She prompted with a glow in her eyes, shedding the sadness from her face.

"You need to drink a gallon of wolf juice a day," he joked with a throaty voice and turned over to stare at the overpass above his head. "Yep, I think a gallon of wolf juice a day would turn you into...wolf-rack."

"Hell yes, I would lure them in with my fantastic breasts and then rip them apart like a ragdoll," the plumber stated with an emphatic chuckle.

"Excuse me, young lady," the man taunted in a snide fashion, "but we have manners in this household...overpass-hold. We don't just rip our guests apart without first offering them a warm bottle of water."

"So what is it that inspires you to rub your magic lamp, Mr. Norway?" Litz questioned in an unbridled display of audacity.

"Oh geez, well that might be embarrassing to answer," he expressed in a sarcastic tone. "Let's see...the sound of manufactured cheese being unwrapped...that gurgling noise a pipe makes before water comes out...and the back seat of a police car."

"Holy romantic butt clippings, Oslo," Litz agreed with a giggle. "Those are all things that do it for me too! Oh, my dear friend, how long has it been since we were at that boarding school? I still remember when you beat up that sixteen-year-old who tried doing naughty things to me. When all the other kids hated me, my sweet Oslo came to the rescue."

"Well, only eighty percent of them hated you; that's hardly a majority," Oslo deadpanned in a dramatic tone. "Yes, my job as a school counselor was never complete until I hit one of those little sociopaths. By the way, you never paid me anything for those heroics; I'm still waiting on a check."

"Oh, yeah, and what address should I mail that check to?" She teased with a transparent grin.

"Let's see, you could send it to the Hudson River as the crow flies; turn left at the green dumpster – the one with the orange graffiti. Stop when you hear the ice cream truck that sells meth," the homeless man uttered with his hands in the air as if they were gripping a steering wheel.

"Yep, and if you see a freeway sign with a pig eating a donut, then you've gone too far," Litz added in a cocky tone. "You know, Oslo, I really don't know where to go from here. I had another episode in Houston, but I was able to get some things done that were long overdue. They arrested a man with Sunset Syndrome at my hotel."

"Just one?" He asked in a more serious manner. "Yeah, Sunset Syndrome sounds so much nicer than 'crazy older person who can't deal with fate and keep their mouth shut.'"

"You should've seen the Memorial Towers in Texas," Litz conveyed with a somber voice. "There were more than ten black skyscrapers, each over 1,500 feet high. They cast long shadows over the city in the morning – the effect was creepy."

"You're creepy," he said with a smile of deep affection. "You're creepy, and you smell like barbecues and baby showers."

"Yeah...baby showers – the theme for this century." She emoted in a state of deep thought. "I love you, Mr. Norway," the steadfast woman said as she made eye contact with her longtime friend.

"I love you too; my dear, as much as any homeless person ever loved a middle-class female plumber with a severe anxiety disorder," he announced with a broad grin, laughing in silence at the speeding cars overhead.

Canarsie Park – Brooklyn, New York

The pale German sat with his arms folded taut against his chest on a bench in Canarsie Park. He wore black carpenter jeans and a soft white sweater with a Dallas Cowboys logo on the front. An opened bag of chocolate-covered raisins was between his legs, balanced on the faded green paint of the wooden bench. His demeanor was the epitome of exhaustion and contempt. He had never cared for American football teams, but the clothing seemed to make him more approachable.

A mother was talking on her phone with her back turned to three children that were playing in the sandbox. The German predator watched as the mother walked away from them one step at a time, opening up an opportunity. One of the children had already asked him for some chocolate, but he wasn't able to give her any thanks to the black man.

The enraged German put his head down and placed his left palm against his forehead. He had been excited when the black man stopped coming to the park and watching him while he observed the children. But the police showed up to patrol the park every day after that, and they paid close attention to what was happening in the play areas. After over a week of watching and waiting, he was still no closer to getting his prize.

CKB glared at the German from across the play area with unflinching eyes. Stoney had asked the local police precinct to check his background, but the man's criminal history was clean, and there were no outstanding warrants. Although the career criminal had other things to do and deadlines to meet, nothing was more important than the safety of the local children.

He had considered threatening the child predator or giving him a severe beating, but that type of punishment was often taken out on the next child. CKB knew that there were some areas where the legal system had failed, but they excelled in protecting minors from terrible people.

In his boredom, the television star tried to enjoy the small dramas that were played out in the sandbox and other areas of the park. A feisty little blonde girl had an older brother who wanted to take away her red plastic shovel, but she gave him a beat down every time he tried. Another small, rebellious Hispanic boy kept trying to get on the merry-go-round with the older kids, and his mother had to tow him away to safety.

The muscular man leaned forward over the wrought iron railing and clasped his hands together in a contrived state of amusement. As a boy growing up in poverty, Cody never got the chance to play with toys until he was twelve years old. CKB wondered how these parents would react if he told them that owning toys wasn't possible for him until he sold enough drugs to buy them. It was a curiosity to him that clean-cut Wall Street traders were welcomed into every home, even if they were high on cocaine. However, the man who sold that trader the cocaine could not be trusted to walk past a minivan without the locks being engaged.

CKB smiled at himself and realized that he was being cynical. Those people were smart to lock their doors because he had an automatic weapon under the folds of his jacket for protection. And if his competitors decided to stage an ambush in a clean suburban neighborhood, the bullets would be indiscriminate in their lethality.

The stoic man gripped the cool iron railing in a moment of holistic reflection. He thought about the bullet wounds in his right leg and shoulder. During the party back in Houston, Stoney had told him about a few bullet wounds from action that he had seen. But most of the police officer's 'scar trophies' had come from people with Sunset Syndrome, or while he was trying to prevent a suicide attempt.

CKB glanced at the toys with which the children were playing. He took in a deep breath of the warm spring air and pondered his chances of opening a custom toy store. It had been a while since he revised his business plan, but the man knew that he was close to earning the investment capital needed for a decent operation. During his downtime on various jobs, he had sketched out concept artwork for new toy designs. CKB chuckled when he thought about getting arrested with drawings of toys in his pockets. He thought it would be hilarious if the police sat him down for hours of questioning about a trampoline half-pipe.

The career criminal stood up tall when he noticed that the German was giving up for the day. Cody watched the man cast a bag of chocolate-covered raisins into the grass, and he seemed to be mumbling something on his way out of the park.

"I'll get you, dude," CKB said to the open air of the play area while watching the stranger depart.

When the German had disappeared from the grounds, the mother put away her satellite phone and turned to check on her three children. She then displayed a devilish smile and walked toward CKB with a dutiful stare.

"Thank you for what you're doing to help our kids," the young blonde conveyed to CKB as she brushed back her hair in a flirtatious gesture. "Are you sure this is the best way to get him?"

"Yeah, the cops can't do anything until he makes a move," CKB replied with a yawn of exhaustion. "We need to catch him in the act and let the system do their thing. After he has something on his record, it will be easy to keep him away from your littles."

"Do you want to get some coffee today?" She asked with a conspicuous wink from her gleaming blue eyes.

"That would be amazing!" He answered with a charming smile as his hands dropped off of the railing, and he started walking backward. "But I want to get this done first. Let's keep a clear head and see if we're a good team." The muscular man winked back at the mother before turning away to resume his duties for Mitch Gentile.

"See you around, Cody," the woman expressed with pride and watched his backside swagger before attending to her children.

The Shots Fired Loft – Manhattan, New York

Fassim lowered her head almost to her knees as she sat across from Jennifer Priest in a small corner office of the penthouse. The paparazzi photographer removed a pink hijab from her head and straightened her body to engage the aggressive television producer on her own turf.

"It's racist for you to ask me to tell that story," Fassim surmised through gritted teeth. "What is wrong with you television people? When I signed the contract, I didn't know that you had this much information about my life. How did you get access to something that isn't public record?"

"It doesn't matter, Fassim," Jennifer claimed with a casual demeanor, "our contract allows us to refuse your weekly paychecks and to litigate if you don't deliver. We knew that it would be difficult to tell these stories, which is part of the reason you got the job. Mike and I wanted people of diverse backgrounds who could say witty things and think on their feet. But we also wanted some heartbreaking emotional stories that could be shared with our audience. That is the heart and soul of television." The producer finished with an exhausted gaze, though her stamina seemed steadfast for arguments of this type.

"You know, I could protest and say that television doesn't have a soul," the impassioned photographer relayed with her hands resting in her lap, "but you wouldn't hear anything that I said. I can look into your eyes and see that you're the type of person who would eat your own kind to survive. And although you should be ashamed of yourself for what you've asked me to do, I'm certain that it's far from the most terrible thing you've ever done."

The chubby blonde twisted her neck after this verbal assault from the Muslim and pulled the cap off of a silver fountain pen. She then held the pen in her right hand as though it were a knife and leveled the tip of the writing end with Fassim's face.

Fassim felt sick with fear and began to tug at her tan dress and green blouse in a state of sudden anxiety. The television producer was wearing a black pinstripe suit with a red power tie and looked just like a man, save for her face and hair. But there was something about this silent threat that resonated terror within the young woman. Somehow the paparazzi photographer knew that she had seen this type of evil in the world before today.

"You're going to tell the story with all the relevant details," Jennifer ordered with a disgusting snort from her nasal cavity as she dropped the pen on her desk. "And let me tell you something else; your co-stars are also going to pour their hearts out on this show. We're going to squeeze your hearts from the bottom up like packets of ketchup, if necessary. Because you're right; I'm not afraid to get my hands dirty. If an animal is suffering, you need someone like me to put it down. If a man is getting too proud, you need someone like me to remind him of his mortality."

"I think we've all been reminded too much about our mortality," Fassim muttered in defeat as a tear spilled over her eyelid and dripped from her cheek. "So you're going to make Jazzy talk about being raped the same way that you forced Stoney to come out as gay? We have no idea how the other police officers are treating him at work today. It's something that could get him killed! And what about Richard, Litz, and CKB; do they all have to humiliate themselves for your ratings?"

"What did you think this job was, Fassim?" The older woman challenged with a mighty voice of cynicism. "Did you think that we run a day spa around here where you get fresh clothing and makeup, and everyone adores you all day for no reason? Do you think that television stars ever get an easy ride? For everything in life, there is a pound of flesh to be paid, and I don't think it's too much to ask you to tell a story and shed a few tears. Look at you now, you're bawling like a champ and not even getting paid extra. Do you think the construction worker who has to shovel frozen mud on the side of the freeway feels bad about your cozy existence? Don't you think he'd like to bare his soul for five minutes to make ten times his annual salary? No, Fassim, we're not giving any of you a pass on this, so suck it up and do your job. Our sponsors have paid for you to give us the meat of your sorrow. I don't recommend that you disappoint them. You can tell the story any way you want. Get it over with fast – I don't care. Just get it done and stop crying about it," she commanded with a gaze of unshakable scrutiny.

"You're terrible people," the paparazzi photographer emoted in an impulsive display of repressed anger.

Fassim wiped off her face and placed the hijab back on her head as she stood up to depart the office. On her way out, she glanced at the silver pen on the desk and then into the dead eyes of the woman who sought to change her life forever.

Pier 81 – New York

Ned Jones turned on the water of a three-headed shower in the master bathroom of his seventy-five-foot yacht. He wasn't surprised when the water came out at precisely seventy-eight degrees, but had been dismayed that his boat captain neglected to order the proper amount of red wine. Were it not for this moronic act, he wouldn't have had to subject himself to drinking champagne before bed.

The thirty-one-year-old billionaire decided to shake off these difficulties from an otherwise standard day. He looked down at his pot belly and smirked with a deep level of self-adornment. There was nothing better than knowing that he could get as fat as a house and still maintain a steady stream of beautiful women. The hedge fund manager put his right hand under a motion sensor that released a perfect dollop of lime green soap into his palm. He then began to finesse the soap through his incredible dark hair in a passionate state of gratification. Ever since childhood he had loved having a clean body, and mother had always told him that important people should be cleaner than everyone else.

The fanatical billionaire ran his fingernails down the contours of his thighs, leaving light red scratch marks on the skin. He breathed out in a spasmodic display of dominant grace and wondered if David had wept at the sight of his own perfection.

Ned felt his inner musings interrupted as the bathroom went dark. He heard the shower door open and wondered who would dare intrude on his most beloved ritual of the evening. Something popped a few inches from his face, and he felt a stinging sensation near the right side of his chest. In the next instant, his body convulsed as a substantial electrical current traveled through a pair of wires into his chest.

He gritted his teeth in a state of unbearable pain while the electricity seemed to issue bites all over his body. In addition to that sensation, his muscles tensed and released simultaneously. It was as though every inch of his muscle tissue, other than his heart, was going into a deep spasm.

Ned felt his body slide down the corner of the shower walls in a rush, and he was soon in a sitting position on the grainy, non-slip surface of the floor.

Litz flipped the lights back on to see CKB standing over the naked billionaire with a Taser in his right hand. Thanks to her suggestion, he had the presence of mind to wear an insulated glove in the event of any water splashing him from the shower. The emboldened plumber walked with the swagger of a gangster as she took a position at the left of CKB.

"You know that woman who is lying in your bed right now?" Litz inquired with a wily gaze of satisfaction. "We hired her to let us know when you were getting in the shower. She also helped us to get on the boat – right in front of your bodyguards. I think they're still eating the pizza that we brought."

"Why are you doing this?" Ned demanded with a panicked expression as he pounded his fist in the water at the bottom of the shower.

"You raped our friend," the woman replied with a ruthless gaze of contempt. "In the next few hours, you're going to find out how huge a mistake that was…"

XII. Tragic Appetizer

Ned Jones lamented the heavy whitetail deer antlers that were fixed to the top of his head. He saw a seventeen-year-old redheaded cheerleader dancing seductively just two feet below him on a white platform. The adolescent woman was clad in an Abraham Lincoln High School uniform of traditional blue and white colors. She held a black can of pepper spray in her right hand, which had been used on the billionaire's eyes throughout the morning.

There was a one-ton pickup truck beneath a makeshift float, and its sole deck was broad enough to hold six cheerleaders. The platform had been fashioned from pieces of lumber and wooden supports that were painted white. As a final touch the students had glued blue and white streamers to the float, giving it a more authentic appearance. The high school marching band played brass horns and snare drums in a spirited song as they paraded in front of the float. They were followed by the Lincoln Railsplitters football team, which jogged behind the vehicle while it made wide circles in the Abraham Lincoln High School parking lot.

A group of high school students stood at the edge of the parking area, enjoying a deep belly laugh at the colorful spectacle. It was early enough in the morning that the administration staff had not arrived to see their 'Rape Beer Float.' The teens marveled at this moment of rebellious protest, and most of them had never dreamt of serving up mob justice to a billionaire. They cheered as the marching band led the float across the asphalt while six popular cheerleaders performed antics atop the unit. The football team followed close behind chanting, "Rape is bad, rape is wrong; just say no with a good fight song."

Ned felt cold atop the rickety float with nothing covering his body other than a deerskin loincloth. His hands were shackled to a steel chain that fed through a hole in the pinewood and connected to a hitch on the back of the truck. The students had painted the word 'rapist' on his forehead in their school colors, along with a blue broken heart symbol on his right bicep. A blonde cheerleader was standing behind him with a Taser in her right hand, which she had used multiple times to make him submit. Between the pepper spray and moderate voltage shocks, Ned had elected to endure his punishment in silence.

He thought about the powerful black man that had removed him from his yacht and the mouthy brunette who played along with the crime. They had loaded him into what looked like a cheap rental speedboat and cruised to a dock in the Brooklyn area. From there, the mysterious couple had offloaded his naked body to some high school football players in the middle of the night. Ned scowled as he considered how the duo had provided the minors with beer, money and non-lethal weapons to teach him a lesson. He then spent the remainder of the night in a garage watching dozens of drunken young men putting together a haphazard float. As the drinking intensified, someone had the moronic idea of strapping deer antlers to his head and wrapping him in a loincloth made from the same animal.

The parking lot was littered with cheap beer cans that had been crushed underfoot by the group of demonstrators. In their drunken state of celebration, the teens felt invincible and had no idea how dangerous their prisoner could be under different circumstances. They continued their unsanctioned rally as their peers recorded videos and shared them with the world.

It took less than an hour for a police car to show up, which caused most of the teens to abandon their posts. A brown-haired policeman got out of his patrol car and scratched his head in confusion. He read the words 'Rape Beer Float' on the side of the colorful vehicle a few times, but didn't understand what was happening.

The driver pulled the truck to a halt when the police officer approached, and the squad of cheerleaders stared at the ground with inebriated guilt. All of the band members, football players, and spectators had sprinted across a nearby soccer field to escape the wrath of school administrators and the authorities.

Ned began to tremble with joy when he saw the police car coming to his rescue. The skin around his eyes was red from pepper spray, and his muscles were sore from the recurring onslaught of Taser shocks. He reflected for a moment on his abduction in lucid detail, hoping to learn the identities of the perpetrators. However, as the police officer came toward him, all he could think about was getting home for a warm shower.

Canarsie Park – Brooklyn, New York

'Today is the day; I can't wait any longer,' the pale German thought to himself while stalking the green grass of Canarsie Park. He swore under his breath when noticing the many attentive mothers that were watching their beautiful children. The child predator had decided to wear faded jeans and a short-sleeve flannel shirt to blend in with other dads that came to the park. His heart was pounding as he watched for the black man when taking a route through the play areas.

He knew that more than one pass would arouse suspicion, but there were dozens of children from which to choose on this special day. One of the mothers had confused him for a single father and gave him an invitation to her little girl's birthday party. To his delight, the party started two hours before the black man would show up to spy on him. Although the nosy man had shown up at varying intervals, he had never bothered coming to the park at nine in the morning. His absence gave the crafty German plenty of time to complete an abduction and make it back to the city across the bridge.

The kidnapper grew impatient as he strode through the ranks of children at the birthday celebration. He spied many angelic faces that were only inches from his desperate fingers, but the women were alert and ready to protect them. The man's pale right hand began to tremble at the thought of defeat with such a gratuitous event.

A little black girl with pigtails was throwing a ball in the air near an empty swing set. The predator traversed across the sand near her with rapid footsteps, trying to keep his feet from making too much noise. He began to raise his hands in a steady path above his prey, glancing around at options for a swift exit.

"Hey, sir, what the hell are you doin'?" An African-American woman shouted from behind a large wooden information sign that was just seven feet away. "I see you walkin', loser. You just keep walkin'!" The woman stopped talking on her satellite phone and bolted over to the play area, scooping up her daughter in a vicious display of protection. "Yeah, you keep walkin'; my husband will kill you!"

The ashamed stranger could not vacate the area fast enough. His steps were longer and faster as adrenaline surged through his body, making him more aware. After the woman's death threat processed in his mind, it put him in an instant state of survival. He felt like an enemy combatant that had just been caught on the wrong side of a battlefield. His fingers began to tighten as the fear of lost opportunity was beginning to bite at the back of his neck. 'I just need one to get me through the year,' he internalized with a feeling of panic and sadness.

The forlorn kidnapper was on the verge of crying when he saw a chubby girl with black hair playing alone near a patch of pine trees. Although she wasn't his first choice, the German's legs began to carry him forward out of compulsion. He could feel darkness creeping through his bones and the foul thoughts that entered his mind made him wince. The man quickened his pace like a wild beast in the forest and snatched up the little girl, almost unaware of what he was doing. His right hand covered her mouth as the center of his stomach became nauseous, and they disappeared together through the pine trees.

He pressed forward through the park with an overwhelming feeling of guilt, pretending that he was taking his daughter home to her mother. The chubby man removed his hand from her mouth and held the girl tight against his right shoulder, allowing the child to kick and scream.

"No, you can't stay and play," he repeated every few steps, "mommy needs you at home to get ready for the wedding. I'm sorry, my little Susan, but we have to get to your uncle's wedding. I understand that you don't want to go."

He got bolder in playing his role as her father, and they made good time in getting away from the play areas of the park. After a few minutes of walking, they were nearly a hundred yards from where he had found the girl, and the twisted German felt that she was his property. He saw his white pickup truck in the parking lot at the far end of the park, which helped the man to relax. The girl was writhing in his arms with all her strength, but none of the onlookers knew what he was doing. Some people stopped and looked at him with caution, but he bought them off with a charming smile, and they let him pass.

The pale man began to smirk with wild satisfaction as he admired the prize in his arms. She was dressed in a white jumpsuit with a red undershirt, and her hair was tied up with a little red ribbon. A torrent of delight pulsated through his gut when he considered the heartbreak her mother would experience in the park. His mind was ablaze with the omnipotence of knowing that someone would feel the stabbing pains of loss and hopelessness.

There was an abrupt sound of footsteps pounding the earth as he approached the tree line near the edge of the park. He made an about-face turn to see if someone was coming, and his mouth opened in shock. A bulky figure with a black ski mask was rushing toward him. The mysterious perpetrator kicked the German in the right shin and pried the little girl from his arms with ease. He cried out in agony and dropped to the ground as his prize was wrenched away by the aggressive newcomer.

"Finders keepers!" The man taunted him as he sprinted toward the city.

The German kidnapper got to his feet with dozens of thoughts racing through his mind. Although the logical side of his brain told him that this scenario was impossible, his addictive pathology demanded that he retrieve the youngster. He stood and watched with a perplexed expression as the stranger jogged away with the girl bouncing on his right shoulder. His adversary was dressed in a solid black sweatshirt and sweatpants, which matched the ski mask. A tremendous amount of conflict entered the pale man's mind, and the loss of his prize seemed to make him short circuit.

He exhaled with desperate gasps as the girl gradually got smaller in his field of vision, and the predator found himself trailing behind the masked stranger. His better judgment told him that this was a setup, but he saw no harm in following from a safe distance. The man's legs carried him forward at a frantic pace, inspired by an arrogance of needing to know the fate of the child. For a brief moment her destiny had been under his control, and the power he felt was tremendous. Now that power was sprinting off toward Brooklyn with unknown motivations. The pale German began to move with a rapid gait, realizing that he was in the same position as her mother. If he never knew what happened to the girl, then he was no better off than her grieving parent, and this concept ate away at his core like a bad virus.

The masked stranger sprinted ahead at a faster pace, and the hefty kidnapper found himself losing ground at an unforgiving rate. There were streams of sweat cascading down the microscopic valleys and imperfections of his skin. It seemed as though someone had poured a bucket of water over his head. He tried to keep up for two hundred yards but doubled over with a severe ache in his side. The man was in poor shape, and his muscles were starting to cramp. He knelt down on the grass and lowered his head to catch his breath.

After several seconds of punishment, the pale German looked to his right and noticed a woman in a green hijab filming his movements with a small device. The woman seemed out of breath as if she had been following him from the beginning. He felt a rush of panic in his chest and forced himself back onto his feet. But this action was futile when he noticed that half a dozen police officers were surrounding him and encroaching on his position. All six lawmen encircled him, and it took them less than sixty seconds to handcuff the kidnapper and read him his rights. The German wasn't surprised when he saw the masked figure return to where the police had detained him on the grass.

When the police lifted the kidnapper off of the ground, he saw the black man remove the ski mask and glare at him. The muscular man cradled the little girl safely in his arms, and she didn't seem afraid. A Japanese police officer approached the mighty African-American and put his arm on his unoccupied shoulder in a gesture of celebration.

The kidnapper began to weep, realizing that his fate was set when he accepted a birthday invitation from a seemingly absent-minded mother. He turned his head to the right and watched the Muslim woman getting closer to the site of his arrest. The man shook his head, fearing an uncertain future and cursing his lack of self-control.

The Shots Fired Loft – Manhattan, New York

"Look, Richard, I'm going to make this really simple," Mike articulated with his hands held high. "All of you signed contracts stating that you're going to share some intimate details from your lives on our show. Stoney has done his part, and Fassim is going on the air in about five minutes to do hers. So why do you think that I'll give you a pass? Because you're Richard? Do you think you're more special than everyone else? Frankly, Jennifer and I are sick of these conversations. There's nothing to negotiate, and besides, I doubt your alcoholism is much of a secret after the party at NASA."

Richard gripped his forehead and stared at the fancy wooden desk that was between him and the director. He had told Mike that unveiling his past as a playboy would hurt his chance at running for political office with the Republican Party. The disgruntled man tugged at the jacket of his dark gray suit, which blended well with his white dress shirt and navy blue tie.

His brown eyes locked on the director in a moment of heated disdain. The man who sat across from him was wearing a bright white suit and black tie that would have been the envy of any 1920s gangster. Richard decided that every man who held sway over his life had been a bully, and Mike was no different.

He recalled growing up with alcoholic parents that never wanted a second child. The couple had exhibited severe favoritism toward Richard's younger brother Thomas, and as a result, nothing he ever did was worthwhile. This perception led to Richard being raised in a household with three bullies; all of them self-righteous and unyielding.

When he was old enough to attend college, Richard sought comfort in the arms of different women every week. He found himself descending into a downward spiral of hard alcohol and gorgeous females. This hedonistic phase of his life proved treacherous when Thomas came to visit on Christmas Day, and Richard gave him a beating that left him hospitalized. He spent the next thirty days in jail as his brother began the painful physical therapy needed to heal a broken right leg. Richard found himself shunned by the rest of the family and was kicked out of college for committing assault in the dormitories.

He recollected getting a job as an editor at Feature Films for Families and scoffed at the owners for their Christian beliefs. Richard had spent many Sundays playing pool at strip clubs while his colleagues were going to church. However, his life remained incomplete until he got arrested for public intoxication. The troubled man was certain to lose his job and get ousted from the community, but the owners showed compassion instead of aggression. They took the time to understand his problems, and helped him to forgive his family. He was then able to disseminate his anger in peace and live a more constructive life with a group of people that accepted him.

"Whatever, Mike," Richard replied after a thoughtful pause, focusing back on the conversation, "you can force me to share my demons with the world, but my story is about redemption. I can't say that the same will be true for you with all of your little…secrets. What is it that you're into, anyway? Is it drugs?"

"Okay, Richard, that's enough; I've had it with these conversations," Mike confessed as he slammed his right fist on the desktop. "Fassim, CKB, and Stoney got back from Canarsie Park thirty minutes ago, and they should be getting out of makeup. So I need to get you and your self-righteous attitude out to the set. And believe me when I say this, but I appreciate the drama. However, that said, I need the drama to stay in the show where it belongs and away from my office. Now, we need to get up and move to the set; I have a television show that's going live without me. Should you decide to breach your contract and go rogue - that's fine. Go ahead and ruin yourself financially for the next twenty years." He held up his right index finger and gestured toward the door. "Look, I'm done talking! We need to go."

Richard sneered at Mike and shook his head with deep regret. He decided that being away from the man for a few hours would be a good change of pace and took his leave from the office as instructed.

When he stepped into the living room, Richard saw Fassim surrounded by the camera crew and other cast members. She was sitting at the center of the sofa wearing a yellow hijab and conservative fuchsia dress that reached all the way to the floor. Stoney and CKB sat directly across from her on tall barstools and seemed genuinely attentive. They had not changed their clothing since the incident at the park, but their hair and faces looked fresh. Litz was seated to the right of Fassim on the sofa clad in a little black dress, maintaining a gaze of compassion. Jazzy occupied the spot at the photographer's left and wore a royal blue miniskirt with a matching blouse.

Richard rolled his eyes at Mike when the director pointed to an empty barstool near Stoney.

'Oh, you mean the empty chair?' Richard mouthed to the director as he motioned toward the set with a blank expression. Mike became more animated after this response and gestured with both hands toward the seat. But when he noticed that the television star was mocking him, the director raised the middle finger of his right hand and ushered Richard to take a seat with his left.

Richard chuckled after this small victory and made his way onto the set, unenthusiastic to hear his colleague humiliate herself for a paycheck.

"So, I was living in Saudi Arabia with my boyfriend Kujhad and we were thinking about getting married." Fassim spoke into the camera with an innocent demeanor. "He was very romantic and would often take me out for walks at night, or to swim in the river. Kujhad had been studying to become a doctor but was working as a stonemason to pay for school. After a few months of saving, he was able to propose to me with a new engagement ring, and I accepted. Since he had a strong body and was fearless about doing most things, a terrorist group called Bojihat approached him to join them. When Kujhad refused to help their cause, they threatened to behead him and his family." The brooding woman paused and took a drink out of an open water bottle from the coffee table before continuing.

"So, my Kujhad joined the Bojihat terrorist faction, but he also contacted the CIA before his training began. A man from the CIA named Paul told my fiancé that he would protect us and help us to escape from the terrorist cell. We were excited by this news, but the CIA wanted Kujhad to get them detailed information before they would agree to help. So he did as they asked for three days, and then a war broke out between Saudi Arabia and Israel. The Israeli army was extremely efficient in destroying the terrorist group, and within less than a week the faction had lost most of their soldiers. But the Bojihat refused to die quietly, and they asked my fiancé to wear a suicide bomb to a hotel where members of the international press were staying. Again, he went to the CIA for help, and Paul agreed to replace his suicide backpack with one that was harmless. The agent promised that Kujhad would be arrested in the hotel lobby, and we would be taken to freedom." She dipped her head for a moment as the pain of these memories caused her voice to crack.

"So, the next thing I know, the CIA is flying me off to safety in India," Fassim announced with tears falling onto her face. "I was told that Kujhad would meet me there the next day after completing his mission, but it was the last time I saw him. The terrorists sent my fiancé into the hotel café where all of the journalists were enjoying coffee and speaking with their crews. Kujhad ran into the crowded place as fast as he could and pushed a button to trigger the bomb. When it went off, it sprayed confetti and glitter all over the patrons in the café. There were even a few of those...what do you call them? Trick snakes? These yellow trick snakes flew out of the backpack, and the CIA was filming the entire incident. Apparently, they wanted to use this failure to humiliate the Bojihat leaders. And their plan worked, except the CIA had to evacuate when the Israeli army started a raid. They didn't have time to get Kujhad on a plane."

"Wait a minute," CKB began with an enthusiastic gleam in his eyes, "your fiancé was the confetti bomber? I mean, the confetti bomber that everyone was laughing about in their video feeds?"

"Yes, but-" Fassim tried to elaborate more details, but the rest of the cast began to laugh and howl with memories from the viral video.

Fassim kicked over the coffee table and shattered the glass near the legs of her three male co-stars. The drinks that were balanced atop it spilled on the gray shag carpeting, soaking it around their feet. She then stood with a look of pride and stomped off toward her bedroom with a demeanor of incredulous hatred.

"Fassim, Fassim!" Mike called out from the corner of the room. "Everyone be quiet, and please show some respect." The room returned to silence as the other five cast members took a few seconds to gain control of their laughter. "Fassim, we apologize for this response and mean no disrespect. Please finish the story." He pleaded with a gracious hand gesture to the Muslim woman.

"Well, the CIA achieved their goal," she stated with a posture of deep sorrow and looked down at her hands while rubbing them together. "Kujhad had made a fool of Bojihat to the whole world. It was such an embarrassment to the terrorists that they planned to change their name. But when they captured my fiancé, they decided to end him using the four hells. In the tradition of ancient laws, he was eviscerated, emasculated, drawn and quartered. They ripped him apart with their trucks, and that's how…the love of my life died."

Fassim looked pale and nauseated when these words escaped her lips, and she almost fell over from telling the story. The panicked woman grabbed her abdomen and stomped away from the television set to the safety of her bedroom. From their seats in the living room, her co-stars could hear a wail of terrible agony and longing. They each closed their eyes and made an effort to show some belated respect.

Highway Junction – Brooklyn, New York

Litz moved with a spirited gait through the slums of Brooklyn toward the overpass where her friend Oslo was staying. Although the men from her security detail had tried to make excuses to stay away from this neighborhood, she reminded them who was in charge. It had been less than an hour since she had witnessed Fassim's heartbreaking revelation, and Litz needed to have some laughs with an old friend.

The young woman froze in her tracks when she saw a homeless black man sprawled out in Oslo's thick canvas hammock. The man was relaxing and reading the pages of a tattered magazine. He was wearing an orange winter hat and a green army jacket with matching cargo pants.

"Where is Oslo?" Litz asked the man with a confounded expression as she walked up to the makeshift sleeping area. "Why are you in his bed?"

"What do you want from Oslo?" The man replied without looking up from the pages of his magazine. "You don't belong in this part of town."

"Oslo is my friend," she declared with contempt and stuck out her chest to indicate an unshakable resolve. "When will he be back?"

"They took Oslo…to Camp Paradise." He replied with an icy stare. "But there are plenty of poor white folks around here that would like to be your friend. As for me, I'm out of the friend business. You have yourself a good day." The man suggested with a dismissive wave of his right hand as he reached up and turned a page in the magazine.

Litz spun around and put her hand over her mouth. She stepped away from the abrasive homeless man as though his negativity could smash her into the asphalt.

"Are you okay?" Bulky Kevin asked when he saw how distraught the television star appeared. "Do you need to-"

The security guard stopped speaking when Litz began to sprint away from the overpass at top speed.

"Where's she going now?" William asked his colleague as he saw the athletic woman ambling across the asphalt with incredible force.

The two men looked at one another in bewilderment and pursued their client with haste. However, she was in much better shape than them and ran like a championship boxer until they lost sight of her.

XIII. *Angry Potatoes*

The air over Zackenberg, Greenland had relaxed its lethal, freezing grip from the mountains for the afternoon. This small window of time had allowed fourteen-year-old Holloss to put on his wool facial coverings and go exploring the majestic mountain springs. He had argued with his mother when she forced him to take their American Husky, JoHann, for protection, but Holloss was thankful to have the dog as company. The brown-haired teenager was thin for his age, which meant that he had to cover himself with more insulation to leave the house. He checked his right pocket for what must have been the third time, confirming that he had everything required to build an emergency fire.

When Holloss and the dog reached an altitude of only four hundred feet above their small town, the rare grandeur of the landscape began to reveal itself. There were formations of ice over which fresh waterfalls spilled into a valley of immaculate beauty. The land here had remained untouched for thousands of years, and only the most brazen settlers would call it a permanent home.

Holloss admired the divide where the mountain landscapes gave way to solid ice formations, and he found his favorite nook to be unoccupied. There was a tall stretch of solid rock that jutted out atop a brilliant waterfall. He and the dog climbed the rock formation with ease as though it were a natural concrete staircase. This area was a perfect vantage point for sightseeing since reflected sunlight from the rocks had a warming effect, and he could spy on the glacier without endangering himself.

The inquisitive youth knelt down at the top of the rock formation and admired the frenzied energy of water escaping over the smooth edge of the white ice. There was a massive bowl of glacial ice with unusual jade green colors at its center that became pure white at the outer edges. The water swirled and gurgled in this ice bowl with a hypnotic appeal, and Holloss began to meditate above the tranquil scene.

Something caught the young man's attention in his peripheral vision to the right, and Holloss focused on the movement, turning his body toward the grand valley. He opened his mouth in awe as a small storm of fiery debris rained down from the heavens. At least two dozen objects were leaving smoke trails as they appeared through the low clouds and shot toward the earth. The sheltered adolescent licked his dry lips in fascination as the flames burned hot all the way to their impact with the ground. To his delight, a thirty-foot-by-thirteen-foot section of steel smashed down on the mountain ridge just a hundred yards from where he stood. The massive blackened object was still smoldering when it landed, and white smoke emanated from every corner of its surface.

Holloss gazed with regret at a logo embossed at the center of the steel, which read 'USA' in big, bold letters. The light show took only fifteen seconds to cascade down from the upper atmosphere, but it would take the boy much longer to understand what he had just witnessed.

Your Stay Inn – Brooklyn, New York

Litz Eliza Rack scorned the New York City skyline through the eighth-floor window of a cheap hotel. Her eyes had become dead and frigid with sorrow, which had been a preeminent theme in her life since she was a teenager. The troubled woman watched the Memorial Towers as the sunset passed behind their hulking black structures. There were over a dozen skyscrapers built in Jersey City to take on the burden of New York's portion of an event known as The Passing. Litz thought that this simple phrase was a clever and tidy way to describe something wretched in the history of mankind.

The orange sunlight cast long shadows across the bay, and at times they passed over The Statue of Liberty. She felt trapped by the power of the shadows, and it seemed cold in her lonely hotel room, although the temperature was adequate. Litz used her right hand to explore her face and inhaled with apprehension. She plucked her right eye from its socket with the same delicate movements someone might use to diffuse a bomb. There was a familiar discomfort when the bulbous glass became unstuck from the clingy surfaces inside of her skull, and Litz was careful to handle the aesthetic placeholder. The glass eye felt light and fragile as she turned it over in her hand. It looked pale in the reddish hues of the sunset that protruded through the cheap blue curtains.

"Ten cups of dust per urn and ten urns per drawer," Litz said to the empty hotel room as she looked out upon the Memorial Towers. "Fifteen drawers from floor to ceiling, and over one hundred and fifty rows of drawers per floor. One hundred and sixty floors per tower, and fifty-six towers built since 2033. Not enough storage space in Houston, New Jersey, Los Angeles, and Portland to last until the end of the century." The haunted woman grew silent and closed her eyes to recollect when it all began.

TWELVE YEARS EARLIER

"I'm scared, mom," Litz said to her mother Martha as she stared at the floorboards of a gray Chevrolet Corvette. "I don't understand why this has to happen; we already lost dad and Jimmy. Why can't that be enough?"

"Sweetheart, I asked you to be strong and try not to think about those things." Her mother answered with a wink from her left eye. "We have seven months to enjoy the time of our lives and over two hundred and fifty thousand dollars. Most people never get a chance to experience the things that we've done this year. Look, just stay positive today and we'll talk about sad things later tonight, okay?"

Litz nodded at her mother and forced a smile to emerge from her otherwise mundane face. They had just finished a shopping trip at The Venetian in Las Vegas and were on their way to the attractions of New York-New York. She and her mother had worn identical baby blue T-shirts and stonewashed pink coveralls for a fun display of solidarity.

Martha was an attractive forty-four-year-old woman with dazzling blue eyes and long, dark hair. She drove the powerful sports car with determination and always appeared ladylike, even when shifting gears with the temerity of a professional race car driver. Litz began to giggle as her bum slid back and forth on the black leather seat when the car turned into the casino's parking structure.

At the age of fifteen, Litz was just beginning to develop into a woman. She had been homeschooled since her mother retired at the age of forty, which is when the two embarked on a grand road trip across the United States. Although the bond she made with her mother was priceless, there were times when Litz longed for friends of the same age. It was also impossible to start meaningful relationships with boys given such a fast-moving lifestyle. The mother and daughter pair had been inseparable since her father Ross had a heart attack while driving home with her little brother Jimmy in the car. This tragic event led to a severe automobile crash from which neither of their loved ones would recover.

It took Litz many years to gain perspective on the loss of her father and brother. She and her mother had grieved in ways that they could never have anticipated. At one point, they found themselves watching The Godfather movie trilogy while eating ice cream. Somehow the onscreen tragedies of the characters and their enduring love of family were oddly soothing. Litz recalled how the ambush of Sonny Corleone in the first film had given her peace after her father's passing. At that moment, she witnessed how life could get taken from even the most powerful and passionate of souls.

Litz and her mother made their way to the Coney Island section of the New York-New York casino. Martha gestured for Litz to follow her to a game called Drown the Clown. The simple venue consisted of a long row of tacky blue water pistols retrofitted to a stainless steel countertop. There was a squishy red barstool bolted to the floor in front of each water pistol, and the women took their seats at the center of the attraction. Her mother paid an aloof teenage male vendor some cash to get the game started, and grabbed a squirt gun with a glow of excitement.

Litz mimicked her mother's actions by raising the small blue gun from its holster, noticing a long black rubber hose connected to the base of the unit. She looked at the ghastly row of clowns in the target area. Their heads moved back and forth in a smooth and predictable pattern. Each of them had their mouths open with sickening expressions of joy, all seemingly eager to receive gallons of water from ardent players.

"I used to play this when I was your age," Martha said with a smile of youthful delight as she twisted in her seat with anticipation.

When the vendor hit the bell for the game to begin, Litz began spraying her female clown in the mouth and watched a green balloon expanding from the top of its head. Her mother was dousing a male clown with forceful accuracy and a dark blue balloon swelled from above his hairline. Although Litz was ahead of her mother from the start, she let off the trigger when the balloon was about to burst. Two seconds later, her mother's balloon popped and sprayed water all over the rotating heads of the clowns.

"Okay, it looks like you win Mr. Frog," the male vendor said as he handed a green stuffed animal to Martha. "If you want to play again, maybe you can win Mr. Rabbit."

Martha stood up and looked at the awful artwork of the square black pupils painted on the frog's eyes. She knew that Litz had let her win and presented the stuffed animal to her daughter in a silent display of affection. Litz chuckled when she realized that her mom had busted her and accepted the ugly toy with a rueful smirk.

"Let's go on the roller coaster," Martha proposed with a spark of enthusiasm. "It's not as big as the others we've tried, but it should still be fun."

Litz smiled and nodded when she saw how exhilarated her mother was from this plan. It took them less than two minutes to locate the entrance of the outdoor attraction, and the observant youth watched a group of makeshift yellow taxicabs barreling across the red steel structure. The roller coaster had just over a dozen passengers, but they screamed loud enough to emphasize every curve of the track.

It was a slow Wednesday afternoon at the casino, and the line was short enough to guarantee them a spot in the next turn. After delivering a bumpy ride to its passengers through a scaled-down version of New York City landmarks, the roller coaster came to an abrupt halt using a series of industrial air brakes.

Litz grinned when she saw the heads of the passengers tilt forward in unison and then back upright. They rolled to a slow stop at the beginning of the track, and the ride operator issued instructions through a PA system for them to exit the attraction. When the cars were empty, the operator walked over to the head of the line and opened a small black gate to allow another set of passengers onboard. The petite blonde could not have been more than twenty years old, and she yawned with a blank stare as she opened the gate for her patrons.

Martha and Litz clambered for a position near the back of the roller coaster, but people ahead of them occupied those seats in a hurry. Litz grimaced when she realized that the cars were filling up and that the front seats were their only option. When they got to the head of the unit, Martha shrugged and gestured for her daughter to get in on the left, and then took the seat beside her. Once they were seated, the women secured their seatbelts and pulled down the black, padded overhead bar until it locked in place just above their legs.

The diligent ride operator started at the rear of the unit as she walked from car to car, tugging on all of the safety bars. It took her less than a minute to confirm that everyone was secured in their seats, and she returned to the control booth.

All of the passengers were talking and laughing with anticipation while the ride operator mumbled obligatory safety instructions through a terrible audio system. In fact, the only words Litz remembered understanding were 'enjoy the ride.'

The roller coaster came to life on the red tracks with a powerful lurch. An industrial-strength chain knocked and hummed underneath the unit like some medieval torture device. Litz reached out and grabbed her mother's left hand with her right and squeezed it with building anxiety. Everyone in the passenger seats had become silent when the roller coaster reached a forty-five-degree angle. The yellow taxicab designs no longer presented as foolish or innocent when the chain forced the unit upward with incredible might.

All of the passengers seemed to hold their breath as the last few feet of track disappeared beneath them. Litz felt her mother let go of her hand, and she turned to her with a smile, realizing that this was a signal to conquer her fears. The teenager froze in her seat, and her gut became tense with panic. Martha was slumped over with her mouth open and eyes closed.

"Mom! Mom! Mom!" Litz shouted as she attempted to rouse her mother awake by gripping her left leg and shaking it violently. "Mom! Mommy..."

Litz began to scream when the roller coaster topped the first hill, and the rush of fear that came with falling was a poisonous jolt to her mind. She continued to grab her mother and tug at various areas of her body, trying to elicit a response, but there was no movement. Her hand darted up to Martha's nose, but the coaster went into a barrel roll on the track, forcing her hand to drop near the black plastic seat. Litz felt an explosion of grief and wanted to be free from her restraints. She cried out in terror and tugged on the safety bar, but it was locked in place.

When the cars leveled out, she placed her hand in front of her mother's nose and couldn't feel any air pressure.

"Help! Help! I need help!" Litz screamed when she realized that her mother wasn't breathing. "Get me off of this thing! Get us out! We need to stop!"

Her pleas were drowned out by the screams of other passengers that were clueless to her plight. The roller coaster began a second lap and Litz placed her hands over her ears and closed her eyes. She couldn't bear the sight of her best friend in the world being bounced around like a ragdoll when she needed urgent care. All the distraught adolescent could do was scream and rock back and forth in denial of the horrid event.

When the screaming didn't ease her pain, she lashed out with raw aggression at the safety bar. The teenager felt as though her arm muscles were on fire when she began to pound and scratch the steel that held her in place. There were jagged areas where the metal had been welded, which delivered some nasty cuts to her hands and forearms.

By the time she heard the air brakes bring the roller coaster to a halt, Litz was attacking her restraints like a laboratory animal. Her head shook back and forth like an attack dog that had been abused and caged all night. When the ride operator removed the restraints, she allowed herself to be bathed in the darkness of reality.

"Help her! Help her! Help her!" Litz repeated as she stood up too fast and fell on her right side, knocking her head against the safety bar. "She needs, she needs…she needs help!" The panicked youth stuttered with uncontrollable terror. "I-I think…no breathing. There's no breathing." The teenager pleaded with her eyes shut tight to block out everything around her.

"Call the paramedics and get an ambulance!" The ride operator shouted to her colleagues at a nearby attraction as she attempted to get Martha to respond. "Can you hear me? What is your name? Ma'am, can you hear me?"

Litz opened her eyes and felt like she was going to vomit. Her mother's head was tilted back against the seat of the roller coaster and the ride operator was tapping her on the right cheek. A group of bystanders had gathered on the platform behind the operator, and they gazed at the unconscious female with expressions of shock. Litz felt like her insides were being raked apart with gravel, and she turned away from their ignorant faces. Many of the bystanders had their mouths agape, and some showed genuine concern, but more than half seemed to be grateful that this wasn't happening to them.

"Get them out of here! Make them go!" Litz began to bawl and twisted further away from the horror on her right side. "Are you going to give her CPR? Please give her CPR!" She pleaded with the ride operator in a passionate tone.

"I don't want to move her, sweetheart; the problem might be with her spine." The casino employee stated with a hopeless gaze. "The paramedics should be here soon."

"Oh my God, mom!" The teenager began to wail as she reached out and grabbed her mother's limp left hand. "We've got seven more months! You need to be here. We've got seven more months!" She repeated and shuffled about in the cramped car as her right hand began to tremble.

"Is she breathing?" A twenty-eight-year-old paramedic asked as he ushered the ride operator out of the way. "Have these people get back; they don't need to be here. Sweetheart, does your mother have any medical issues that you can tell me about?" The man inquired as he pushed a pair of sunglasses close to the bridge of his nose.

Litz looked up at the skinny paramedic and admired the soft brown curls of hair on his head. He seemed to be speaking to her in a dream, and she could barely understand what he was saying.

"She's in shock," the paramedic said as he turned his attention away from Litz and back to Martha, "let's get her out of the car and start performing CPR."

The ride operator and paramedic were careful to remove Martha from the roller coaster. They set her body down on the concrete platform, and the man began to breathe into her mouth and perform chest compressions in an alternating pattern.

Litz stood up in the roller coaster car and vomited all over the front of the unit. She felt dizzy, and her arms were shaking in a fit of unfiltered horror. A few small streams of blood had run down her arms, and she used her coveralls to wipe it away. There were pieces of food mixed with stomach acid that dripped from her mouth, but she didn't care about her appearance. The young woman felt such a terrible pain in her stomach that she was forced to crawl out of the car onto the concrete platform. When she was free of the roller coaster, Litz remained on all fours, watching the paramedic perform CPR.

The world had become a blur of things that she didn't want to accept. Litz began to think about how long it had been since her mother stopped breathing and her stomach jolted with a series of dry heaves.

After several minutes of resuscitation efforts, a team of senior paramedics arrived from an ambulance. They performed tests for vital signs after using a defibrillator and applied a breathing bag to Martha's mouth, but she remained unresponsive.

Litz cowered against the concrete when the paramedics put the paddles on her mother's chest and applied electrical current to her heart. Every muscle in her body was convulsing, and the look in her eyes was beyond wild.

"Okay, we need to stop," a thirty-eight-year-old paramedic said when he looked at Martha's driver license. "She's forty-four years old and has a cyanide implant. It looks like someone screwed up and set it for June instead of January."

"No, no, she has seven months left," Litz pleaded as she scrambled across the concrete toward her mother's body. "She has seven months left with me!"

"I'm sorry, sweetheart, but she's gone," a senior paramedic said, placing his hand on the grieving girl's shoulder. "The moment that cyanide implant went off, she was gone. That's what they're designed to do. I'm sure she didn't feel any pain."

Litz stood up and pressed her right hand hard against her forehead. She felt confused and betrayed by the group of strangers that were watching her actions. The grief-stricken teen returned to the roller coaster car out of compulsion and hung her head inside where her mother had been sitting. She spotted the green stuffed frog on the rubber flooring of the unit and grabbed it with a voracious swipe of her right hand.

When the reality of her mother's death struck, she curled up in the fetal position on the cement with the frog pressed to her abdomen. Although the four strangers seemed desensitized to the tragedy at their feet, they let the forsaken youth mourn in silence. Litz put her head down and tried to muster some strength to honor the memory of her mother. In her despair, she vowed to dedicate her life to preventing this from happening to others.

PRESENT DAY

Litz walked into the bathroom of the low-quality hotel with the glass eye in her right hand. She washed it off under the faucet and was careful to put it back into its socket. Her stomach was burning with wounds reopened by the disappearance of her friend Oslo.

The callous woman looked at the glass eye in the mirror and marveled at what a fantastic job the doctors had done in matching the color of her real eye. She recalled her tumultuous journey from the boarding school and the leap she took off of the seventy-five-foot cliff into a large pine tree. Although the branches had caught her body and prevented a deadly fall, one of them struck her in the right eye and created a permanent disability. Fortunately, she had been too high on cocaine to feel much of the sting.

Litz looked down at a bottle of blonde hair bleach on the bathroom counter with a wicked smirk. She remembered escaping from a boarding school in Utah and luring a perverted drug dealer into giving her a ride in his Chevrolet Corvette. The television star snorted aloud as she thought of the stupid look on his face when he saw her pulling away from the gas station. Litz surmised that he must not have been much of a drug dealer, failing to recognize that a runaway would steal his car at the first opportunity.

"You know what, Oslo, I've decided that you're not going to die," Litz announced to the empty hotel room as she scooped up the bottle of hair bleach. "In fact, nobody that I ever cared about will die again. I'm implementing a strict no death policy and plan to live that way for the rest of my long life. So, what do you think of my hair? Do you think I would be cute as a blonde? Oh, Oslo, of course you'd have something snarky to say. Well, look at your hair, it isn't much better. I know that you don't have access to a shower or money, but that's hardly a viable excuse."

The lonely woman continued talking with her friend as she turned on the shower and began to moisten her long brunette hair.

XIV. Bridge of Bodies

Richard awoke and rubbed his eyes as he looked at the scarlet numbers illuminated on his alarm clock. It was 3:45 am, and the video editor sat up in bed, trying to confirm that he heard someone rummaging through the kitchen. The television star shook his head with doubt and considered that this was probably a dream. There were enough security staff in the loft and lower building that even a government agent would have trouble getting into the penthouse.

The disturbance got worse as Richard heard what sounded like tools or pieces of metal slamming about in the penthouse. He scratched his chest during a moment of denial and then jumped out of bed like a man on a mission. It took less than fifteen seconds to traverse from his bedroom through the dark hallway, and to the pale ambiance of the kitchen.

When his bare feet reached the smooth, cold surface of the kitchen tiles, he opened his eyes wide and blinked a few times. Richard felt confounded as to why Litz Rack was tearing apart the plumbing underneath the kitchen sink at such an early hour. The crafty woman had tossed aside all of the cleaning supplies from the cupboards and was busy dismantling their drainpipe and water supply.

"Did we have a plumbing emergency?" Richard asked with a gruff voice, bringing his right fist to his mouth as he yawned. "Oh, wow, you changed your hair color."

"There's a leak somewhere in this pipe," Litz replied with certainty as she brought up a large red pipe wrench and went to work on the drainpipe. "I don't know what the origin is, but I can hear water dripping from somewhere when I walk in this kitchen."

"So did you feel any moisture or see anything that was dripping?" He contemplated aloud and stepped over near the wall to his right, using the switch to turn on the brighter commercial lights. "How far back are you going to take that thing apart? The camera crews and makeup people will be getting out of bed in a few hours."

"I need some vitamins," the aggressive plumber stated without answering his question.

Richard noticed that her hair was tied up in a ponytail, and it was an orange-like blonde color from being dyed in the past few hours. He was shocked when Litz opened the lid of the garbage can and snatched half of a banana from the trash. She then stomped back over to the kitchen sink and plopped down on the floor with her legs crossed to enjoy the fruit. The film editor scratched his head out of instinct and made a face at a bunch of six fresh bananas that were on the kitchen counter – just seven feet from the garbage.

"You know you're eating a banana out of the-"

"Yes, I know that I'm eating a banana from the garbage – I'm not stupid!" Litz lamented without hesitation and began to eat the brown and yellow banana peel in addition to the fruit that was within. "Thank you, my Republican overlord, for your witty observations on life. But if you people wouldn't throw so much food away, then there'd be more for the rest of us." The young woman burped as if to emphasize her point and wiped the side of her mouth like a cave dweller.

"So where do you think the leak is, Litz?" Richard prompted with a twist of his neck.

"Why don't you like garbage banana?" Litz mocked from her position on the tiled floor. "Garbage banana has just as much to offer you as a fresh banana. In fact, I'll bet that I can get you to like garbage banana," she said with innocent eyes, and stuffed a large piece of the banana and peel into her mouth.

Richard became mystified and repulsed at the same instant as the agile woman stood and walked toward him like a runway model. She teased the man with her electric blue eyes and embraced him before he could protest. The uninhibited vixen pushed her ample chest against his pectoral muscles and forced his right hand to grip her bum.

The conservative pulled away, but Litz gripped the back of his head and thrust him into an open-mouthed kiss. She pushed the heat of her body against his pelvis and used her tongue to shove some of the discarded banana into his mouth. He winced in immediate discomfort but realized that the banana tasted good, and the lips that delivered it were a new definition of delicious.

The television stars embraced and kissed for several seconds, and Litz inadvertently crushed the remainder of the banana and peel onto the back of his white undershirt. She pushed him backward with her hand on his chest, realizing that he was trying to engage in a feeding frenzy of lust.

"I think you like garbage banana," Litz confirmed with a playful wink as she tapped the front of his boxer shorts with her right hand. "Are you going to help me find the wet spot?" She tempted the man with a broad grin of dominance. "Just listen when I walk in this part of the kitchen, and you'll hear dripping water," the plumber suggested in a more businesslike way, taking a position closer to the kitchen sink.

Richard could feel his heartbeat pulsating at the front of his pelvis, and although finding a leak was the last thing he wanted, the stunned man obliged his colleague. He listened in silence as the spirited blonde shifted her weight back and forth on the kitchen tiles in a repetitive pattern.

"There, did you hear it? Listen again," she instructed, and began a sort of tribal dance on the shiny white floor until it made a few dripping sounds.

"That's coming from the floorboards, my dear," Richard scoffed with a hearty chuckle. "I can't believe you shut off our water and took apart our plumbing over a creaking sound in the floor." He began to laugh harder until he saw an expression of pain and shame on her face. "Come here, crazy girl, let's do something more constructive." The man said with passion as he marched over and grabbed his co-star with a firm hand in the small of her back.

Richard gazed into her wild eyes for a moment as if to tell her that everything was going to be all right. He paused until the heat of her body had brought him to a full state of desire, and then they devoured one another on the kitchen floor.

Richard's Bedroom – The Shots Fired Loft

"Litz, Mike wants to see you in his office," a bearded stagehand relayed through the cracked door of Richard's bedroom. "Hey, Litz Rack, did you hear me? The director wants to see you in his office. By the way, thanks for turning off the water – the bathrooms smell great!"

"It looks like I've been called to the principal's office," Litz declared with a short giggle as she rubbed her right hand across Richard's somewhat muscular chest. "I guess everyone in the loft is going to hate me this morning – other than you."

"So are we exclusive now?" Richard suggested with a romantic gaze and tried pulling her closer to him.

"Okay, that's enough! I need to get up anyway." The unpredictable woman erupted in a panic of confusion as she jumped out of the bed and grabbed her pajama bottoms. "Richard, I know you're feeling deep and romantic and…whatever," she began with her right index finger held up in a warning, "but I can't. So just think of last night as your sole opportunity to take advantage of me while I was vulnerable. Who knows, maybe I'll go through a crisis again before my girl dries up and you can have at me for another night."

There was an awkward silence after these statements, and Richard sat up in bed to think about a response. Although Litz didn't have her top on all the way, she made a fast exit from the bedroom. Richard heard hoots and catcalls from members of the camera crew after the unpredictable blonde left his living space.

Litz embarked on a short journey to Mike's office as she finished pulling her pajama top on and hiding her breasts from the world. However, the director was on his way to Richard's bedroom, and their paths met halfway into the living room.

"For hell's sake, Litz, keep your breasts covered," Mike chastised with the tone of a responsible parent. "What did you do to my kitchen? I had to call in an emergency plumber to put everything back together."

"I want to double check his work," she argued with an expression of fiery outrage.

"No, you can't check his work because it's already done, and he left an hour ago," the director informed her with a slight flaring of his nostrils. "Of course, it took him a while to get started after he found some boxers and a bra and panty set on the floor."

"I don't want to talk about it," she said in a dismissive fashion and began to walk away from Mike toward the kitchen.

"Well, you do need to tell your story, and so does Jazzy," he insisted with a sober demeanor and followed her toward the kitchen cupboards. "People will want to hear about how you wrecked a sports car and climbed a cliff in the middle of a snowstorm. Look, only Stoney and Fassim have given their testimonials, and the rest of you are going to get yours done before the end of the season," Mike announced with increased power in his voice when he noticed a few other cast members looking for food in the kitchen.

"Yeah, well we're not doing it today," Litz declared with a prideful gaze and stomped through the kitchen like a queen bee. "In fact, we're having lady's night tonight. Jazzy, Fassim, Stoney and I are going to Mud Rituals to blow off some steam."

"No, you're not going to the mud tournaments, Litz, I need-" Mike stopped talking and considered the entertainment value that Mud Rituals would add to the show. "That's right; you're going to Mud Rituals for lady's night, so make sure that you have a camera crew and your security detail with you." He nodded with a hint of restored pride and began to walk away from the charismatic diva.

"Way to put your foot down, Mike," Jazzy shouted toward the director before he disappeared around the corner en route to his office. "I've never been to Mud Rituals; is it fun?" The comedian asked as she fished in the cupboards for a morning snack, attempting to keep her bum covered with a small pink nightgown.

"Well, let me put it this way," the adventurous plumber conveyed with expert salesmanship. "What is your favorite sexy costume?"

"I don't know; I've always thought about being a vampire," the comedian replied as she removed a strawberry breakfast bar from its box.

"Turn off the cameras," Stoney said to the crew as he stepped closer to the pair of women in the kitchen. "I need to talk to them in private," he added while scratching his stomach through a plain white tank top.

"What's up, Stoney?" Jazzy mused with a twisted smile, watching the police officer as he stumbled across the tiles in his boxer shorts. "Did you skip a few steps this morning?" She inquired after seeing that the man's hair was messy and his eyes were half-open.

"Litz, I had some officers show up yesterday from a precinct in Manhattan," he relayed with a sober gaze. "They were asking questions about the Ned Jones abduction."

"Do you know what he did to me, Stoney?" The comedian prodded with a pensive demeanor. "He's lucky that Litz and CKB didn't dump him into the ocean."

"Yeah, yeah, I know," the Japanese officer responded and held out his right hand with the palm facing forward. "Look, I empathize with you as a victim, and I'll do what I can, but they'll catch up to you eventually. I'll try to stall them if they come back."

"Thank you, Stoney!" Jazzy exclaimed with a smile of jubilation, and gave her co-star a tender embrace.

Mud Rituals – Newark, New Jersey

The atmosphere at Mud Rituals was filled with pulse-pounding excitement as a team of men dressed in traditional Mayan loincloths wore face paint and banged on war drums. There was a mud pit at the center of the amphitheater, and it was surrounded by a dining area that stretched up over eighty feet to rounded black walls of concrete. The mud pit was enclosed in Plexiglas like a hockey arena and featured lavish decorations such as gargoyles and Tiki torches. Fires burned throughout the establishment within concave pits of rock, and clusters of yellow and orange lights emphasized this effect.

There were four sections of the dining area, each using a color to represent one of the combatants for the evening. The four divisions of the arena were: red, blue, black, and orange. During the event, members of the audience could use their phones to control the water cannons and mud pipes in their quadrant of the arena. Each audience member would cast a vote on their digital device during a live countdown. A majority vote would cause staff members to shoot a chosen enemy combatant with their water cannon, or to cover a colored section of the platform in slick mud. When a champion won the event, the audience members seated in that combatant's section would be awarded a free meal.

Litz wore a black ninja outfit and stood atop the black quadrant of the platform. She looked up at the foreboding mud pipes that stretched above all four sections of the combat area. Each mud pipe was retrofitted with a black skull that displayed an open mouth as if in mid-scream. When mud flowed from their mouths, each skull's eyes would light up blue and white like oxyacetylene torches. These pipes were mounted over the stage at odd angles and had varying ranges of mud flows. The curious woman raised her head to see four water cannons, each five feet in length, mounted on the ceiling at the center of the arena. One water cannon was designated to each section of the platform and painted with the same color as its combatant. The water cannons could shine green lasers, allowing employees to target combatants with pinpoint accuracy. However, staff members were only permitted to target combatants when the crowd voted to douse them with water. The arena had four screens to display points, and there were countdown clocks that showed the audience when they could release a mud flow or fire their water cannon.

"Welcome to Mud Rituals, ladies and gentlemen," the announcer began when a spotlight shone down on the center of the stage, and a plume of white smoke emerged. "I am your host, Thor, the god of thunder, and we have a special show for you tonight. All of our combatants are stars of the hit television series Shots Fired in the Melting Pot." When the smoke cleared, a muscular man with blonde hair was seen posing at center stage in a Norse demigod outfit. "In the black corner, we have everyone's favorite hot plumber, Litz Rack, and she will be performing as the ninja." The host spoke into the top of a large plastic hammer that was equipped with a microphone and gestured toward Litz after the introduction. "In the orange corner, we have our sexy punk rocker, and one of New York's finest, Stoney Akuda."

Litz and Jazzy smiled when Stoney raised his hands to gain applause from the audience. He was dressed in a wild black leather outfit, sporting a pink Mohawk hairdo, and his face was adorned with gothic black and white makeup.

"In the red corner, Mud Rituals salutes our sexiest vampire of the year and a comedian that will make your heart bleed, Jazzy Auburn Michelle." The announcer played to the desires of the audience and bowed slightly toward Jazzy with his hands raised toward the ceiling.

Jazzy shifted her hips in a bold bad girl pose and let the crowd take in her athletic body beneath a bright red vinyl suit. Her face was brushed with the finest pale colors of death, and she blew a kiss to the audience from her bright red lips before showing off some impressive fangs.

"And, last but not least, we have a rapper from the Twentieth Century, who never died." Thor beamed with his left hand held high to build excitement in the crowd. "In the blue corner let's welcome Tupac Shakur, as embodied by the stunning Fassim Johnson." He broadcast from his powerful throat until the crowd roared with anticipation. "Now, before we begin, I want to give a quick recap of the rules. Hitting or grabbing the face is not allowed. You have only one objective, which is to knock your opponents off of the platform into the mud pits. When there is only one challenger left on the platform, they will be declared a winner. If you get knocked into the mud pits, you can climb back up, but only if there are at least two challengers remaining on the platform. Please wait for a count of ten, and when you hear the war drums pounding at full speed; it's time to stop being friends. Are we ready to do this?" The performer asked with both arms outstretched toward the crowd, resulting in a unified cry of 'yes.' "Okay, everyone start clapping with the beat of the drums. It's time to begin Mud Rituals!" He finished with a bow and hearty smile, and then the stagehands lowered him until he disappeared into the center of the platform.

Jazzy felt her body tense as a series of drum beats echoed through the arena from the Mayan performers that sat just outside the Plexiglas barrier. She decided that the vampire teeth could injure her during a fall and elected to zip them up in the outfit between her breasts. Her heart began to pound when the drum beats commenced like the intro music for a giant marching to his or her death. The comedian glanced around the platform and saw square holes where competitors could fall through into the mud. She tried to memorize their positions but realized that they were opening and closing at random intervals.

The other combatants were poised to attack, and before the comedian could form another thought, the drums surged to life in a barrage of tribal thunder. Jazzy sprinted toward Stoney, who stood in the orange quadrant to her left. The punk rocker turned to face her, but he also saw Litz Rack running up to engage him in her ninja outfit from the opposite direction. Stoney looked across to the far end of the arena and watched Fassim running in her Tupac Shakur outfit toward Litz. He decided to distance himself from Litz and barreled across the non-slip orange rubber tiles to take on the vampire.

Litz turned to her left when she heard an aggressive war cry coming from Fassim. She began to laugh when her co-star emerged as an iconic rapper. The moderate Muslim had on a blue do-rag partially concealed under a black baseball cap, which she wore backward in the tradition of hip-hop music. Her oversized black T-shirt depicted a portrait of Dr. Dre, and she moved with a spirited gait in a pair of black cargo pants.

A two-foot square panel slid out from under the path that Litz was traversing, but she was able to leap over it in time. Fassim saw the panel open and adjusted her route to gain some ground on the agile ninja.

"Ten. Nine. Eight. Seven. Six." The crowd started counting down with voracious authority, which caused the combatants to freeze in their tracks. "Five. Four. Three. Two. One."

A buzzer sounded, and Stoney looked upward in unison with his co-stars to see the eyes of the skulls glowing with blue and white fire. The mud pipes shook all around the arena, and the colored padding that enveloped their steel cores emphasized this effect.

Jazzy looked up and noticed that she was standing directly beneath an orange mud pipe, having only enough time to cover her face before the warm earth-tone liquids drenched her. Stoney took this as an opportunity and got into a position behind the vampire, waiting for the mud flow to stop. When the mud ceased raining down, Jazzy cleared off her face, but she felt someone shove her in the back and slid off of the platform in a daze.

Litz had crouched down and covered her head when the mud pipes began to drench the black platform. She raised her head and saw a green dot appear on her chest from the red water cannon across the way. The limber woman did a somersault and laid flat on her back. After a brief pause, the water cannon soaked the entire left side of her body but washed away the mud in a three-foot area of the quadrant. Litz could feel intense water pressure threatening to wipe her off of the platform, but her body resisted its push.

Fassim danced around the spray of the water cannon on the black section of the combat area, waiting for Litz to be vulnerable. After the water had halted, the rapper engaged her co-star with aggression. The ninja began to crab walk backward in a rush until she noticed a green dot from a laser sight that appeared on her assailant's neck. Her retreat then slowed, and the plumber pretended to be injured, lying on her right side and dragging herself across the rubber tiles.

The paparazzi photographer hunched down and pretended to threaten Litz like a gangster, but a water cannon shot her in the chest, and she exploded off of the platform into the mud ten feet below.

Litz turned to see where the other combatants were, and discovered that Stoney was almost on top of her. She reacted by raising her feet and using them on his stomach to catapult him to the far corner of the black combat area. Stoney landed hard on the rubber surface, and the back of his pink Mohawk became saturated in mud.

This allowed the clever ninja to get on her feet to gain an advantage before he could recover, but then she saw another green dot on her outfit. The nimble woman dropped to her knees on the muddy platform and felt herself slide forward – almost off the edge. Litz then knelt down with her knees clutched to her chest as a water cannon blasted her again in the left abdomen. The concentrated torrent hit like a hurricane-force wave and the young woman sensed that she was going over the edge. However, Litz was able to lean into the spray and maintain her balance.

The ninja got back to her feet despite the chilly water that saturated her sore muscles. Litz then closed her eyes in a grimace of exhausted disdain. She noticed that Jazzy had already climbed out of the four-and-a-half foot flows of mud below the platform, and Fassim was ascending one of the yellow padded ladders.

"Enjoy your mud bath!" Stoney shouted as he lunged toward Litz in an attempt to knock her off the edge.

The police officer was shocked when the ninja blocked his maneuver with her forearms. She then danced backward with graceful arrogance across the muddy platform, taking three large bounds away from him. During the third step she slipped in the mud, and her right knee buckled, smacking against the black synthetic surface.

Stoney signaled for help from the other women; however, Jazzy seemed to want revenge and was in pursuit. He smirked at the ravenous vampire and gestured for her to come forward, but a water cannon shot him in the center of his back, and he dropped to his belly on the slimy platform.

Fassim climbed to the top of a ladder and planted her feet on the non-slip surface of the combat area. The crowd began to count down from ten, and the prudent Muslim looked upward to see where the mud pipes would be spewing their payloads. When she lowered her gaze, Fassim caught a glimpse of Litz in the ninja uniform and felt herself being shoved hard in the chest. The humble woman couldn't help but smile in acceptance of her short roundtrip back into the mud pits.

Jazzy saw that Stoney was vulnerable and crept up behind him with a devious gaze of premeditated humiliation. But her focus was broken when she heard the mud pipes rattling throughout the arena. She braced herself for a torrent of sticky liquid to douse her costume in another coating of light brown. The alert woman heard footsteps approaching from behind and glimpsed an image of Litz coming at her through the mud.

When the mud flows stopped, Jazzy watched Litz drop into one of the square openings in the floor. The comedian then pulled her right fist to her stomach in celebration. However, this gesture was for naught as she witnessed the ninja avoid a fall by keeping both arms outstretched. Jazzy's eyes opened wide in awe when she saw Litz use her upper body to rise out of the hole in the floor until her knees reached the platform.

The comedian turned just in time to see Stoney trying to push her off the edge. She dropped to her knees and put her arms out straight, which forced the punk rocker to alter his course and slide in the mud. Stoney faltered for a moment and tried to regain his balance, but fell nonetheless.

Litz engaged Jazzy from the woman's right side with a fierce look in her eyes. Her ninja outfit was now mostly brown and soaked all over. Jazzy smiled when she noticed a green dot shining on the abdomen of the ninja costume. But to her dismay, Litz grappled Jazzy around the chest and pulled the comedian up to a standing position. The water cannon fired and hit Jazzy in the gut while the merciless ninja used her as a human shield.

When the water cannon lost pressure, Stoney emerged through the waning stream and tried to shove both women off of the platform. Litz sidestepped in a motion that looked instinctive and watched the punk rocker toss the vampire into the mud. She then pivoted and used Stoney's momentum to guide him off the edge as well.

The arena exploded with a satisfied cheer and Litz held her arms high in a display of victory.

Jazzy stood in over four feet of mud below the champion sporting slicked back hair that was gritty with debris. The skeptical woman scowled and folded her arms in disbelief after witnessing the efficient display of acrobatics. She then exhaled and glared at the crowd, feeling mud seeping into places where it didn't belong.

Stoney emerged from the small lake of mud and wiped his eyes with an expression of defeat. When his gaze met with Jazzy's brazen stare, the stars exhibited solidarity in their experiences. The mud tournament no longer felt like a fun night out; it seemed to have deeper implications.

A tall figure gazed down at Litz amid the screams and cheers in the arena. He had wanted to get a table closer to the action, but due to short notice had wound up in the second row from the back. The athletic man admired her body in the muddy ninja outfit, and his biceps shook with desire when he thought about being close to her. In his mind, the crowd was there to cheer him on and advance their closeness in the bonds of fate. He saw the beating of the war drums as a serenade of their hearts joining in rhythm. The passionate stranger was overwhelmed with desire and began to hate the crowd for coming between them. His arms rose toward the ceiling, and he shook his fists in contempt at everyone. After this wicked display of longing, he blew a kiss to the victor on the stage and made his way toward the exit.

XV. Punchy the Predator

"Look, I know that I screwed up in Houston, but I can handle a plumbing call, guys," Litz pleaded with her security team as they traversed a staircase made from concrete slabs toward a yellow townhouse in Brooklyn. "I appreciate the show of solidarity, but you don't need to be with me all the time." She snorted after a length of clear snot emerged from her nose and cursed herself for not canceling work for the day.

The adventurous plumber felt exhaustion and pain in her joints from a cold that came on after her appearance at Mud Rituals. She detected a slight fever and hoped that the rainclouds would give way to warmer afternoon weather. Litz looked around at the neighborhood to assess any threats from dogs or desperate characters. Her eyes locked on the concrete slabs ahead and she surveyed the moist areas left behind from a recent rainstorm. The weary vixen dragged herself up the last few steps and onto the concrete porch, feeling grateful to be on drier ground.

She inspected the pristine entryway and admired the cleanliness of the home. These signs gave her a feeling of confidence that the inside might be just as tidy as the exterior, which would be a welcome benefit to her during the repair work. Litz rang the doorbell and raised her eyebrows at the two men standing beside her.

A muscular thirty-year-old man with extensive tattoos on his arms opened the dark cherry wood door. He was tall and lean with large biceps and magnetic blue eyes. The smitten woman was enamored by his brown leather vest that was draped over a white T-shirt and faded blue jeans.

"Hi, I'm Aron Woolsy," the homeowner said as he reached out with his right hand toward Litz. "Are you here to fix my water heater?"

Litz smiled at her customer with curiosity, watching him flex his toes in a pair of new white socks. She looked at a silver crucifix necklace that the man wore and smelled his fantastic cologne, but couldn't make out the brand.

"Yeah, I'm here to take care of your repairs," she replied with a wry smile and reached out to shake his hand. "And these are my escorts. I call them bulky Kevin and William." The young woman gestured to the men in dark suits to her right as if they were benign tumors.

"Well, that's real cool; why don't you come on in?" The man invited the trio with an expression of formal hospitality, taking a few steps backward. "The lights went out in the basement, but I have a flashlight at the bottom of the stairs."

"What happened to the lights in the basement?" Kevin pried with an expression of mistrust as he stepped across the threshold toward the stranger. "Why don't you have proper lighting for the job?" He added with a callous stare.

"Look, I hardly use the basement," Aron explained with his hands on his hips. "I didn't know that my water heater was going to fail, or I would have gotten the lights fixed. Do I need to call someone else?" He asked with skepticism and walked backward to a dining room that featured mellow décor.

"No, it's nothing to worry about," Litz interrupted before Kevin could speak. "I'm sure my security team isn't afraid of the dark," she challenged with an expression of annoyance at her colleagues. "Would you guys mind checking for spiders down there?" The plumber joked as she placed her hands on her hips over a pair of gray coveralls.

"Would you like a bottle of water?" The homeowner suggested and pointed to the entrance of a kitchen in the next room.

"I would love a bottle of water, Mr. Woolsy," she responded with a hearty smile and teased her blonde hair, reaching back to adjust the ponytail. "Just lead the way."

"The water heater is down those stairs and to the right," Aron instructed Kevin with a lackadaisical wave of his left hand. "Do either of you want a bottle of water?"

"No, we're fine," Kevin answered with impatience as he approached a light blue door just six feet in front of the entryway. "Keep an eye on her," he said to William in a whisper.

Litz walked through the interior of the townhouse with an attitude of optimism. She admired the white walls with pink seashells airbrushed on their surface, and the door frames painted in bright orange. The entire home was carpeted in a thick gray shag material, save for the white tiles near the entryway. There was modest furniture in the living room made of cherry wood. A darkly stained coffee table was positioned in front of a tan sofa, and it faced a seventy-two-inch television mounted on the opposite wall. Two end tables were on either side of the sofa, both matching the coffee table in design and color. There was also an odd, black, old-fashioned weight bench at the far end of the room.

The considerate plumber followed her customer through a sizeable orange door frame that led to a quaint kitchen. He walked over to a black side-by-side refrigerator and retrieved two bottles of water from the door on the right. Litz found Aron's kitchen to be unremarkable, save for an orange countertop and a medieval mace mounted on the wall above the cherry wood kitchen table. She admired her host's high school charm as he stepped over to the table and set down the bottle of water. The table featured six matching cherry wood chairs, which was the same material used for the kitchen cabinets. All of the appliances were black and seemed to be new.

"So how is your TV show going?" The cheerful man prompted as he snapped the cap from his water bottle and took a drink. "You seem like quite a character."

Litz was about to answer when she heard the sound of a body tumbling downstairs in the next room. She felt a spike of fear travel down her spine and turned to see William standing in the entryway.

The security guard held up his right hand toward Litz and moved closer to the entrance of the basement staircase.

"Kevin, are you okay?" William inquired with blind reverence to the darkness as he began to descend the staircase for a better view.

"Is everything okay?" Aron prompted with a worried look and moved his face closer to Litz.

The vulnerable woman jumped back and grabbed her chest after the man invaded her space without making a sound. She exhaled in exasperation and took another step backward near the wall of the kitchen. When she realized that there was no danger, Litz nodded and smiled at the homeowner. Her chest was thumping with irregular heartbeats, and she sensed that perspiration was about to come on from her fever. She turned her head to the left, waiting for William to make an appearance at the top of the stairs, or for any signs of Kevin.

Litz turned her head to the right to speak with the customer and got a glimpse of his powerful fist careening through the air toward her jaw. She felt hot pressure on the left side of her face, and her body slammed against the wall like a truck had hit her from the front. The young woman detected instant pain in her neck and shoulders. It seemed like the man was trying to remove her head with one punch. She turned over onto her right side and watched Aron run over to the basement door and slam it shut. There was no sign of Kevin or William when her vision blacked out.

"One punch, one punch," Litz overheard a man repeating when she awoke to find herself lying on something soft. "Punchy, punchy. Punchy, punchy. One punch, one punch." She took a moment to inventory the pain in her body, which included a terrible headache, a throbbing jaw, and ringing in her left ear. "Punchy, punchy. Punchy, punchy. One punch." The man's voice seemed close, but she couldn't be certain with the ringing in her ear.

Litz opened her eyes to find herself face to face with the tattooed brown-haired predator. She detected bindings on her hands made with something elastic, and her coveralls were gone. The disoriented woman became horrified when she discovered that Aron had stripped her down to a red bra and panty set, and tied her up with bungee cords. Her captor was snuggled up beside her with a vindictive sneer of triumph on his well-groomed face.

She glanced around the bedroom and wondered if they were upstairs. There was a tall oak dresser near the wall, which was tan-stained like the rest of the furniture in the room. The concerned woman felt a chill on her bare skin and saw a large mirror mounted on the wall behind her assailant. An oak chest of drawers was next to the wall under the mirror. There was a ragged green sweater on top of the unit with a framed photograph of a young blonde woman nestled within its folds. The picture frame was a cheap, tacky bronze color and the glass was dustier than anything else in the room.

Litz turned her chin downward to look at a pair of glass closet doors just beyond the foot of the bed, but the man jabbed her twice with his right hand in the mouth.

"Punchy, punchy," Aron announced when his fist connected with the jaw of his captive. "Punchy, punchy," he repeated in a reserved tone of voice, striking Litz with less force on her left eye and the side of her head.

"Ow, stop doing that!" She complained when her face began to report a plethora of new pain. "What the hell?" The half-naked plumber protested, but her cries inspired a new combination of punches and she decided to remain quiet.

After delivering another four blows to the face of his attractive blonde victim, Aron snuggled up close to her. His body pressed up against her right side, and he put his face close enough to Litz's head to hear her breathing. The man seemed to enjoy the frustrated sounds that she made when he hit her with varying degrees of force. Aron grinned in silence and observed her movements as though he were waiting for her to cry.

"Punchy, punchy." He taunted his captive in a whisper and watched her head shake back and forth in disagreement. "Punchy, punchy," Aron threatened in a louder voice as he delivered another four punches to the face of the television star.

Litz held back a flood of despair as the brutality visited on her nose and eyes was causing tissue damage by the stone-like knuckles of the man. After a few seconds, she felt a small stream of blood and snot trickle from the left side of her nose.

Aron stopped hitting her and snuggled up closer to the restrained woman, waiting for her to break down.

The terrified plumber didn't want to consider what his attack was doing to her face. She recognized his disturbing pattern of violence and knew that the next round was coming soon. Her fingers detected a loose steel hook near her bare belly button, and the tenacious blonde was careful to maneuver the hook out from under the lengths of bungee cord. Litz closed her eyes and gritted her teeth in anticipation of another beating, but somehow Aron was uninterested in hitting someone that was prepared. Her hands fumbled through the loops of heavy-duty elastic cord, and she dropped the steel hook.

Aron delivered another series of four blows to her face; each of them softer and more targeted than before. He seemed to be toying with Litz and trying to build her disenchantment to a level that was acceptable to him.

Litz attempted to remain silent during this round of abuse, but she couldn't help groaning in disdain. Her nose and eyes were becoming red and raw from the constant barrage of violence, and the man was picking some tender targets. While his punches were landing, she worked the bungee cords with eager hands and maintained a stoic face. The television star was delighted when the bindings came loose from her lower torso, and then she ripped off the bindings from her upper thighs in one motion.

When he saw this movement, the muscular man's eyes seemed like hateful blue orbs that one might see on a predatory lizard. He swung down with the jackhammer that was his right hand, forcing Litz to use her arms and abdominal muscles to avoid the punch. His fist crumpled the white pillow next to her head, and Litz used her right arm to elbow him in the center of his back.

Her counterattack added to the momentum of his body, and the muscular psychopath fell forward with his face on the pillows. Litz leapt from the bed and began to look around the room, but she was dizzy from the assault and had to freeze in place. The lightheaded woman took in a deep breath and grabbed her knees, trying to stabilize the spinning motion that she felt.

Aron shot up out of the bed like a bull with a rider on its back. He came toward her with a face of hunger that she had only seen before on trolls in books as a child. The man swung his anvil hand at her again, and she jumped to the right, which caused him to strike the center of the large mirror.

The spirited blonde grabbed her ears and put her head down when shards of glass exploded all over the room from his punch. Her mind filled with desire for survival, and she forced herself to open her eyes. There was a long, sharp piece of the mirror at her feet and she retrieved it from the floor without another thought. Although she was handling the mirror by the larger end, it still cut the skin between her right thumb and index finger. Litz ignored the pain and turned to see that her kidnapper was inspecting his bloodied right hand.

She took the opportunity to assert herself and jabbed him three times in the back of the head. The man wailed in pain as the plumber tossed the improvised glass knife aside and bolted toward the bedroom door. Litz scrambled across the room in a panic, feeling her breasts bounce under the tight bra. Her face screwed up somewhat as a few pieces of glass found their way into her bare feet. She grabbed the door handle as if in slow motion and felt relief when it twisted open.

The television star burst through the door with all her strength, doing damage to the drywall in the hallway. She saw a staircase leading down to the main floor and found herself rocketing through the house to the front door. Her body slammed against the entryway wall, and she saw streaks of blood from her feet on the tiles. Litz began to unbolt the locks with impatience. She thought of bulky Kevin and William in the basement but heard Aron stumbling through the hallway upstairs.

"I'll send the police to get you; I promise!" Litz shouted toward the basement as she opened the front door in a daze and saw the blinding light of day.

The liberated woman ran down the cement slabs as if in a dream. There was an older woman with thick eyeglasses standing on the opposite side of the street. She had on a green and white flower print dress that covered her bulky body.

Litz ran across the street despite the cars that were coming from the east. Pieces of asphalt tore at her bare feet and found their way into the fresh cuts therewith. The elderly pedestrian stared at her with an open mouth as Litz began to scream for the police. But the woman didn't respond because she wasn't real.

The perplexed blonde felt herself sink out of her fantasy of escape and back into bed with the abusive stranger. She closed her eyes and held her breath as the punches kept coming in odd patterns. Litz knew better than to fantasize about characters that couldn't exist in this world and regretted the end of an exhilarating escape.

She began to focus on what was real in the room and what had taken place. Aron hadn't been saying punchy, punchy or one punch. In fact, he had been silent during the entire assault. Litz didn't understand his need to hurt and dominate her, but the smile on his face indicated unnatural gratification.

The young woman had felt a spike of hope when Kevin and William fired their pistols from somewhere in the house, but then everything went silent. It had been over five minutes, or three hundred seconds by her count since the last shot went off. Litz was hopeful that the police would soon arrive, but her captor wasn't concerned with the gunfire.

She looked over at a tall, dark cedar dresser on the right side of the room. There was a framed photo of a redheaded woman with a beautiful smile atop the dresser. The photo frame was gold and its glass free of dust like the rest of the house. She tried getting a glimpse at the matching chest of drawers to her left, but Aron thumped her in the right eye with his fist again. The television star winced for a few seconds and then gazed at the chest of drawers, which had a large mirror mounted above its surface. There was a brand new brown sweater on top of the unit, in front of the mirror.

Litz saw her half-naked body covered in bungee cords that were tight to the point of slowing the circulation in her extremities. She detected folds of her skin bunched up under the cords and a pitiful redness at each binding. The forlorn woman noticed that her attacker would stop his assault long enough to admire her red bra and panty set, and she feared that something worse was coming. There had never been a moment in recent memory when she wanted her mother so much. Life had devolved to one sprawling nightmare after another since that hellish roller coaster ride. Litz never knew that a person could become ill from a tragedy until her stomach emptied over and over during that awful day. It occurred to the glum woman that her escape fantasy wasn't plausible, and this situation would require a sacrifice.

"You hit like a pansy!" Litz taunted her assailant with a firm jaw and even stare.

Aron reacted to this comment by exhibiting pain in his face and delivered a massive uppercut to the woman that left her ears ringing. She clenched her teeth and took the blow as though it were something normal – a new form of beauty treatment.

"You punch the way a fat guy makes love," her rant continued, and Aron rewarded the plumber with a second uppercut of greater force. "I bet I could hit harder than you, fat boy," she managed to say through a daze.

Litz could feel the teeth in her upper left jaw coming loose, and she knew that her consciousness was fading. There was a stream of dried blood that had run down her face when the assault began, and a layer of clear gunk from her nose topped it off. The cunning woman braced herself for more strikes from Aron, but he was distracted.

She drifted in and out of consciousness for the next few minutes. For a moment there appeared to be a staircase with familiar gray shag carpeting. The dazed woman found herself being carried by someone and hoped that her bodyguards had come to the rescue. This trip downstairs reminded her of that awful roller coaster – a ride she never escaped. There were several flashes of light and darkness, until she felt cold water get splashed all over her face.

Litz became conscious from the immediate shock of the chilled water. She felt violated and tormented in the same instant. When the water cleared from her eyes, she saw the muscular man standing across from her in the kitchen. There was an empty gray mop bucket in his hands, which he had used to douse her in water. Litz leaned back in her seat and noticed that the water had also soaked a section of the cherry wood table.

"So you think you can hit harder than me, b****?" Aron swore as he set the mop bucket on the floor and stared at his captive. "Don't worry about your bodyguards, there's a half-inch steel plate inside that door. They can shoot at it or through the walls; it doesn't matter. So what do you have to say now? Acting like a tough girl isn't going to stop any of this."

"I can hit harder than you, pansy," Litz replied through a fog of pain that was engulfing her face. "Let's do this," she muttered in an awkward fashion and tilted her head to the right.

Aron exploded with his strength across the surface of the table, knocking over two chairs on the long side of the serving area at his left.

"You're a liar!" He said, pointing his right index finger at her chest. "You can barely sit up in that chair. But I'll humor you for a minute. I'll humiliate you, and then we'll go back to bed for more playtime," the man threatened with a wicked grin that made her shiver.

Litz looked down at her body and noticed that she was free of her bonds. The optimistic woman tried to move her jaw from left to right, but felt something pop and chose to be cautious.

"I'll bet you can't break a dinner plate," she challenged her captor, raising her swollen eyelids.

The powerful man pursed his lips together and blew air into the spacious kitchen, mocking her with dominant authority. He shuffled over to the kitchen cupboards and retrieved two white plates. His face was flushed and red when he returned to the kitchen table and slid a plate across the surface. It flew with unexpected force and slammed into her right breast. Litz grimaced and reached out to take the plate in her hands.

"Go ahead and break it," Aron ordered as he stood at the other end of the table with another plate in his right hand. "By the way, if you try to hit me with that, I'll just make it so you can't walk or stand up."

The plumber looked down at the glossy, white plate and was disheartened to read the words 'microwave safe' on its reverse side. She flicked the center of the object a few times with her right hand and then held it against the edge of the table at a forty-five-degree angle. Litz then took the meaty part of her right hand and smacked it against the portion of the plate that was hanging off the table. The leverage of this maneuver snapped the plate in half, and she set the jagged pieces on the table in front of her captor.

Aron waived his right hand at her in disapproval and slid the jagged pieces of the plate out of her reach. He then balanced his plate against the top of the table at a forty-five-degree angle and hit it in the center, which broke the object at an odd angle.

"See, that's how a man breaks something," he boasted with his chest puffed out. "We don't rely on the edge of the table to do the work for us."

"I'll bet you can't break a bowl," Litz contested with a bit more pride.

The man shook his head and took a moment to put all four pieces of the broken plates into the mop bucket. He then moved the bucket over to the kitchen counter and fished in the cupboard for two white soup bowls.

"You first, tough guy," he mocked with a smirk of superiority and slid a bowl hard across the surface of the table.

Litz was ready for his cruelty the second time and caught the bowl before it could wound her chest. She turned the object over in her hands and looked at the concave shape that reinforced its structure. The literate woman knew better than to attempt to break something so durable, but wanted to put on a good show. She placed the bowl against the edge of the table and feigned a hard strike to its surface with her right fist. The television star screamed in agony and dropped the ceramic dish to the shag carpeting below her chair.

"Do you think I'm stupid?" Aron asked with an indignant expression. "I'm not going to break my hand on that so you can escape. I knew it was going to hurt before you even tried."

"Why? Are you afraid of pain?" She challenged with a cocky stare. "I'll bet I can handle more pain than you."

"Sure, why not," he agreed with a satisfied shrug, "I'll watch you hurt yourself. What did you have in mind?"

"Let's see who can put a flame closer to their eye," Litz suggested with a determined gaze. "All you have to do is get it as close as you can handle."

Aron rolled his eyes and stepped over to a set of drawers next to his stove. He opened the top drawer and brought out a long burgundy lighter that one might use for lighting gas appliances or grills. Litz put up her hands to catch the device, but her captor shook his head in disagreement.

"No, I think this is going to be fun," he said with a face of stoic amusement, "I'll do the honors."

Litz felt her insides shaking as the man flicked the lighter several times until it sparked to an eerie glow. He brought the flame close to her left eye and then waved it over her right. His excitement seemed to grow with anticipation as he switched sides again, and moved the fire closer to her left eye.

The guarded woman detected that the warmth was drying out the surface of her left eye and her breathing started to intensify. Litz remained steady as he moved the fire back to her right eye and brought it closer to the surface. She sensed a high temperature on her eyebrows and a burning sensation at the front of her eyelid, but everything else was cold. Aron seemed amazed when he brought the flame within a half-inch of her pupil and held it there for almost five seconds.

Litz let out a scream and protected her face, pretending to be in agony. The man laughed at her and shook his head again. He walked over to the kitchen sink with the other bowl and filled it with cold water.

"You know, when I saw you at Mud Rituals the other night," Aron began with a smile as he set the bowl down on the table near her, "you seemed special. But now that I've watched you cowering and whimpering, it just doesn't have any appeal."

Litz took the bowl of water and used the fingers of her right hand to dab little droplets of cooling liquid onto her injured eyelid.

"Do you actually think I'm stupid enough to do that?" The man inquired with contempt and sat down in a chair at her left with his arms folded. "Why would anyone hold a flame up to their own eye?"

Litz started to laugh in a manner that was slow and humble, but built up to a cackle of mockery. She looked at Aron's enormous muscles with their tattoos of knights from the middle ages and giggled harder.

"You know, I have a few friends that are nurses, and they told me that guys with tattoos are always the ones who are afraid of needles." The vigilant woman laughed in a hysterical manner and slapped her left hand down on the table.

"Oh, you think a little fire next to your eye is a big deal?" He prompted with a stare of almighty hatred. "When I was in prison; the things they did to us... I'll tell you what; you keep your hands up in the air, and I'll do your little gypsy trick. If you so much as move, I'll break your neck right here."

The television star gazed at the floor for a moment and then raised her hands above her head. She felt exhaustion and pain all over but managed to keep them up for her captor.

Aron stared at Litz for a few seconds and then brought the lighter up close to his face. He flicked the igniter a few times until the flame danced back to life, and then gazed at his prisoner with distrust. The willful man inspected the small fire as though it were a meaningless gesture, and seemed like he was going to douse it in the water. But after some consideration, Aron moved the burning object a half-inch above the surface of his right eye.

Litz counted to three before shoving her foot the rest of the way into the center of his crotch. She then scooped up the empty bowl with her right hand and jumped out of her chair.

Aron screamed when the flame brushed across the surface of his right eye. He felt a terrible pain in his groin and scowled at the sneaky woman. The man raised his hands in defense as she struck him in the head with the bowl five times. With each blow, his skull was knocked back and forth by the durable ceramic object.

Litz watched him drop to the floor and cover his head from the immense pain. The panicked blonde set the bowl on the table and grabbed one of the heavy wooden chairs, which she hefted down against his body several times.

After confirming that the man was too injured to move, Litz set the chair down and ran to the entryway of the home. She walked up to the blue basement door, breathing heavy from exertion, and released the deadbolt lock before twisting the door handle to free her companions.

"Kev, Will-" she attempted to say when the door was flung open, but found herself too exhausted.

There was a long moment of silence, and she heard a groan coming from the kitchen. Litz shuddered at the thought of having to battle the maniac again in her condition, but her fears subsided when both security guards emerged from the basement.

"Oh my God, Litz; are you okay?" Kevin asked with an expression of shock after inspecting her face.

"He's in there," Litz answered with a nod and an expression of pride. "Be careful."

XVI. Abortion Street

"Do you know what could happen if people saw me having coffee with a cop?" CKB asked his companion with a reticent stare.

"What would they think about coffee with a gay guy?" Stoney offered with a smirk as he took a sip from a large, tan, steaming cup.

"I could have coffee with twenty gay guys, and nobody would flinch," CKB said with a brief belly laugh. "They'd probably think that I was trying to pick up some new drug clients."

"Hector left me a warning yesterday," Stoney began without being prompted. "Three cars were set on fire outside of our building in the middle of the day. I was gonna' tell you about it, but after what happened to Litz, it slipped my mind."

"How is she?" CKB fished for details with a subtle recklessness that broke through his otherwise stoic gaze. "Was that the guy who was writing the death threats?" He thought aloud, and took a sip from a similar large coffee cup.

"I don't know; she gave him a concussion, and he might have a hematoma," Stoney remarked with a cautious gaze. "After going up against her at Mud Rituals, I'm not surprised that she took him out. Look, I know you have a thing for Litz, like the rest of the country, but we need to talk about Hector," the officer suggested with a raise of his eyebrows.

"Oh, Stoney, don't be a b**** just because you ain't the pretty girl at the prom," CKB lamented with a genuine smirk. "I have something planned for Hector, but my boss won't let me get by without that video being uploaded. I'm in as much danger as you if I don't cooperate with him: he already paid me to get it done and it's been two weeks."

Stoney set down his coffee cup on the black, round steel table and folded his arms as he watched New Yorkers walking past a short iron fence that surrounded the seating area. He was wearing a navy blue muscle shirt and black jeans with matching walking shoes. The police officer exhaled with what sounded like strained lungs. His demeanor was getting darker as the moments passed, and he refused to look at his companion.

CKB seemed like a preacher in his white turtleneck sweater with a golden crucifix necklace resting on his heart. His black cargo pants and red and white basketball shoes made him seem prepared for action.

"Hey, Stone, everybody has a boss," CKB added in a more comforting tone. "I never said I was gonna' hang you out for the crows. The last thing that I want is for The Templars to come crashing down on you and your boys – especially after you helped me with that creep in the park."

Stoney refused to speak and turned the bottom of his coffee cup counterclockwise with his right thumb and index finger. He ran his tongue over the front teeth on his upper jaw, enjoying the clean smoothness of their surface.

"You do know that the guy I work for makes people disappear every day, right?" CKB fenced with his silent coffee buddy. "Okay, I'll admit that this is a screwed-up situation, but you should've never followed me that day. What the hell were you thinkin'? Why didn't you stop to take a crap?" He asked with a restrained chuckle.

"I've been asking myself that for two weeks," Stoney pondered aloud with a rich outburst of laughter. "I can't believe I took him hostage." He contemplated in embarrassment and covered his eyes somewhat with his left hand.

"You should've seen the look on your face," CKB reminisced with a hearty grin. "Your gun was in that dude's chin like a goatee on a hipster. I think he had to s*** more than you." The career criminal giggled with enjoyment and scratched the underside of his chin with his left hand.

"What are we going to do about Hector?" Stoney challenged with a serious gaze, taking a swig from his coffee.

"What are we gonna' do about Mitch?" CKB fired back with an expression of regret, wishing that he hadn't shared the name of his employer. "Stoney, I've got a plan to get this out of our ball court, but we'll have to bend a few rules. All you've gotta' do is tell Hector that he can come and get the video at the subway station."

"Which subway station?" Stoney coerced his companion with interest, leaning closer to hear the details.

"Any subway station that he wants outside of The Templars' territory," CKB projected with pride. "I want him to feel comfortable. He needs to think that he's in control."

The Shots Fired Loft – Manhattan, New York

"You're so bad," Litz flirted with Richard as she sat beside him on the comfy living room sofa. "I'm not changing my company name to Great Raccoon Plumbing," she said with a warm smile and massaged her injured right eye with self-conscious tendencies. "Besides, everyone loves Great Rack Plumbing; even some of the ladies."

The video editor smiled at her like an adoring puppy. He wore a white dress shirt and black slacks, both pressed into perfect form by the wardrobe people. The television staff had chosen a similar white blouse and a long orange sundress for the plumber. It had taken most of the morning to get her blonde hair pulled up in a bun with what they called the bangs of a baroness. She also had to spend extra time in the makeup chair to cover the wounds on her face.

Fassim sat opposite the doting couple on one of the barstools. She felt uncomfortable and out of place on the wooden seat, and hated that Litz and Richard were holding hands. Every cute moment that they shared was like an overheated grill, leaving black marks on her soul. She sensed turbulent emotions that caused her stomach to build up with volcanic guilt. The incensed woman wondered if anyone else had to fight back a smile when they heard about Litz getting served with some karma. She recalled Jennifer Priest giving the news to all of the cast members and having to fake a look of shock. Fassim knew that it was wrong for her to wish that Litz was out of the picture, but she had no desire to lose Richard to Bathsheba.

The paparazzi photographer sought refuge in Jazzy at her right, but she also wanted to pull the lime green headscarf down over her face in embarrassment. Unfortunately, her comedian friend seemed supportive and intrigued by the romance between Richard and Litz.

Jazzy watched the odd couple indulge in a small breakfast of bagels and fresh fruit with the foolish expressions you might see on great apes in a small cage. The comedian was wearing a red scarf with a tan blazer, making her seem like a tourist among the other New Yorkers. Her matching skirt and blue high heels made her appear out of place, and Fassim had detested the wasted photo opportunity.

It took a moment for the Muslim to quell her anxiety, and she gazed down at her body with dissatisfaction. Fassim had selected a pair of white dress pants and black high heels to help her get more attention from men. At the suggestion of her mother, Fassim had bought a light blue button-down blouse. It was a traditional garment with large marble-colored buttons, but somehow it made her feel inadequate. The envious woman glared at Litz and her perfect breasts; endowments that many women weren't fortunate enough to share. She thought of them as fruits that were overripe and hoped that they would begin to sag when the plumber hit her thirties. The photographer had recent memories of Jazzy's somewhat saggy breasts, which made her smile, and she took a moment to envision what older breasts would look like on Litz.

"Okay, let's call for a commercial break," Mike stated from off camera as he stepped onto the shag carpet of the living room set. "Fassim, you can't be daydreaming while we're shooting an important story like this," he protested with a gentle shake of his head. "Jazzy just poured her heart out to everyone, and then we turn the camera to you, and you're in another damn world."

Mike had thick stubble, and his hair was out of place, with subtle streaks of gray all over. He seemed to have thrown his outfit together without thinking for the first time in weeks. His muscular, tan legs were showing underneath a pair of black running shorts that went to his knees. The black, long-sleeve mock that adorned his abdomen illustrated that he had given up wearing suits for the immediate future.

"Well, what about you, Mike?" Jazzy scorned the director with flared nostrils. "When Litz came back from the hospital, all you could say was, 'It looks like you survived.' You're like the greatest prick on the east coast. Do you have feelings, or are you waiting for a new shipment from orange-cream-stick?"

"Jazzy, I'm not here to live life to your standards," Mike retorted with a tired gaze and grabbed at his hair. "The studio provided Litz with security and she got into a bad situation. And if I recall, you were one of the people who complained about the security escorts. So how about saving that passion for when we're on camera?" He proposed with a roll of his eyes.

Jazzy bit the center of her lip and stared at the floor as if to summon a mighty earthquake. She let her disapproval be heard in a deep sigh and turned her body away from the director.

"Hey, I came over here to give you some bad news, but I'm not sure if some of you can handle it," Mike stated with an irritable expression. "Look, I'm not great at sugarcoating this kind of thing, so I'll just get it out. The space shuttle was on its return flight from the moon, and it exploded due to a malfunction. There was a bunch of debris found in Greenland, and it matches up with the one that went out. I'm sorry for your loss."

"Oh my God! Litz, I'm so sorry," Jazzy reacted aloud in a soft voice. "I know that Jason-"

Litz closed her eyes and clutched her stomach with her right hand. She hadn't felt such pain and sickness since the roller coaster ride with her mother. The plumber started to shed tears, covering her face with her left hand.

"I told him," the heartbroken diva stated with a voice choked by agony. "I told him not to go on that mission. But then I saw his wife and kid in the car, and I didn't care anymore." Her hands began to tremble, and she leaned forward to hide her face from everyone.

"I'm sure it was a quick death," Richard offered with a delicate gaze of empathy. "It was probably one of the better ways to go – crushing pressure and insane heat."

"You always know," Litz berated Richard as she raised her head and glared at him with raw hatred, "exactly the wrong things to say. You want me to be grateful that he burned up in an instant because you're jealous that he was inside of me? Well too bad, Richard, I had feelings for him, and it's something you'll have to deal with." She lowered her gaze and stared at the video editor like a lioness on the prairie. "In fact, when he was inside of me, I felt much more like a woman."

Jazzy and Fassim turned to look at one another with their eyebrows raised and mouths open. Litz stood up from the sofa and leered at Richard with the entitled body language of a conquering emperor. She then turned and walked out of the room without looking at anyone else.

Fassim got up from her chair and walked over to sit beside Richard, which caused Jazzy to shoot her an insubordinate gaze. The comedian became more disturbed when the paparazzi photographer placed her hand on Richard's right knee.

"Why does this happen when we're in a commercial break?" Mike jested as he made an about-face turn and walked off the set.

Subway Platform – Brooklyn, New York

CKB watched the stairs for incoming foot traffic from his position on the subway platform. He had guessed that Hector would pick the first stop outside of his territory to make the exchange, and knew the man wanted this affair kept close to his chest. His hands shook with anticipation and paranoia was beginning to get the better of him. There were a lot of entrances and exits in this public arena, and he knew that The Templars could be upon him in seconds.

He gripped the back of his neck with his right hand and began to massage the deep tissues. The strength of his hands was encouraging, despite the impending threat of death that could be coming around any corner. CKB knew that The Templars had no intention of letting him leave, regardless of how many copies of the video he provided to them.

Cody jumped multiple times and swung his arms to limber up for the exchange. He was careful not to dislodge a black pistol from beneath the waistband of his pants. The career criminal looked up at the stairs and spotted three Templars descending them to meet with him. He took in a lot of oxygen and tightened his muscles, mimicking a behavior he had seen whales exhibit before going hunting.

When the men got closer, Cody was unsurprised to see that Hector was not among them. They each wore a small patch of a red cross on their leather jackets – a sign of Templar membership. All three of the men were of Hispanic ethnicity, and two of them seemed somewhat subdued. The alpha emerged from the pack and stroked his spiked brown hair when he spotted CKB. This gang member had a tattoo of a shrieking mother on his right forearm, which was indicative of a higher rank.

"Yo, are you CKB?" The alpha asked when he got within ten feet of the black man.

CKB didn't respond right away. He looked the three gang members over for a moment and then gave an abrupt nod.

"Hector wants you to come back and answer some questions." The alpha instructed with a demeanor of dominance. "Let's go."

"Don't you want your video?" CKB suggested with a sarcastic smirk. "It's right over there." He pointed to a section of the floor next to a gray garbage can at something black and shiny.

The alpha jutted his chin upward to the other gang members, and they walked toward the garbage can to his right. When one of the men bent down to pick up the object, CKB pulled on something invisible to the eye. The black device shot out of the gang member's fingers and dragged across the floor toward the television star. CKB turned and ran behind one of the support pillars on the platform with the device trailing behind him, attached to a thin fishing line.

"Get back here!" The alpha gang member shouted and reached for a pistol under his jacket, but thought better of it when he noticed the thick rows of bystanders.

CKB retrieved a black pistol from under his white sweater and fired at his pursuers, but the non-lethal pellets of pepper spray jammed in the chamber. He began to sprint and tried the weapon several more times, but it was useless. His heart was fluttering when he heard the danger on his heels. The criminal wasn't sure if he could outrun the younger men.

He felt the fishing line tighten in his right hand, catching on something solid that snapped it a moment later. CKB noticed that one of the men circled back to pick up the black object, but the other two were gaining ground on him. There was an escalator coming up with a line of at least a dozen subway patrons in his path. He turned and pointed the weapon at his pursuers, which caused them to stop and take cover.

The savvy criminal then barreled his way through the crowd and down the escalator, shoving past anyone in his path. CKB tossed the weapon aside when he got to the next platform and took a moment to catch his breath next to an empty train. After a short break, he gathered his wits and began to amble in a casual fashion across the concrete.

The Templars followed close behind him and were quick to catch up. CKB turned to see the alpha approaching him with a wicked gaze, and he used his right fist to deliver a stunning punch to the gangster's gut. The wounded man's gang companion reached for a pistol beneath his leather coat and drew it out to take aim at Cody's chest.

However, the gangster failed to notice a group of police officers to his left, descending the stairs with their guns drawn. CKB pointed to the officers with his left index finger and the gangster's mouth opened in shock. He tossed his weapon aside and put his hands behind his head to surrender.

"We need to question this one," Stoney explained as he led the pack of ten officers to where the alpha and CKB were standing. "Let's get him on the train," he suggested, and grabbed the gangster by his collar to guide him into the empty rail cars.

"Sorry, I think there were reports of a black man in a Templars' jacket setting fires in the subway earlier," CKB explained to the alpha gangster. "Politicians get really nervous when transportation is threatened, and the next thing you know, there are cops everywhere."

When the men were inside of the empty train, Stoney forced the gangster to sit down on the far passenger bench. CKB frisked the man with flippant authority, removing his satellite phone and pistol. He then handed the weapon to Stoney and sat on the passenger seat opposite the gang lieutenant to enjoy the show.

"Okay, here's the deal," Stoney began in a tone of reason. "This is a copy of the video that Cody took of Hector to humiliate him. I'm giving it to you." He placed a small memory drive in the gangster's right hand and then stood up straight. "We swear on our honor as men that this video will never be uploaded to the Internet. Hector's reputation is safe, and we can end this thing right here. Or you can go to jail with your buddy."

"How does Hector know that you got rid of all the copies?" The alpha gangster questioned with a hard look from his brown eyes.

"He doesn't," CKB interrupted from a standing position and punched Stoney with ferocious energy in the right side of the jaw. "You can still get out if you run that way. Go through two train cars and up the stairs to the left," he added, and gave the satellite phone back to the gangster.

The alpha watched CKB with interest, but when he saw police officers scrambling toward the train in the background, the man became light on his feet. He jumped up and ran through the train cars as instructed. Cody stood up with a smile and watched the gangster disappear out of the train, across the platform and up an unguarded set of stairs.

"What the hell are you doing?" Stoney shouted as he stood up and pointed the pistol at his co-star's head. "You let him get away before I could resolve anything."

CKB put his hands on his head and sat back down on the opposite side of the train.

"Are you okay?" Another officer inquired as he stuck his head through the sliding train doors.

"I'm fine," the Japanese man confirmed with agitation, "just go after him and bring him back. I've got this under control."

"Okay, well the transit authority needs to get this train back in service," the other officer said with a suspicious expression. "The captain wants this platform clear and back up in a few minutes."

Stoney gave his fellow officer a fierce look and gestured with his chin for the man to depart.

"Why did you do that?" He asked CKB through gritted teeth with the gun pointed at his co-star's forehead.

"I used his phone to upload the video," CKB confessed and lowered his eyes toward the floor of the train.

"Are you stupid? Are you trying to get me killed?" The police officer roared, feeling the pistol shaking in his right hand.

"No, but you are," the criminal said with a disappointed glance at Stoney and leaned back on the seat, folding his arms. "I uploaded it using his video channel, from his device."

Stoney stared at the floor for a moment and allowed the rage to subside long enough for him to think. He inspected his blue police uniform as though it would provide him with the answer, and then started to laugh.

"Yeah, that's right," his companion confirmed with satisfaction. "I uploaded it with his video channel from his phone. The other gangster already got out with a copy, so Hector will know that we did right by him."

"You know what's frustrating about this whole thing?" Stoney challenged with a moderately wounded chuckle.

"You can't press charges on me?" CKB boasted with raised eyebrows.

"No, that's not it," the police officer said as he dropped the pistol on the opposite bench.

Stoney turned toward his co-star and struck him on the right cheek, causing CKB to hit the floor on his butt.

"Thanks for taking care of that," he stated with affection and helped the career criminal back to his feet.

XVII. Eyes on Toothpicks

Stoney leaned back against the weathered blue stucco on the outside wall of a rundown apartment complex. He clutched a 9 millimeter semi-automatic pistol in front of his chin and listened to a group of Rain Bird sprinklers that danced and clicked their way through repetitive cycles. The apartment community was like a ghost town during the midmorning hours. All manner of beer bottles and cigarette butts littered the property, along with the occasional syringe.

"We're going to breach in thirty," Troy Mickelson called back to the Japanese officer as he stuck his head around the corner. "Stoney, are you good?" The tall policeman asked and turned back to look at the older man through his mirror sunglasses.

Stoney nodded at his partner and sucked in a deep breath, preparing to backup another unit for a drug raid. The Japanese man looked at his partner's spiked blonde hair and lean figure. He was grateful to let the twenty-four-year-old take the lead in this operation. His companion seemed eager to make an arrest and kept stroking his goatee and mustache. Troy was lean and brawny, but by Stoney's estimation he didn't have the patience to survive for more than two years in the vice unit. He and Stoney had instructions to stay back from the door of the suspect's apartment since their blue uniforms made them unworthy of a covert raid.

Although the official name of the apartment complex was '75th on the Brooklyn,' the police often called it 'The Laundromat.' This nickname was due to the number of drug busts resulting in fatalities over the past five years. These incidents had inspired a campaign by the chief of police to have the property condemned.

"Let's go!" His partner shouted and galloped around the corner to a metal staircase with cement steps.

The Japanese police officer followed his partner with reluctance and witnessed his younger colleagues charging through the door of an apartment at top speed. He heard shouting and orders for people to get on the floor as he strafed twenty feet at a time, stopping to ensure that nobody was watching from the street or courtyard. Stoney climbed the stairs at just above walking speed and felt his body shivering from the threat of death all around him. His veteran status allowed the man to conserve energy and be more conscious of foolish mistakes that the others might miss.

Stoney stepped through an open apartment door from the second-floor concourse. The apartment smelled awful from drug abusers with body odor and some food that a resident had burned in a frying pan. He brought his pistol down to waist level and moved in a cautious sweeping pattern across the brown shag carpeting.

It was a small apartment with a kitchen and living room that merged into one space. Just off from the living room, an opened sliding glass door led out to a small concrete balcony surrounded by a brown wooden railing. Stoney saw his partner questioning a tall, heavy suspect that was kneeling on the cement with his hands behind his head. The man had a thick beard and long, matted brown hair. He was wearing a white tank top and cheap khakis with what appeared to be black hiking boots.

Stoney smirked at Troy and watched him reply with a middle finger from his left hand. His gaze shifted away from the balcony, and he was careful to navigate through the piles of garbage and contraband that littered the floor. There was a black oak coffee table with ashtrays and needles near the wall in front of the entryway. It was adjacent to a brown leather sofa that featured burn marks and soda stains.

The rest of the area was unremarkable, and Stoney noticed that there were dishes in the sink and on the counter that hadn't received a proper cleaning in months. Aside from these repulsive features, there was a modest poker table with mismatched barstools and chairs used for meals and other activities.

"Coming back," Stoney called out to the undercover officers who had made the initial breach. "Are you all clear?"

"Yeah, we're good," an officer shouted in a deep African-American voice, "can you cover the front door?"

"No problem," he acknowledged, exhibiting a smirk of vindication for being slow enough to get the easiest job. "I just need to get eyes on you."

"Come on back; we're decent," the other officer joked, causing his partner to chuckle.

Stoney stepped with caution down the narrow hallway to a single bedroom and saw two officers questioning an obese redheaded woman. She wore handcuffs that were a snug fit and sat upright on a bed with surprisingly clean sheets. A thin black officer was standing beside her with a notepad and pencil, taking notes as the woman mumbled phrases that were somewhat coherent. His heavier white partner was overturning items in the room, searching every viable hiding place for paraphernalia.

The Japanese officer waved to his undercover colleagues in a melodramatic pantomime and then turned back toward the entryway of the apartment. He heard a male voice scream from the balcony and rushed through the small piles of garbage in the hallway to investigate. Upon entering the living room, Stoney saw the bearded drug addict choking his partner and slamming him against the wooden railing. He readied his weapon and crept closer, aiming his pistol between the shoulder blades of the suspect. The officer stood just inside the open glass door, wanting to shoot the man without following police procedures.

"Let him go, or I'll shoot you in the knees," Stoney threatened with a wild gaze, watching Troy's face turning red from a lack of oxygen.

The bearded criminal twisted around in a rapid fashion and held Troy hostage in front of his chest. His body was massive in comparison to the thinner police officer, which allowed him to drag the man like a vacuum. Stoney held his breath and tried to find an area of the drug addict's body that was open for a nonlethal wound. He checked the meaty portions of the abdomen, along with the man's extremities, but could not find a safe target.

Stoney cursed his partner in silence and then saw the man release Troy's throat. There was an instant where he felt relieved until he realized that the attacker had shoved the blonde officer toward him. The television star felt Troy's body slam into him as if it had been thrown off by a bull. He winced immediately when the younger man's head smacked against his, and Stoney found himself falling to the floor.

The older police officer cringed in disgust when he felt dusty junk mail and empty fast food containers sticking to his skin. He ignored the discomfort and reached up to check Troy's pulse. His body relaxed when he noticed that his partner was still breathing.

Stoney gave Troy a gentle push and rolled his partner's body away to the left. He looked down near his feet where his pistol balanced against the side of his right shin. The Japanese man went cold with despair when he witnessed the bearded criminal reaching down to grab the weapon. His right foot shot sideways and moved the pistol aside out of instinct. This maneuver allowed Stoney to get to his feet and confront the drug addict.

Despite the officer's efforts to keep the firearm away from his assailant, Stoney observed in shock as the man scooped it up with his right hand. During a moment of pure inspiration, Stoney made a running leap onto the criminal's back. The officer then wrapped his arms around the suspect's throat, attempting to make him yield.

"Put the weapon on the floor, or I will shoot you!" The African-American officer commanded from behind the poker table in the kitchen. "Look, man, we're not playin' games here; you need to give up now!"

The massive crook went silent for a moment, breathing in a heavy rhythm that made his belly bow in and out above the coffee table. Stoney relaxed his grip and sensed that the man was about to give up, but his body tensed when he saw the 9 millimeter pistol pointing upward. His eyes looked around the room in a panic, and he tried to restrain the right hand of the suspect.

The drug addict began to spin in a clockwise circle and fired the pistol over his shoulder several times. Stoney felt pieces of the ceiling dropping on his forearms, and he watched the awkward aim of the gunman line up with his face several times. He grabbed at the throat of his attacker and wrenched his left forearm against the man's windpipe. His bicep was pulling with desperate aggression like an animal that a hunter fired upon in the wild.

When the suspect felt his airway closing off, he fired the pistol in desperation and Stoney used his unsteady right arm to keep it away from his face. Every explosion from the gun was another attempt to remove the police officer from the planet. Each time the ringing got louder in his ears, he felt farther away from his beloved fiancé and the dreams they were bold enough to share. He saw the pistol moving closer to his forehead and wondered if any of this life had been worth his time.

Something long and black swung through the air, forcing Stoney to close his eyes. He heard an impact and opened his eyes to see a collapsible baton strike the suspect in the back of the hand. The pistol flew as though lightning struck it away, and the drug addict cried out in agony.

Stoney turned his head further to the right and saw the African-American officer answer the criminal's cry with another blow to the back of his right leg. The Japanese officer felt the massive body collapse beneath him and released his grip to slide away from the offender. He got to his feet and stopped to catch his breath, but refused to take his gaze off of the ruthless criminal.

"I've got this, Stoney," the other officer assured his colleague with a solemn expression, "you can relax. Hey, Stoney, I've got this…you need to go relax. If he moves, I'll put two in the back of his head," he added with a wink and a smile.

The television star stood up straight and took a moment to get his bearings. He then leaned down toward Troy to check his vitals again.

"I'm okay," Troy spoke in a weak tone before Stoney could bend his knees. "My throat is worked over, but I think it'll be okay. I'm sorry, brother," he muttered in a state that was somewhere between consciousness and death.

Stoney patted Troy's right leg as if to acknowledge that the apology was enough. He then stumbled out to the concrete balcony and rubbed his eyes in the sunlight. When Stoney saw how beautiful the day was from this vantage point, the television star sensed a surge of emotions. He asked himself why someone would try to end it all for another person who was just doing their job. Stoney's stomach became nauseous as he imagined the simple mechanics of a weapon that could fire a projectile at 1,000 feet per second.

"The finger squeezes the trigger," Stoney said to the courtyard between the apartment complexes, "and the pin hits the back of the round. The round explodes; the bullet spins...destroying everything."

The Japanese man thought he heard the sound of a rifle in the distance and dismissed it as an eerie coincidence to his last statement. Something struck him in the chest and broke a rib on the right side of his body. Stoney was in immediate shock and felt confident that this was all part of his imagination. In his mind, an object hit the outside of his uniform and got caught in his bulletproof vest. But he knew that it was impossible. Even when his body slammed against the floor and he heard the other officers scrambling around him, it seemed like a dream.

"Where the hell did that come from?" The portly, white undercover officer asked his partner in a state of raw fear.

"I think it came from the courtyard," his partner remarked with a tinny voice of doubt. "Get your head down and call for an ambulance."

Stoney closed his eyes with a smile as his consciousness drifted; he knew it had to be a dream.

The Shots Fired Loft – Manhattan, New York

"Cut the cameras and go to commercial," Mike said as he stepped onto the set in the middle of the living room. "Stoney was shot this morning during a drug raid. I don't know many details, but they said it happened at 75th on the Brooklyn and caught them by surprise."

Fassim closed her eyes and put her head down until her face disappeared underneath a pink headscarf. Jazzy put her hands over her mouth and shook her head. She then leaned back into the sofa, forgetting that she was about to divulge the story of her sexual assault on national television.

"Is he going to be okay?" Richard inquired with a perplexed expression. "Stoney always seemed so tough; I can't imagine somebody..." The film editor trailed off and had a difficult time forming another thought.

CKB stood up from a barstool near Jazzy and walked over to the kitchen counter with his head hung toward the floor. He seemed to be trying to work something out. The powerful man appeared defeated in his black muscle shirt and white cargo pants. His left foot dug into the carpet in an anxious manner, and he gave off the ambiance of a haunted man.

"We need to go to the hospital," Jazzy stated with urgency as she adjusted her black skirt and stood up tall in a pair of matching high heels. "Where is Litz?" She looked around the room and tugged at her lime green blouse in a nervous way.

"I think Litz is on a plumbing call," Richard contemplated aloud and stood up from the other barstool.

Fassim glared at Richard with confusion but knew that her jealousy was misplaced. She watched his black and red tie swinging across his white button-down shirt and seemed hypnotized by his appeal. The man had been wearing tighter pants lately, and the black jeans he had on today were impressive. A sensation of pure guilt crept over the woman, and she leaned back into the sofa as if to disappear.

"I have to go," CKB announced in an abrupt fashion and turned on his heel toward the exit.

"What the hell, CKB?" Jazzy demanded with outrage, placing her hands on her hips. "You're leaving, and Litz isn't here: doesn't anyone care about Stoney?" She gestured to the room with her hands outstretched, but everyone seemed to have other priorities.

"I'll go with you," Fassim answered as she jumped up from her seat and made quick strides in her gray sundress to stand near Jazzy.

"Yeah, I'll go too," Richard agreed with a perplexed expression and watched CKB leave the loft in silence.

Jazzy glared at Mike and folded her arms, which caused him to lower his head and blink with exhausted eyes. The director appeared to be thinner than normal in a pair of blue jeans and a gray two-button dress shirt with white stripes.

"Yes, of course; why don't I drive?" Mike responded like a man who had just spent the last four days shoveling coal at a prison. "Let's go see how he's doing," the executive conceded and began to shuffle toward the front door.

Jazzy shook her head and raised her eyebrows, electing not to say anything due to the director's cooperation. Fassim and Richard seemed to share her sentiments, and they communicated their solidarity with expressions of disgust.

"Why don't you stop marveling over what an a**hole I am and keep your minds on your friend?" Mike called back to the group without turning around.

Although this statement tempted the group to share another round of disapproving glances, none of them wanted to make him look smarter than before. The three cast members bowed their heads with disappointment and followed Mike in a silent march of uncertainty.

Warehouse 38 – Brooklyn, New York

CKB tugged on the handle of the bulletproof, tinted glass door of his employer's warehouse, entering the facility like an elephant ripping a tree from its path. He knew that Stoney's near-death experience had nothing to do with fate, and two men had threatened his friend's life in the past few weeks. The career criminal moved slower upon entering the warehouse and decided not to let his rage play against him. CKB's better senses told him that Hector had initiated the shooting, but making assumptions about the enterprise of crime was an amateur's errand.

The muscular television star began to move between racks of spring clothing but froze in place when he laid eyes on the head of the timber wolf. There was something odd about the piercing gaze of the animal, and it made him reconsider the nature of his employer. CKB retrieved a satellite phone from the right pocket of his cargo pants and began to type on the display.

'I'm here.' He texted and stared at the rough birch door with its chipped brass handle that stood between him and Mitch's deadly enterprise. 'We need to talk about the cop.'

'What is there to talk about?' Mitch responded within a few seconds. 'I thought you were on our side. Or is this some other cop?' There was a brief pause before the conversation continued. 'Why don't you come in and we'll discuss?'

'Why don't you come out?' CKB suggested, and fixed his gaze on the aged interior door of the warehouse. 'I've never known Hector to use The Laundromat to do business-' His rapid typing was interrupted by the sound of the interior door opening.

CKB crouched down when he noticed that the lights were out in the security office. He knelt toward the floor until his right hand touched its warm, dark hickory surface. Just ten feet behind him and to the left, he heard the sound of a steel tumbler turning as the front door lock was engaged. His body became overwhelmed with anxiety and everything seemed to be moving too fast. CKB glanced up at the wolf above the door and cursed his employer in silence for his ruthless way of doing things. He looked around for a weapon and saw a rack of metal baseball bats hanging down from a shelving unit to his right. The career criminal chided himself for not finding a way to smuggle a firearm into the warehouse. It would have been simple to use a piece of lead to fool the cheap X-ray security system on his way through the front door. His hands shook when he considered that staying outside of the building would have been the better choice.

"I got your video uploaded," CKB confided under his breath as he strafed toward the shelving unit. "Then you have the balls to accuse me of becoming an informant because I was nice to a cop for five seconds?" He let these thoughts fuel his actions, using caution and patience to pick up a blue and gray metal baseball bat without making a sound.

Cody became nervous as the seconds went by with no movements in the warehouse. He removed a glossy, black wireless video camera from a small case in the left pocket of his pants and clipped the unit to the neck of his muscle shirt. The young man squatted again and transferred the baseball bat to his left hand, feeling the rubber grip with pensive authority. His right hand fished for his satellite phone in the right pocket of his pants, and he clicked the 'quick record' button on top of the unit. A small red light illuminated on top of the camera, and he gripped the steel baseball bat with both hands, preparing himself for action.

The warehouse lights went out, and his breathing escalated to a state of mortal terror. He forced his eyes to stay open, trying to adjust to the blackness as quick as possible. A shotgun fired twice into the racks of clothing from just inside the doorway of the security office. CKB put his head down and held his breath, ignoring the temptation to run for the exit. He knew that the front door was formidable with layered bulletproof glass, and the locking mechanism had three steel cylinders. The explosive sounds of gunfire seemed to be amplified by the enclosed space, and all he could hear was ringing in his ears.

CKB saw the barrel of a shotgun protrude from the doorway of the security office and was grateful that his vision had adjusted to the darkness. He waited for the security guard to emerge, but knew that the man was unlikely to make his day by being stupid.

The guard panned across the entire space from right to left, listening for any signs of his target. After this brief interlude, the shotgun swung in a wild arc back to the right and was fired at random two more times.

CKB closed his eyes and inhaled until his lungs filled with oxygen. A fifth shot went off and hit the back of the shelving unit behind which he was taking cover. His legs began to cramp under his weight, and he noticed sweat forming on his brow. The television star knew that Mitch had trained all of his men to use patience to their advantage. He thought about the blocked escape route through the front door and lamented his decision to enter the building before knowing the truth.

"You stormed in here like-" CKB started to criticize himself but was interrupted by thunderous gunfire.

Two more shots went off as the security guard pulled back on the pump action to eject the spent shells. CKB got to his feet and tripped on the corner of the shelving unit, causing a factory-packaged basketball to fall from the top shelf to the floor. Although this object made enough of a sound to alert the guard, Cody knew that the man needed to reload his shotgun. He imagined the heavyset man with his unkempt black hair and dead eyes, trying to force shells into the magazine of the weapon in total darkness. CKB smirked and dodged between the racks of clothing, but his victory was short-lived. At least one thug would be waiting outside the front door, and CKB's survival depended on several factors that he didn't want to contemplate.

The inundated man made his way to the winding staircase that was made of stainless steel and ascended the stairs as if his body were on fire. When Cody reached the second floor, he dodged past several display racks with fishing poles and kayaks. Although his eyes had adjusted to the dimness, he stumbled several times over boxes and steel shelving units. In his mind, these small sacrifices were worth the effort, because CKB knew that the gunman below would soon exit from his hiding place.

Once CKB reached the far right side of the room, he tossed aside some archery targets that were covering up a pair of decorative windows. He then twisted his head to the right when noticing how small the windows were in comparison to his memories of them. Every part of him was protesting the concept of leaping off of the floor to climb out of windows that were only two feet high and positioned near the roof of the building. CKB gripped the steel baseball bat with both hands and smashed the glass out of the window frame from the outside edges inward. The decorative glass was thick and broke into sharp pieces that spun on the smooth hardwood flooring. Cody unclipped the small camera from the collar of his shirt and put it back in the case, which he stuffed into his right pocket.

After clearing pieces of glass from the windows, CKB removed his black muscle shirt and used it to wipe away loose shards and particles from the black steel frame. He then whipped his shirt in the air a few times to free it from debris and pulled it back over his powerful torso. With the window frame free of sharp objects, he was able to stand on the tips of his toes and thrust the baseball bat through the small space. CKB pulled the steel cylinder tight against the outside of the building and used it as a handle to haul himself up. His left foot anchored him away from the wall, and he leveraged his considerable upper body strength to pull himself through the window on the right.

The television star froze when he heard the sounds of heavy footsteps thundering up the stainless steel staircase less than thirty yards from his position. CKB's gaze shifted to a distinct shadow cast on the interior wall by his body and the baseball bat. He bit his lip with regret, realizing that his figure had become the easiest target in the world; a moving shadow outlined by a rectangle of sunlight. If he didn't escape soon, Mitch would make him disappear with his other victims.

The athletic man felt his legs dangling above emptiness when he emerged fifteen feet above the ground. CKB was forced to grip the edge of the window frame and let go of the baseball bat. The television star felt fresh cuts in his hands and fingers despite all he had done to clean the sleek, black surface. There was a dull ringing sound when the baseball bat bounced on the concrete slabs below, and the daylight blinded him.

Although he wished for more time to plan his descent, the pain in his fingers was too irritating. Cody let his body hang from the full length of his arms and then dropped the remaining ten feet. He allowed his knees to take most of the impact with the cement, but it connected harder with his body than anticipated. This impact forced his rear end and lower back to smack the solid surface while his body rolled backward until he was lying flat.

CKB detected alarming pain shooting through the center of his anus and lower back. While he was grateful that his head was uninjured during the fall, the pain from his tailbone didn't seem to be a fair tradeoff. The uneasy man took a few deep breaths and inspected the cuts on his hands. He gazed up at the window high above him and shook his head at his apparent lack of sanity. Experience told him that the gunman in the warehouse wouldn't bother poking his head through the window for fear of becoming an easy target. Nobody wanted to die for a pitiful hourly wage.

Cody reached out with his right hand and felt a large piece of glass on the concrete. He pulled his arm away with an immediate sense of danger and decided to use his stomach muscles to get to his feet. The television star felt hellish bells of pain ringing in his anus again as he rolled his body upward from the ground. CKB used his legs to steady himself and rose to his feet. Although he wanted to take a moment to rest, he knew that time was against him and started to weigh his options. As he was contemplating his situation, he removed the small camera from the hard case in his right pocket and clipped it back onto his shirt.

The criminal leaned down to pick up the baseball bat and looked to his right toward the loading docks at the rear of the warehouse. This option was appealing, but the area had security cameras and was monitored by guards. CKB gazed at the building next door and tried to find a point of entry; however, it only presented another fifteen-foot surface of faded steel panels. The adept man sighed and heaved his shoulders with reluctance, deciding that the front parking lot was his best escape route.

When he reached the corner of the warehouse, CKB peered around it to scope out the situation. There was a large black pickup truck parked at an angle fifteen feet in front of the building on the cement pads with its engine running. Cody saw two men leaning over the bed of the truck with black semiautomatic pistols in each of their hands. He crouched and sprinted toward the driver side of the vehicle, hearing gunfire ricochet off of the concrete. The television star began to run a zigzag pattern when he approached the truck, throwing off the aim of his enemies. His body rocketed toward the large vehicle, building momentum for a running leap, which allowed him to find cover behind the unit.

CKB ignored the scrapes and pain in his bones after his body dropped to the cement a second time. He used his powerful abdominal muscles to rise from the ground and sneaked into the cab of the truck through the driver door.

"Why the hell did you leave the truck running?" A tall brown-haired gunman shouted at his stout companion.

"I didn't know he could run that fast! It would have been easier just to shoot him, throw him in the bed, cover him up and then take off to the cemetery!" The shorter man exclaimed and clutched the top of his shiny bald head. "I mean he just…shot out of there like a damn circus performer. And I didn't think he'd be coming from the alley."

Cody put the automatic transmission into drive mode, checked the parking brake, and then slammed on the gas pedal after verifying that the brake wasn't engaged. The vehicle roared to life, and its tires squealed across the concrete, producing small wisps of steam.

When the truck lurched forward, both gunmen stepped aside, and the taller of the two took aim at the rear of the cab. His brown eyes watched the driver's head, and he sensed his insides going calm in preparation to fire.

"Don't shoot at my truck!" The bald crook warned his companion and swatted the taller man's forearms to throw off his aim. "That's an eighty-thousand-dollar truck! You don't need to shoot at it; we can find him later."

"You better hope you're right," his taller colleague answered in pronounced disagreement. "If Mitch finds out that your truck was more important than getting this done…I wouldn't wanna' be you."

"Where's he gonna' go, huh?" The shorter man prompted with his arms outstretched. "I have a GPS unit welded into the frame of that truck. It would let me find him at a gas station in China if I wanted. So relax, I think Mitch just wants him to have the fear of God again – the guy is getting too loose."

Mount Sinai Hospital – Brooklyn, New York

"Are you sure these are the guys that shot Stoney?" Troy Mickelson prompted Cody for confirmation as he rubbed the back of his neck. "It looks like you've had one hell of a day," the tall blonde said as he watched CKB through his blue eyes with admiration.

"I think so," CKB uttered with a demeanor of caution. "There's a chance that Hector and The Templars were involved, but after all this, I doubt it."

"No, Hector and his lieutenants are caught up in a pseudo civil war," the police officer explained in a discreet manner. "Your video didn't do him any favors."

CKB was standing in a busy emergency room hallway next to Stoney's younger partner from the police precinct. The man was lean with spiked blonde hair but seemed to have good judgment for his age. Although their impromptu meeting had been short and interrupted by constant hospital codes from loudspeakers, Troy was able to learn a great deal. Cody had shown the officer text messages from his employer and allowed him to watch the video that his phone captured from the incident.

"Is that everything?" Troy asked after he finished watching the video.

"No, there's a stolen truck in the parking lot," CKB admitted with a smirk and dangled a set of keys in front of the officer. "I hope you can make that disappear. How is Stoney doing?" He asked with genuine empathy, bracing himself for bad news as Troy took the keys from his hand.

"Well, the bastards shot him with a high-powered rifle, but the round didn't get through his breastplate," the policeman confirmed with a smile. "It did break two of his ribs; they're patching him up now, and he should be able to get back to your TV show in a few hours. Go ahead and say hello," he said with a friendly expression, and reached out with his right hand toward the criminal.

CKB held his breath when the uniformed lawman offered to shake his hand, but he decided that diplomacy was the best option and friends like this would be useful.

"Thanks again for taking the risk so that we could get these guys," Troy said in the spirit of comradery as the two men shook hands. "I'm on my way to make it happen."

Cody nodded to Stoney's partner as the man took hurried steps toward the exit of the emergency room. He shook his head and smiled, thinking that he would never have visited a cop in the hospital three weeks ago.

The athletic man strolled into the outpatient hospital room and saw three of his co-stars standing around a pristine bed where his friend was resting. It would have made the perfect photo for a hospital recovery, except that Mike was seated in a padded chair at the corner of the room wearing a sour expression. CKB moved closer to the bed and saw a smile form on the Japanese man's face. The criminal smiled back and nodded as a sign of mutual respect.

Stoney was shirtless in the bed, and a clean white blanket covered his legs. There were lengths of gauze wrapped around his chest just above the man's small beer belly, which met under his armpit with some white medical tape.

"Troy is on his way…to get the bastards," CKB said as he admired the healthy appearance of his co-star. "I'm glad you made it, brother."

XVIII. A Mother's Wrath

Stoney had a difficult time adjusting to the new level of pampering and attention provided to him by his co-stars. The Japanese man couldn't comprehend surviving such a treacherous afternoon on the job. In over ten years as a policeman, he had never remembered a day overshadowed by more darkness. Officer Akuda was further disturbed by the chilling tactics of the gunman that fired upon him in the ransacked apartment. The assassin would have had to follow him for most of the day with discipline and intent, taking his or her time to choose a position and escape route. Stoney mulled over how the would-be killer had chosen a vantage point that leveraged multiple opportunities to take a shot. His abdomen was burning inside with conflict, and he wondered why the shooter had waited until after they breached the apartment. The perpetrator could have made a clean shot before the police executed their infiltration, but for some reason, they chose to be patient.

"Do you want me to get you a pillow for your back?" Jazzy offered the wounded officer with a dazzling smile. "I know your chest must be hurting."

"No, I'm okay," Stoney replied with a wave of his right hand, deducing that life had given him enough blessings for one day. "I'm just going to sit down and watch something on TV to get my mind off of the world for a while," he admitted with a sad expression and began to massage the back of his neck. "But first, I want to change out of this uniform and forget about being a cop for the night."

"I'll help you get undressed," she said with a delighted expression, somehow appearing vindicated that a man had finally opened up to her. "Don't worry; I'll be gentle."

Richard and CKB smirked at one another as they made their way into the kitchen to unwind. The men admired Jazzy's delicious figure and shook their heads at almost the same moment, expressing a collective mourning for a wasted sensual opportunity.

"Oh, get over it," Fassim fumed when she noticed that her co-stars wished that Jazzy would undress them instead. "By the time Litz walks in the room, you'll both forget that Jazzy ever existed."

Jazzy turned to glance at Richard and CKB as she was helping Stoney back to his bedroom. Her eyes tightened as if she were attempting to singe the men for being shallow, and both of them looked at the floor, pretending to be occupied doing nothing.

"Where is Litz?" Richard inquired and turned his head from left to right, inspecting the loft as if the woman would spring forth from somewhere. "Did she respond to any of your calls or texts?"

Jazzy and Fassim shook their heads and went about their business, showing solidarity in their disdain for the diva. Richard looked at CKB with a curious demeanor, but the muscular man shrugged and began to play with his satellite phone. The conservative film editor glanced at his watch and surmised that they had spent over five hours at the hospital. He gazed at the city through the sliding glass doors of the apartment and saw that the sun was setting.

Richard scratched the back of his head and made his way from the kitchen to the hallway for an inspection of Litz's bedroom. His senses indicated that something was wrong, which caused him to quicken his pace. When he reached the bedroom, the young man twisted the doorknob and was relieved to feel it open. He pushed the sturdy, white door aside and felt guilty that part of him hoped to catch her undressing.

His mouth opened in horror upon an initial inspection of the disorganized bedroom. Richard saw a large man on his knees next to the headboard of the bed. Someone had tied his hands to the bedpost with black climbing rope. The television star twisted his head to the left in surreal confusion from this unexpected scenario and felt uncomfortable all over. A Hello Kitty tote bag had been used to cover the portly man's head, and the handles were wrapped around his chin, secured to his neck with steel wire.

Richard noticed a camera on the bed that seemed similar to those used by members of the television crew. The restrained man moved his head forward and back underneath the tote bag, which made Richard realize that he had been holding his breath in fear. The conservative film editor exhaled with relief and sprung into action, stepping over obstacles next to the cedar bed and its bright pink bedspread.

There were books all over the floor that covered advanced topics in fields such as engineering, physics, thermodynamics, psychology, and military strategy. Richard felt confounded as to how his co-star had found the time to read so many thick textbooks. Notes and drawings littered the room, and it was clear that Litz had engaged in her studies with devotion. He now understood why his colleague had kept her bedroom locked up like a bank vault during the day.

Richard placed his right hand between the shoulder blades of the overweight man and assumed that it was cameraman Doug. The bound man was wearing a large green T-shirt and blue jeans with cheap white tennis shoes. After a bit of effort, Richard was able to untwist the wire from around the handles of the tote bag, undoing it in neat, wide circles. Once the wire was gone, he removed the pink and black bag and saw the familiar face of Doug. The man was pale and had matted hair stuck to his head, saturated with droplets of sweat. There didn't seem to be any wounds to the crew member, other than his pride.

"Thank you, Richard," Doug said in a high tone of voice that was unusual for such a large man. "Litz has gone crazy, man; you guys need to watch out for her!"

"What are you talking about?" Richard protested, recalling how vulnerable the woman had been when he kidnapped her stuffed frog. "Dude, Litz is a pussycat; she can barely keep herself safe in this city."

"Will you untie me, please? I have to use the bathroom!" The cameraman complained with a smidge more masculinity in his voice. "Look, she brought me in here and tied me up, and told me that you guys need to watch the video."

"How the hell did she get you in here?" Richard stated with observant rhetoric as he began to unfasten the knots from the bedpost. "You outweigh her by at least a hundred and fifty pounds. There's no way she could overpower you."

Doug became silent and looked at the floor as Richard kept working on the knots. He turned his face away, but the television star stopped loosening the rope and put his hands on his hips.

"Okay," Doug submitted with a nod toward the bonds on his wrists, "she came out into the living room in a bra and panties while I was filming. I felt embarrassed, at first, but she invited me to her bedroom for an 'amazing experience.' Then I followed her in here like an idiot, and she asked me to get on my knees near the bed. So I got down-"

"I get the idea," the conservative man replied as he continued to untie the ropes, "she promised to play a naughty game with you and tied you to the bedpost. That doesn't show a lot of willpower, Doug."

"You're one to talk, garbage banana," the cameraman hissed back with a hint of jealousy in his bright brown eyes. "I'm sorry. Please don't stop untying me. Yes, I was filming you guys that night, but Mike made me destroy the disk."

Richard finished removing the rope and Doug jumped up from the floor in a hurry. The large man ran past him at a speed that was almost unfathomable. After Doug had vacated the area, Richard looked at the camera on the bed and decided to check the recordings from the past few hours. There was the sound of a bathroom door slamming as Doug scrambled to the toilet. Richard felt as if the room was spinning around him, and he could only focus for a moment at a time after so many disturbing revelations. The film editor picked up the camera by its black strap and carried it out of the bedroom toward the living room.

When he entered the living room, Richard saw Stoney lying belly down in gray sweatpants and a white tank top on the sofa. Jazzy had mounted his rear end and was busy giving the man a deep tissue massage. The Republican winced and smirked at the thought that she might be trying to convert the Japanese man from being gay.

CKB stood next to the kitchen counter and was busy making peanut butter sandwiches for himself and Fassim. The paparazzi photographer made eyes at the ripped criminal, but also stole a moment to stare at Richard when he entered the room. She then turned her attention back to CKB and put her left hand on his right bicep, leaning forward to tell him a joke.

Richard noticed that a mindless cartoon with mature themes was playing on the 3D hologram television. He used the remote control to change the video source, awaiting protests from his co-stars. The film editor then set the camera down on the carpet and connected the audio and video cables to the front of the display unit.

"What the hell are you doing?" Jazzy asked with outrage as she continued to massage her co-star. "Stoney is trying to relax after the hospital. Next time you get a broken rib, you can decide what we all watch."

"Something has happened to Litz," Richard announced without turning around as he finished setting up the device for playback. "She tied up cameraman Doug in her bedroom, and he says that she recorded something for us on this camera."

The room went silent after Richard relayed this news to the other cast members, which inspired them to focus on the television display area with stoic anticipation.

When the video began to play, it showed an image of Litz in a white bathrobe, and she jumped back from the camera as if just having pushed the record button. The diva stepped back a few paces and sat on the sofa in the living room. Everyone turned their heads to the sofa where Stoney was relaxing, confirming that it was the location where Litz had made the video.

The blonde plumber crossed her left leg over her right and leaned toward the camera with an expression of deep purpose. Her hair was pulled back in a tight blonde ponytail, and she seemed like a different person than the one they had known while filming the show.

"First, I want to thank Doug and all of the other men for thinking with their balls," Litz began with a tone of brash superiority. "When I was young, my father and brother were killed in a car accident. I was an awkward girl; an intellectual, so I didn't have many friends. When dad died, mom couldn't afford the house, and we moved around a lot. She retired a few years later on a government subsidy and began her Golden Years Tour of the country. We had a lot of laughs and got to be really close; it was marvelous. But then one day, we were at a casino riding a roller coaster, and she died right next to me. My best friend in the whole world – the center of my universe. I could tell you a lot about what that day did to me, but I'm sure you're about to figure that out for yourselves." She paused and stared into the camera lens with a mystique of extreme hatred.

"So we've come forward twelve years from that tragedy, and none of you are paying attention," the introspective woman expressed with a sneer of deep shame. "When I look around today, I don't see appreciation for the sacrifices that were made during The Passing. You keep going about your lives without taking the time to have regard for anyone else, and that's how this problem started. You knew that only so many people could live on this planet, so why did you keep having children? Why did you think it was okay to get lost in your own worlds... to forget what others gave up so that you could live? Those people whose ashes are stored in the Memorial Towers made the most heartbreaking choices," she said, pointing at the windows, "so that you could fulfill your dreams. And what are you doing with your time here? Have you become better? Have you gotten stronger and wiser? My mother died six months early because someone put the wrong date on her easy-out implant. I lost the most wonderful person in my life because someone couldn't think twice to check a f***ing date!" The unhinged woman swore and began to cry.

"Let's face it; you've taken a lot from me over the years," Litz continued as she wiped away tears from her eyes. "But now I've taken something from you, and I hope you feel the sting of this national tragedy. A few weeks ago, I entered the headquarters of NASA in Houston. I seduced one of their astronauts and got right up close to the space shuttle. Just like the rest of you, the fool was too trusting and told me everything I needed to know to sabotage the sensors. He said that a little bit of clear tape in the wrong place could lead to a catastrophic failure upon returning to earth. And you know what?" She asked and leaned toward the camera lens with a demented grin. "He was right! That man really knew his s***, and the shuttle exploded on reentry exactly the way he described." The television star put both of her legs flat on the floor and clasped her hands together to continue speaking.

"So now you've taken from me, and I've taken from you," Litz said with careful conviction, expressing an unforgiving mindset. "You might say that we're even, but I don't want to be even. I don't want to live in a world where politicians decide who lives and who dies, and when and how that is supposed to happen. You make me sick with your lack of consideration for the world and the damage you've done. But your lack of thought is a sin that I intend to exploit. Rest assured, I'm far from that sweet, giggly woman you saw on the television show. This nightmare won't end until I see a dramatic change in the way you make choices. You'll be seeing me again soon. Oh, and by the way, Mike and Jennifer – your talented director and producer of the Shots Fired television show - are both over the age of fifty. They've been buying prosthetics and injections to make their faces look younger. And, I might also mention that they used to work for the CIA. As for my co-stars, I love each of you a great deal. I'm sorry to put you in this situation. Goodbye." The preeminent woman got up from the sofa and walked toward the camera, bending forward as she got closer to the unit, and the projected image went black.

"What the hell was that?" Jazzy lamented with a sad expression. "I don't even recognize her with all of the things she was saying." The comedian had gotten off of the sofa after the video began and now stood in the center of the room with her arms folded across her abdomen.

Fassim and CKB had joined Jazzy in the middle of the room while the video was playing, and they both seemed stunned. CKB put his head down, and Fassim looked at Richard as if he could answer why these events had taken place. Someone stuck their head around the corner from the hallway, causing Jazzy to look back, but they disappeared before she could identify them.

"She's a very disturbed woman," Stoney suggested from his position on the left side of the sofa. "I feel bad for the astronauts; they never did anything to her. She even used Jason and pretended to be in love with him. Litz is just another criminal!"

Richard gripped his knees and watched the gray carpeting for a few seconds. The softness of its texture seemed to sooth the high tide of emotions that were wrecking his insides. He wondered how someone could appear infatuated with Jason and manage to let him burn up in the atmosphere. The entire premise made him numb from his core to the nerve endings in his feet. In that instant, his toes felt vibrations through the floor, and there were sounds of people shuffling about near the offices a few doors away.

"She's a terrorist," Fassim said after a moment of contemplation. "We need to call this an act of terror and forget that she's white. I don't care what they did to her mother; I never hurt anyone after my lover was killed."

There was an odd suffocating sound from the sofa, and everyone turned to see Mike strangling Stoney from behind. Before anyone could react, Jennifer entered the room with a nickel-plated, semiautomatic pistol and pointed it at each cast member in succession. The pistol had a matching silencer affixed to its barrel and looked menacing in the producer's hands.

"What are you doing?" Jazzy demanded in a soft voice, appearing horrified by the situation.

"Come on, big boy," Mike said to Stoney with his right arm pulled tight around the officer's neck, "where is your gun? I know you must have your secondary weapon with you."

"What the f*** are you doing?" CKB asked as he turned toward Jennifer and Mike with an expression of betrayal. "I'm gonna' take you apart; he's got a broken rib!"

"Get him into submission!" Mike ordered Jennifer as he grappled Stoney's throat with his right hand and frisked him with the left. "In fact, get all of the men into submission; I want to leave this place without an incident."

"Damn you, Litz; nosy little b****!" Jennifer swore and walked toward CKB, urging him forward with the barrel of her pistol. "Get over to the corner, CKB; this can all be over fast if you walk the line."

"He's clean," the director announced as he let go of Stoney's throat and shoved the officer hard into the cushions of the sofa.

Stoney jumped upward with a grimace and tried to take Mike's pistol away, but the older man jabbed him in the chest near his broken rib. The wounded man cried out in pain and continued his attempts to overpower the director.

"Stop fighting me! Stop fighting me!" Mike repeated and shoved the Japanese man back into the cushions of the couch.

From the waistband of his jeans, the director removed a nickel-plated, semiautomatic pistol that had no silencer. In a moment of shocking ferocity, Mike's face turned red, engorged with blood, and he struck Stoney three times in the mouth with the barrel of the pistol. Stoney screamed in anguish and grabbed his lower jaw as a flood of tears emerged from his eyes. He fought through the pain in silence with an occasional moan as blood began to stream through his fingers.

When Jazzy saw this demonstration of violent behavior, she got down on her knees and raised her hands in the air. CKB protested the treatment of his Japanese co-star, and Jennifer rewarded him by smashing the butt of her pistol into the back of his bald head.

"Where are our security people?" Fassim thought aloud and glanced around the room.

"Your security people work for us," Jennifer answered in a callous manner. "Now stop with the twenty questions, or we won't be able to end this peacefully."

Several members of the television crew came running toward the living room to see what was happening. The group of over a dozen men and women stood at the end of the hallway with shocked expressions, attempting to understand whether they were witnessing something real. A few of the men became aggressive when they saw the director abusing the television stars, but Mike was quick to train his weapon on them.

"Get back to your rooms, or we'll execute all of them," the director assured the small group of onlookers. "In fact, anyone that gets between us and the door is going to get shot in the throat. Do you know how horrible it is to get shot in the throat? Do you want to find out?" He added through gritted teeth, which caused the crew members to raise their hands and back away.

CKB lurched backward at Jennifer with the hulking weight of his body while Mike was distracted, and used his left arm to swat at her pistol. The producer had been watching the crew members over her shoulder, and the criminal was able to knock the gun from her hands. Cody turned further when he saw the pistol fall away, but the woman exploded back to attention and jabbed him hard in the throat. He began to choke, and Jennifer grappled his left arm with formidable aggression, twisting it around his back at an uncomfortable angle. With a slight amount of pressure, the producer was able to make CKB feel like she was about to dislocate his elbow. The large man submitted and fell to his knees. As a measured response, Jennifer reached over the back of the television and pushed it off of its stand onto his back. The layered 3D hologram screen smashed against CKB's back and shoulders but did little else, other than serving as a garnish to Jennifer's rage.

Jennifer turned to see that Richard was holding her pistol, and the agitated film editor had it aimed at the center of her chest. She exhaled with wounded pride and doubled her hands up into white-knuckle fists.

Richard crept across the room between Jennifer, Jazzy, and Fassim, preventing Mike from getting a clear target.

"Do you think that having your co-stars in my way will keep me from shooting you, Richard?" Mike threatened and took aim at the back of Fassim's head.

Fassim exhibited a paler color on her face after the director uttered these words, and with her eyes, she begged Richard to do something. The film editor locked his gaze on the petrified Muslim and then began to sprint across the living room carpet toward the kitchen.

Mike tracked the fleeing television star across the room with his pistol and waited for a clear shot at the center of mass. However, Richard dove over the kitchen counter like a superhero, taking bowls of fruit and bananas crashing to the tiled flooring with him.

The film editor felt his body smack the cold tiles face first, and he dropped the pistol to inspect his left eye. Richard was relieved when the wounded eye opened and closed without issue. Although his vision was blurry; the damage didn't seem permanent. Richard shook his head and found the pistol on the floor under his right leg. He then used his right hand to pull the weapon up to his chest and slid backward against the kitchen cupboards.

"Richard, if this turns into a standoff between us and the police, it's going to end badly for you," Mike promised from his position at the center of the living room. "Look, everyone, Jennifer and I just want to leave in peace. We came in here to subdue Stoney and CKB because they're the biggest threats to our safety. That's what we're trained to do, and I'm sorry it had to go down this way. But you need to surrender your weapon and let us get out of here."

"I don't think we can trust you!" Richard called out from below the kitchen countertop. "You look like evil people to me."

"Richard, I don't care if I get out that door with fifteen bodies at my feet, or with no bodies, but I'm getting through that door!" The director proclaimed with a roar from his commanding throat, causing his face to redden somewhat.

The television star clutched the pistol tighter in his right hand and looked at the front door to his left. He was confused by this ultimatum from Mike because both exits led to the elevators, but the route from the front door was shorter than the back. Richard tried to recall what was unique about leaving through the front door, but the adrenaline in his veins and a rapid heart rate would not allow him to focus.

"Come on, shutterbug!" Mike demanded with authority from someone in the living room and began to shuffle across the carpet.

The film editor held the pistol silencer close to his cheek in dismay, considering the possibility that the crazed director was holding someone hostage. He jumped backward and almost fired the gun when a woman's head peeked over the kitchen counter at him. Richard bit his lower lip when he saw Fassim's pink headscarf fall from her hair and float down to the tiles on the cool kitchen floor. Someone was squeezing her neck and holding a pistol against her right temple. The helpless woman looked down at Richard with empty eyes that dripped small tears of confusion onto his clothing.

"Since your ears don't work, Richard, let's see how good you are with visual aids," Mike growled as he manhandled the timid Muslim atop the kitchen counter. "In five seconds, I'm going to start with her, and then I'll empty my clip into the rest of your friends. One. Four. Five!" The retired CIA assassin yelled through the loft and watched as the suppressed pistol was tossed gently upward on the kitchen counter. "Jennifer, get your piece," he called out to his companion and yanked the photographer away from the countertop.

Jennifer sprinted to the kitchen and retrieved her pistol from the smooth white tiles on the counter, and then took aim on the crew members in the hallway. The group began to retreat backward, feeling less emboldened with two gun-toting psychopaths in the loft.

"Jenn, you're out the door," Mike barked with efficiency and pointed his pistol at the crew as the producer ducked below his arms, darting forward to open the front door. "We're gone, and you're safe, as promised. But if anyone tries to follow us, we'll put no less than four bullets into you, and we won't care about where they land." The director followed his co-conspirator through the front door, walking backward to keep an eye on everyone in the room.

The front door slammed shut, and the attack was over as fast as it began. Jazzy had tears streaming down her face in perfect, glossy lines, and her expression was that of a terrified animal.

"I think they're taking the stairs," Richard surmised as he got up from his position behind the kitchen counter. "The only reason they would want to go through the front door is so that they could make it to the stairs. I'm going after them."

Stoney wiped his mouth and shook his head from side to side at the conservative film editor. He wanted to speak, but his swollen, bloodied lips were burning with pulsating pain.

"Leave it alone, dude," CKB replied to Richard as he pushed the broken television aside and got to his feet. "Look, if someone is dangerous enough to make Stoney stay put and force me to play dead – it's like a hornet's nest." He finished in an awkward manner, unable to articulate his explanation. "Just stay put and be glad you're alive."

"Is someone gonna' call the cops?" Jazzy asked with subtle sarcasm that was overshadowed by fear. "I appreciate you guys pretending to be macho, but if Stoney and CKB couldn't do anything, then we need more help."

"I'll try Stoney's partner and see if he can send someone over," CKB responded in a manner that lacked enthusiasm. "In the meantime, Richard, just chill out and lay low with the rest of us. Let's find out what's goin' on."

Richard ignored this sentiment and used his right hand to snatch a butcher knife from a white oak block in the corner of the kitchen. He then bolted for the front door and exited the loft in a rush. The film editor felt a surge of horror upon leaving the safety of their living space and wanted to close his eyes. But the hallway near the elevators was empty, and this discovery gave him confidence.

Richard walked past the elevators and confirmed that the lights above the doors were not moving. He smirked to celebrate this small victory, realizing that his theory was correct. After taking a moment to gather his wits, he began to trudge across the tan and brown carpeting of the hallway toward the door labeled 'stairs.' The halls were typical of a hotel layout, complete with a few dark brown end tables with fake fruit and knickknacks atop their shiny surfaces. Richard felt odd running with the butcher knife and tried to conceal it beside his right thigh. His left hand gripped the bronze door handle to enter the staircase, and he pulled the door open in a slow and steady manner.

The heedful man moved his body under the pale lighting of the stairway, keeping his left hand taut against the door. This maneuver allowed him to close the heavy door without making a sound. Richard peered over the stairway railing and couldn't see any movement below, but he suspected that the perpetrators were walking near the outer walls of the staircase. His hands began to tremble when he realized that there was no plan of action if he were to confront the killers. Despite the danger, Richard felt guilty for the events that transpired, and this shameful feeling propelled him down the flights of stairs. The green warning signs and bare gray walls looked identical to the young man, which made it seem like he was descending into hell. Each stairway landing had pitted gray non-slip surfaces, and the stairs were covered in a similar gray color. There was a chilly breeze coming up from the ground floor, which reminded the television star of his mortality.

Richard was sweating by the time he had descended eighteen flights of stairs, but his excitement piqued when he heard movements from a few floors below. His satellite phone began to ring, and the apprehensive man backed against the wall, freezing in the middle of a stairway to fish in his pocket for the device. It rang three times in the menacing tones of an old-fashioned telephone, and Richard answered the call in vain. He placed the unit close to his left ear and held the butcher knife out in a threatening manner. The television star was almost hyperventilating after the obnoxious ringing announced his presence to what seemed like the entire building.

"Is this Richard?" A middle-aged male voice asked through the receiver of his satellite phone. "Don't hang up, Richard. Look up to your left at the camera. We can see you coming, and it seems like all you've got is a knife." Richard turned his gaze up and to the left at a video camera that was mounted high above him on the concrete wall. "Richard, the people you're chasing are assassins – some of the best in the world. I urge you to turn around and go back to where you started. This whole thing is bigger than you think, and they won't hesitate to make an example of you."

Richard looked up at the red motion sensor light that displayed beneath the camera each time he moved and responded by raising his right middle finger from the handle of the butcher knife. He then hung up the phone and placed it in the pocket of his jeans as he sprinted down the stairs toward the ground floor. The defiant man heard a door open and shut on the level just beneath him and felt it was odd that someone would be exiting one floor above the lobby. His body resisted going further, and he felt almost paralyzed with fear, but Richard ignored his instincts and rushed down the next flight of stairs like a wild meerkat. When he got closer to the door, his phone started to ring again, and Richard answered the call out of pure fascination.

"Don't go through that door!" The male voice shouted at him with what sounded like a sincere warning.

Richard dropped the phone on the gray non-slip surface of the landing and used his left hand to tug on the door, keeping his body concealed behind it for cover. For a moment, the film editor thought that he had heard a woman screaming his name, but his senses were overwhelmed by a bright and deafening explosion. The steel door was knocked from its hinges and impressed itself on Richard's body against the stairs. He felt heat and pressure all around him, and the door slammed down on his chest like the foot of a giant, forcing his head to smack the concrete. His vision blacked out under the scorched and twisted metal door, giving him no time to react.

XIX. The Jester's Joker

THREE WEEKS LATER

Something was wrong with his eyelids; the young man had tried three times to open his eyes without success. This revelation gave him severe discomfort, combined with the sensation that he could not move his body. He strained several times in vain to complete this simple task; something he had been able to do since infancy. 'Open your eyes,' the man thought as he worked his eyelid muscles up and down with growing anxiety. After what seemed like several minutes, his right eyelid split open at an odd angle, giving him the ability to see bright indoor lighting. There was a burning sensation from the split eyelid and a trickle of blood, which caused him to wince and hold his breath.

When the man turned his head to the left, he noticed a heart monitor that was beeping in time with his pulse. There was also a tall rack with two bags of intravenous fluids hanging from stainless steel hooks. He could see long, thin tubes extending below the bags of fluid and into a vein in his left arm. A bright white body cast covered every bit of his skin, and it appeared fresh as if fashioned from new material.

Due to the rigidness of the cast, his ability to turn his head or speak were limited. The confused man strained to open his mouth and wanted to call out to someone, but felt a tube between his lips and heard the rhythmic sounds of air being pushed by a machine. He began to writhe within the confines of the body cast, realizing that a piece of hospital equipment was breathing for him.

This fit of rage didn't last long, and his body punished him with pain that was worse than a thousand wasp stings. He stopped moving when his nerve endings began to hurt as if someone was rubbing sandpaper across his muscles and arteries. The burning was severe enough that it felt like he was going to die. He attempted to cry out, wanting to make the agony subside, but chose not to move his body until someone could tell him what was happening.

An alarm sounded from the heart monitor next to his hospital bed, and a twenty-seven-year-old African-American nurse sprinted into the room.

"Oh my God!" The woman exclaimed and partially covered her face with both hands, shocked to see that her patient was awake. "I'll get the doctor right away." She grabbed a paging unit from a black lanyard around her neck and spoke frantically to her coworkers through the device. "Yes, I have a code red situation in the ICU. Doctors needed in room 224."

The nurse fled from the hospital room and returned a few seconds later with a bag of intravenous fluid. Her slender fingers were quick to mount the bag on one of four stainless steel hooks of the medical caddy. She then disconnected a tube from one of the other bags and affixed it to the bottom of the new bag.

"Okay my friend, you're about to feel much better," the wholesome woman assured him in a comforting tone. "This morphine is going to make you a little drowsy, but we need you to rest anyway." She adjusted the flow of the pain medication until her patient's heart rate went back down to normal, and turned around to check on him with a bright smile.

"What have we got?" A thirty-two-year-old doctor asked as he entered the room in a rush. "Oh, wow, he tore through the stitches on his right eye. How are his vitals?" The doctor inquired as he removed a pen light from the pocket of his white coat.

After a short pause, the doctor turned on the pen light and pointed it at the right eye of his patient. He listened to a verbal report from the nurse and seemed calmer after hearing the readouts. The doctor had large hands and was of Chinese-American ancestry. His hair was neat, and he carried himself like the type of person one would trust to save lives in desperate situations. Without looking, he reached toward the nurse with his right hand extended, and she handed him a clipboard with a hospital chart attached.

"Okay, Jason, I'm Doctor Henneman," the medical professional stated with a smile and glanced down at the clipboard in his hands. "You were involved in a space shuttle accident, and you're at the Brooke Army Medical Center in San Antonio, Texas. You and a few members of your crew managed to climb into an emergency escape pod and eject during the explosion. Over sixty percent of your body is covered in burns, and we've already done five surgeries to keep you alive. So, please go easy on your body for the next few days; it can't handle much. I'm sure you have some questions, and the FBI would like to ask you some questions too, but right now we need to focus on making you feel better. So, my nurse is going to give you something to help you sleep through the pain until we feel that you're stable enough to interact with anyone. Your family is being brought down from the cafeteria, and we'll let them see you before you go back to sleep. Don't worry, Jason, you're in the best burn unit in the country," he said with a reassuring smile, and then jotted some notes on his paperwork.

Jason tried to stay awake for his family, but between an overwhelming state of emotional shock and his body being too weak to continue looking at the world, hope was the last thing on his mind. The astronaut closed his right eye, praying that nothing he had just witnessed was real.

Edwina Holtzclaw Boarding School – Lancaster, California

Headmistress Mary sat behind a corner desk within a large mobile classroom, watching television on a black video tablet. With her earbuds in place, she couldn't hear the stories that Satoko was telling the students and seemed oblivious to the activities of the class. There was a show playing on the tablet called Shots Fired in the Melting Pot that featured the survivors of an act of domestic terrorism. She watched the events unfold on the eight-inch screen with an anxious expression.

"Welcome to Shots Fired in the Melting Pot," the European host stated as a camera panned in on his face. "I'm your host, James Iverson. For those of you who are new to the show, let's help you to get caught up. This production used to be a reality television series about six natural enemies who were forced to share a loft together in New York City. But after an act of domestic terrorism just three weeks ago, the show has turned into a study of the nuts and bolts behind terrorism. In fact, all of our recurring guests were victims of terror. Now, today is special because we have Richard Orton joining us after his recent recovery from a local hospital." The camera turned to show a forced smile on Richard's face before panning back to the host. "We also have Jazzy Auburn Michelle, Cody K. Black or CKB, Fassim Johnson, and Stoney Akuda on our panel today. Please welcome all of these brave souls to our show." James Iverson paused for the studio audience to applaud his guests and saluted them with a sharp hand gesture.

The television stars sat around the host at a rectangular oak table. All of them looked healthy and normal except for Richard, who seemed depressed as he stared through the center of the table in a daze.

"Okay, well, let's start with you, Richard," James prompted his guest with gentle social energy. "Litz Rack was someone with whom you had become intimately involved, and it seemed like you cared for her. Then she literally burned you by setting off an explosion in your face. Oh, and let me refresh the audience on the facts. A pair of assassins attacked these amazing people you see sitting at my table, and Richard pursued them. And, during the pursuit, the ex-CIA agents placed a magnetic pod on a metal doorway. The pod was about the size of the palm of your hand and was filled with ANFO. For those of you who don't know, ANFO stands for aluminum nitrate fuel oil. It is very easy to make or obtain, and can blow apart just about anything." The host smiled and turned away from the camera back to Richard, appearing to enjoy the sound of his voice. "So, Richard, this woman burned you and seduced you with her feminine charms; what-"

"Let me stop you right there," Richard replied as he raised his right hand toward the host. "Too many journalists have used the catchphrase that I was 'burned by this woman,' and I find the use of that phrase to be in poor taste. Someone had called me before I went downstairs, and they called me again before I opened the door. The person on the other end of that phone was male, but he warned me about the danger and told me to go back to the loft. Now, for me, the only explanation for that type of a warning would be Litz trying to save my life." He tugged nervously at a black tie that encircled the neck of his white button-down dress shirt and finished his announcement with an expression of deep sorrow.

"So, are you saying that you forgive them for what they did to you?" The television host suggested and cocked his head back in preemptive shock.

"Hell no," Richard answered in rapid fashion. "I spent three weeks in the hospital, and without the protection of that steel door, we wouldn't be talking today. If the door had moved even six inches to the right, my head would've taken the blast. I'm not excusing the behavior of these people, but I don't want any of the facts withheld for sensationalism. Does that make sense?"

"Yes it does, Richard," James answered in a condescending way and turned to face the other cast members. "We appreciate your bravery as much as your honesty. Now, I want to get to Jazzy and Fassim; you ladies were both friends with Litz, correct?" The host continued with a brief hand gesture toward the two women.

"I wasn't her friend," Fassim replied from under a light blue hijab before Jazzy could open her mouth. "She was a very odd woman and not traditional enough to be considered one of my friends. Also, as a moderate Muslim, I am required to denounce all acts of terrorism around the world. While I do understand that this person underwent a severe tragedy, it should never have led to the destruction of her soul. I hope that they capture her and make this right." The paparazzi photographer pounded her right fist on the table and turned to look at Jazzy.

"I was really shocked when we found out what Litz had done," Jazzy stated, and leaned forward in an orange blouse with her hands clasped together. "When she went missing at NASA headquarters, we were worried that someone had abducted her. All of us got together and formed a search party – we were sick. But when I found out what she'd done to those innocent people, I was…beyond sick."

"Thank you for those perspectives, ladies," the host said with a nod and gestured toward CKB and Stoney. "Gentlemen, you lived with Litz Rack for several weeks and got to know a lot about her; what are your thoughts on these events?"

"We need to lock her up in a mental hospital," Stoney conveyed with a shrug that raised and lowered his plain white T-shirt. "I mean, there are two types of criminals in our society; those who know what they did wrong and those that can't tell the difference. I think that she was traumatized to the point where…I don't know." The Japanese officer shrugged again and opened up his hands on the table before letting them drop onto its surface.

"Yeah, and I'd say that everyone deserves a chance at redemption," CKB proclaimed to the camera. "I've seen people come back from worse places in their lives, and - it's just too hard to say. But she needs to stop what she's doing. Making innocent people pay for your pain is wrong. I think that history has shown that when you do right by the universe, it does right by you. But when you mess with the natural system; things catch up to you…eventually."

"Well, there's a lot of mystery surrounding this woman, and the details are still coming in, but the consensus from the public is-"

The television host continued to speak as Headmistress Mary removed the earbuds from her ears and pushed a button on the tablet to turn the screen black. She leaned forward and closed her eyes while taking in a deep breath. The guilt-ridden woman teased her brunette hair during a moment of nervous primping, before sliding the tablet and earbuds into a small drawer in the front of her desk. Her gaze went far beyond the children in the classroom as she leaned back in her chair to reflect on the past.

Mary sat forward in her seat when she saw a man in a gray suit entering the front door of the classroom. A seventeen-year-old girl named Cynthia, who had long blonde pigtails and worked as an aid in the front office escorted the man through the classroom. After walking the length of the room and stumbling a bit in front of Satoko, Cynthia presented the man to the headmistress.

Satoko kept reading to the children about three Billy goats trying to cross a bridge, but altered her gaze to observe the well-dressed man. The thirty-nine-year-old Japanese woman rolled her dark brown eyes at the stranger and pushed a pair of horn-rimmed glasses closer to the bridge of her nose. She then flipped a page in the storybook and continued to read aloud. Her voice was powerful despite the petite body from whence it emerged.

"Headmistress Mary, this is John Butler of the FBI," Cynthia announced with her right hand outstretched as though she were introducing a comedy act. "Someone called him with an anonymous tip about our school, and he wanted to talk to you about it." The office aid shrugged after this brief introduction and gave an awkward bow before vacating the area.

Before Mary could speak, the FBI agent retrieved a photo from his jacket and held it up to compare it with her face. The headmistress' nose and ears differed from the picture of Litz Rack, but her high cheekbones and other features were a close match. The woman also had fifteen pounds of extra weight on her body in comparison to the photo, but it was still a close enough match to investigate.

"Ma'am, I'm gonna' need you to come with me to answer some questions," John commanded from his position in front of Mary's desk and clasped his hands over a large, silver belt buckle. "We need to know if you have any information about terrorist activities in the United States. If we find that you're innocent, you'll be welcome to return to your work at the school."

"That's a bunch of garbage!" Satoko exclaimed when she heard what the FBI agent was saying. "My sister-in-law is no terrorist!" The older woman lamented from her position on a metal stool at the front of the classroom. "Why don't you leave her alone so that she can help these kids that your government left orphaned?" She asked with a shaky lower jaw while using her right hand to ruffle her thick locks of long black hair.

"Ma'am, can you prove that this is your sister-in-law?" John proposed with his right hand extended toward Mary. "Do you have indisputable proof that this woman is your relation? Because if she's not, you'll be considered an accessory after the fact, and we'll put you in prison for aiding a federal fugitive. Even at your age, the law applies, so I hope you have some strong proof." He placed his hands on his hips and stared at the Japanese woman with defiance radiating from his deep blue eyes.

"Why don't you just look at the faculty photos next to her desk?" Satoko offered with sarcasm followed by an outburst of laughter that ended in a cackle. "You people are so good with your hamburger eyes, but mine are better today," she said in a celebration that elicited nervous giggling from the students. "Those photos go back for the past five years, and my sister-in-law is in all of them. Do you really think we'd make someone headmistress if they'd been here for a year or two?" The Japanese woman chuckled and slapped her angular left knee beneath a thick denim dress.

"This isn't going to work," the agent said after a closer inspection, gesturing toward the photos on the classroom wall with his right thumb. "I need to see two forms of identification."

"What a bunch of cow crap!" Satoko lamented as she sat up straight in her blue and white striped shirt with an exaggerated smile to amuse the class.

The FBI agent rolled his eyes as he approached the desk of the headmistress and waited for her to fish two forms of ID from her purse. John ran his fingers through his short black hair and watched the teacher fumble through her personal items for several seconds. Just when his patience was fading, the astute woman produced a social security card and California driver license. He took a moment to inspect the two forms of identification with great care and then gave them back to her.

"Okay everyone, I have a few questions about your teacher, and please answer me honestly," John instructed the class with his hands raised in the air like a politician. "How many of you have been here for over a year?" The agent watched with determination as more than half of the students raised their hands. "Okay, that's great, and how many of you remember Headmaster Mary being here when you first arrived?"

The same group of children raised their hands and kept them up high for the federal agent. Some of the students seemed to be holding back scathing laughter as a result of the man's recent gaff. John took in a deep breath after this reaction from the students and turned to stare at Mary for more than thirty seconds.

"She's the headmistress; didn't you see on her driver license that it says female? Why don't you arrest her already so we can get back to our story time?" The Japanese woman decried as curls of black hair near the end of her bangs bounced around her face. "Just make sure that you have her back in time for our math lesson tomorrow. I don't have the sort of head for math that a man would appreciate – too logical."

"I may be back to ask you more questions in the future," John relayed to the teacher as he began to tread with caution toward the door. "Wait a minute," he said with a sudden hunch, "let me see your right bicep." The agent wheeled around and pointed his right index finger at the headmistress.

The woman shook her head in irritation and turned her body sideways to expose her right arm. Mary was wearing black bib overalls with a white dress shirt, which went well with her black hiking boots. She rolled up the sleeve of the white shirt all the way to her shoulder, displaying pale, bare skin for the man. John looked at her clean bicep and nodded in affirmation.

"Thank you, ladies and students; have a good day," John said with a warm smile as he crept past Satoko on his way to the front door.

The Japanese woman glared at the agent, and he stopped to look at her, raising his right eyebrow. Upon closer inspection, the woman seemed too stereotypical in her appearance and mannerisms - something was off. She smiled with old-world charm and raised her middle finger at him, causing the man to scoff and shake his head.

"You know what, lady-" he began to speak but saw something metallic appear from beneath the woman's dress.

John reached for his gun with precise movements, allowing his training to take over. Although his face was still drawn and pale from discovering that the Japanese woman was dangerous, he was alert.

The FBI agent was shocked when a surgical steel blade penetrated deep into the thigh muscle of his left leg. He cried out from the invasive pain and simultaneously whipped the woman on the left side of her face with his pistol. She fell atop a little boy's desk in the front row, and the student made a panicked exit from the classroom, screaming and running with the rest of the children.

Litz looked up from the desk at the FBI agent with a custom prosthetic mask hanging off of the right side of her face. The man's eyes narrowed when her deception came to light, and he raised his pistol with both arms, aiming at the center of her chest. He glanced upward at the doorway, hoping that his partner was coming to join him after checking the administrative records.

"Drop the knife!" He commanded with a thousand-yard stare, repressing the desire to put pressure on his wound.

In one swift motion, Litz leaped upward and smothered the agent's forearms with her upper body. This counterattack was a mistake, and the man fired three times in succession, causing her to shriek in agony when a bullet tore through to the femur bone in her left thigh.

The wanted felon closed her eyes and dropped to the floor, gripping the front of her wounded leg and floundering among the desks. There was a copper smell from the blood, and it was making a sticky mess all over her fingers. She detected a gaping hole in her flesh and began to convulse as if she would vomit. The wound reported heat and a level of damage to her brain that she had never experienced in her life.

"Oh my God! Litz!" Mary exclaimed from the front of the classroom. "I'm so sorry! You're bleeding! What do you want me to do?" The woman asked after taking a few deep breaths.

"Call Mike-" Litz ordered with her mouth halfway obscured by the tiles on the floor. "Tell him to kill the other agent and get ready to leave."

"You can't-" a weak male voice said through heaving, shallow breaths "-not my partner."

Litz heard the desperate sounds of heavy breathing nearby and forced her body to roll from lying face down to an upright position. Her left leg served up sharp crystals of pain, causing her arms to shake during the strenuous movements.

"Mike, we screwed up," Mary announced into a secure satellite phone. "Litz needs you to... take out the other agent. Yes, I'm sure. I don't know... send someone back here. Thanks."

When Litz heard Mary calling Mike for help, it reminded her of the first time she cried out to him at the orphanage. Before he joined the CIA, Mike had been her protector, the only security guard that could make the ravenous boys behave.

Mary set the phone on a desk and unbuckled her overalls, removing a long-sleeved shirt to use as a tourniquet around Litz's leg. Her curvy stomach and a gaudy pink bra made the situation seem suddenly too real for the new recruit. She looked toward the FBI agent while securing the shirt around her colleague's leg.

John was straining for breath as he pulled at the handle on Litz's stainless steel throwing knife. The blood from his chest caused his fingers to slide all over the handle. He gazed at his pistol on the floor and back to the knife in his chest, trying to decide if revenge was a better option.

"You killed innocent people!" The agent exclaimed to Litz with a passion that caused him fiercer levels of hurt.

"The governmen' kills innocen' people ev'ry day," Litz replied with a pale face and blank stare. "They took my mom."

The agent looked away from his pistol and grabbed at the handle on the knife, pulling it upward with both hands. Mary slid the gun away from him and closed her eyes, grabbing Litz by the right hand. There was a sound of choking and suffering as the man's lungs filled with blood. Without the knife in place to block the flow partially, the life-giving fluid became deadly. Both women turned their faces away and began to cry, breathing in an exasperated rhythm.

"Mother's wrath-" Litz muttered to Mary as she heard members of her team entering the room to provide assistance. "I wan- wand'd to go with her." The young woman felt the world shifting beneath her like the steady jolt of a roller coaster making its first descent, and then there was nothing.

XX. PhD in FML

November 7th, 2056

Richard felt crisp ice snap underfoot as he ambled at a steady pace toward a Brooklyn, New York high school to cast his vote. Freezing rain from the previous night had left the streets glossed over in a thin but sturdy cocoon of white ice. Every step he took reported with a sharp crackle and the air surged forth and retreated in a biting wind chill. He felt his nose beginning to burn inside and wondered if the promises made by his presidential candidate of choice were worth the journey. There was a stagnant resentment that Richard maintained for all liberals. This prejudice haunted him after a traumatic hospital stay, and for the past six months, he had remained wary of anyone who showed too much spirit.

The young man decided that his Nunn Bush walking shoes were a poor choice for the slippery surfaces. Despite the aesthetic appeal of their brown leather, his legs were taking a beating on the sidewalk as he slipped every few inches. The television star was grateful for his gray wool pants and a black hoodie that kept strangers from pointing out his celebrity status. Richard didn't mind being somewhat famous during the first season of the television show, but becoming the survivor of a bombing took matters to a ridiculous level. Although he had found a new friend in weightlifting, the unanticipated temptations led to a new lady friend almost every day of his life. The brawny conservative felt guilty for all of his womanizing over the past few months, but his therapist told him that it was a way to deal with posttraumatic stress. Richard smiled as he wondered what the Catholic priests would say, or how his employer would react if they found out he had become a scoundrel again.

"You're Richard Orton," a forty-four-year-old man stated as he pointed a weathered finger at the television star. "You're the guy that bedded down with that psychopath Litz Rack," he added in a gruff tone and gripped the front of Richard's hoodie with both hands. "She burned Americans alive! How could you be with a woman like that? You disgust me!" The man began to scuffle with Richard on the ice and spat in his right eye.

The television star pulled away from the aggressive stranger but felt his hoodie stretching in his attacker's eager grasp. He blinked both eyes several times, trying to wipe the fresh saliva from his right pupil. The film editor detected a lightning rod of fury moving through his core as the fresh spittle stung the surface of his eye, and he began to manhandle his opponent.

Richard grabbed the stranger's tan jacket near the zipper and felt that the man somehow looked familiar. His assailant was tall with a well-groomed graying beard and deep brown eyes. The young man began to slip on the ice and decided to be mindful of his surroundings, noting that self-defense was more vital than chance memories at the moment. The older man was wearing baggy blue jeans and a New York Knicks baseball cap, but there was something in his eyes that seemed patriotic and distant.

"Litz Rack was a disgrace; shame on you for touching that filthy woman," the angry New Yorker scolded Richard again, and punched him with fierce energy three times on his left cheek. "I think you were in cahoots with her the whole time! How does a man put his hands on a woman and not know that she's evil?" He continued his violent assault until the conservative film editor began to fight back.

Richard had learned some defense moves over the past few months, courtesy of new friendships with Stoney and CKB. He stripped off the black hoodie and allowed his attacker to take it from him. This maneuver left him wearing a thin white T-shirt in the frigid cold. The television star then threw a swift right uppercut toward the vulgar pedestrian, but the older man blocked his fist and stunned him with a head-butt to the nose.

The Republican allowed himself to go ballistic with rage, watching steam rush out of his nose as he used the raw power of his body to flip his opponent onto the ice. Although this move was beneficial, Richard's shoes betrayed him, and the two men fell into a heap on the sidewalk near the curb.

"Litz wasn't bad; she just had a rough start in life," Richard lamented with his face pressed hard into his opponent's chest. "She was the desert rose that survived the blizzard," he added with contempt while his fists pounded the mouthy New Yorker in the kidneys and back of the head.

A red van jolted forward in traffic and stopped at the curb next to the skirmish. Richard lifted his head as the side door of the vehicle glided open, and two young men stepped out onto the concrete. They wore black T-shirts and loose-fitting cargo pants with tan work boots. One of the thugs reached down and pulled Richard up by the abdomen as if he were for sale from a local butcher shop. The other man grappled his legs, and they slid him into the van without gaining the interest of more than a few onlookers.

Richard tried to fight his abductors, but they locked his arms at the elbow behind his back. He started to kick with both legs, using all his strength, and someone responded by tying a seatbelt around his ankles.

"Hello, Richard," a familiar female voice said after he heard the door of the van slide shut and lock. "If you stop fighting, then nobody here is going to hurt you."

The van sped away from the curb into traffic, and Richard felt the back of his head resting on someone's lap. He looked up to see Litz Rack smiling at him in full makeup with her long blonde hair in a ponytail. She seemed mysterious and optimistic, sporting a royal blue dress that someone might choose before going on a date.

"Look, you need to stop fighting, or you're going to break something," the woman instructed in a frigid manner as she gripped the underside of his chin. "I don't want to hurt you, but I'm not taking any s*** from you either." She swore with a loving smile and patted the reddened skin on the left side of his face. "God, Robert, you didn't have to hit him so hard!"

"You told me that he was skinny and timid," Robert protested and folded his arms to pout in the rear seat of the van. "That guy is muscular and ready to dance. All I did was give him a good taste of pain; nothing was broken."

Richard glared at the two men that restrained him like a ravenous polar bear snatched from his icy lair. The television star refused to speak or smile, but locked eyes with his captors using all the pride he could muster.

"Well, you've got your man, Litz," Mike called out from the passenger seat, "and now I want my s***. I'm sure you two will have some time to catch up later," he announced with a sadistic grin and pushed a pair of dark sunglasses close to the bridge of his nose. "Hello, Richard - glad to see that you're in one piece," the ex-CIA agent said in a relaxed manner as he twisted his body around to face the windshield.

Richard sensed himself going numb when he saw that Mike and Litz were riding in the same van together. He stopped fighting his captors and stared at the back of the passenger seat. The film editor could feel his heart pulsating in his head when he took in the vision of his greatest enemy. Mike wore a gaudy black leather jacket that was of the same poor quality as his thick sunglasses. The television star guessed that they had purchased these items during their road trip, along with the cheap black jeans that Mike was sporting.

After observing the pain in Richard's face, Litz lowered her head and fixated on the light gray interior of the van. She had never realized the extent of her betrayal until this moment, and by staring into his eyes, it was like he and Jason were both judging her. The amorous woman's hands trembled as she anguished over Richard's disdain for her and the company she kept.

Litz waved dismissively to the young thugs, and Richard watched the men retreat to the rear of the van to sit with Robert. The nervous vixen then got up from her position in a delicate fashion and let Richard's head drop onto the seat. Litz then sat on the edge of the plush bench near the belly of her former co-star and remained silent while the van rolled forward through traffic.

Richard found himself lying on his back in the middle seat of the large passenger van, and although his legs were bound, his arms remained free to move. The annoyed man turned his head to the left toward the driver of the vehicle and saw long locks of blonde hair. Upon closer inspection, Richard decided that the person couldn't be Jennifer due to the masculine clothing and broad shoulders.

"Aren't you going to say anything?" Litz prompted her former lover with a demeanor of hope.

"I wish that I'd ripped the head off of your frog!" He taunted her with a brazen sneer.

"So, when do you think you'll be able to get those plans to us?" Mitch Gentile pressed from the driver seat of the van, demonstrating an impulsive mood.

Mitch was flaunting a cream-colored suit that complimented his thick blonde hair, and sunglasses that were far more stylish than those worn by Mike. His green silk tie had a faint blue checkered pattern across it, and the fabric swung each time the van made a turn.

When the van was on a straight path with less traffic, Mike pivoted in his chair with haste to look at Litz and raised his eyebrows, awaiting an answer. Litz shook her head with irritation and reached for a big, white road maintenance envelope tucked into a wide cloth pocket on the back of Mike's seat.

"Here you go," she said in a succinct manner and dropped the envelope into Mike's lap, "enjoy..."

"That was behind his seat the whole time?" Mitch assimilated with a friendly smack to Mike's left knee. "She had the plans in the back of your seat all the way from California – in the maintenance records!" He began to laugh in several octaves of mocking harmony along with the other men in the van.

"I can't believe the balls on you sometimes, Litz," Mike scorned with a deep sigh as he opened the envelope and pulled out some handwritten documents to pore over them. "I wish you were a real professional," he added with wounded pride while his colleagues continued to chuckle.

"Do you want me to think of you as my enemy?" The young woman suggested with a powerful gaze and leaned closer to the passenger seat.

"You get that thought out of your head, right now!" The former CIA agent requested in a sudden state of concern. "I don't need you running scenarios through that monster brain with me as a target. We're all friends here, everybody loves you, and you've got your boy toy. Let's just relax and enjoy the road for a while." Mike put up his hands with the palms outward and turned back toward the dashboard.

Richard felt odd seeing Mike show concern over the rambunctious hellcat and was stunned when none of the men questioned her authority. He looked up at her pouty expression and voluptuous figure, sensing that his pelvis yearned for her warmth, but the film editor forced his body to put the hunger aside. The captive man thought about his painful physical therapy and the scars from small third-degree burns on his arms and legs. After a brief moment of recalling the pain that she had caused him, it was easy for Richard to grimace at the duplicitous woman.

"I know that you're angry with me, but I've put a lot of work into this, and you're going to hold me," Litz demanded as she turned her body and tried to lie next to him on the bench seating.

Richard used his left arm to push the blonde woman away and heard two men jump up from their seats at the rear of the van. But Litz signaled with her right hand and waved them off before they could come to her aid.

"Hey, Richard," Mike announced as he removed his dark sunglasses and turned halfway around to face the television star, "we didn't drive all the way here to pick you up for a joyride. You have a role to play in this, whether you like it or not, so put your damn arms around the woman and make her feel at home before I break them!" He growled with a haughty stare of malcontent.

Richard refused to look at his enemy but knew from the tone of his voice that the man was making a genuine threat. After a regretful session of contemplation, he opened his arms and scooted backward on the seat. Litz hesitated at the thought of enjoying this forced companionship, but the journey had been long, and she wanted some affection. The conflicted woman turned to the side and rolled into his arms with guilty optimism.

"That's better," Mike said as he put his sunglasses back on and turned to face the road with the documents in hand.

"What has she got planned for us?" Mitch asked his colleague with eagerness. "Is it going to work?"

"You don't want to know," the former CIA agent responded with a measure of hesitation, "but I think it might. There's no training for something like this." He finished with a sigh, continuing to glance down at the documents and back at the road ahead.

There were dozens of questions on Richard's mind as he held the wild murderess in his arms. A part of him wanted to use his new muscle mass to squeeze her neck until the bones popped. He didn't understand how someone could burn a team of astronauts to ashes and relax with content afterward. His throat tightened with the thoughts that came forward while his sworn enemies drove the family van toward the weak sunlight of winter. Richard wasn't certain at what point these deviants began working together, but he knew that any chance of vengeance would require him to be a whore. So, he smiled with primal optimism, praying in silence to survive long enough to repay their kindness with blinding hellfire.

"I like when you're happy," Litz remarked in a whisper after turning her head to gauge Richard's expression. "And you can fantasize about hurting us, Richard, but I won't end you for hating me like a monster - I'll turn you into one."

THE END.

Please take the time to leave a short review of this novel if you feel that it has been worthy entertainment. A few small sentences will be much appreciated.

Other books by Travis Adams Irish:

Dividers (eBook, print, audiobook)

She is Risen (eBook, print, audiobook)

The Golden Goose of Los Angeles: Extended Edition (eBook, print)

Isiah's Skirmish (eBook, print)

Other books by T. C. Clover:

Ashes & Raven Feathers (Fall of 2017)